What Reviewers Say About BOLD STROKES Authors

❧

KIM BALDWIN

"*A riveting novel of suspense* seems to be a very overworked phrase. However, it is extremely apt when discussing Kim Baldwin's [*Hunter's Pursuit*]. An exciting page turner [features] Katarzyna Demetrious, a bounty hunter…with a million dollar price on her head. Look for this excellent novel of suspense…" – **R. Lynne Watson**, *MegaScene*

"*Force of Nature* is an exciting and substantial reading experience which will long remain with the reader. Likeable characters with plausible problems and concerns, imaginative settings, engrossing events, and a well-tailored writing style all contribute to an exceptional novel. Baldwin's characterization is acutely and meticulously circumscribed and expansive. It is indeed gratifying to see a new author attempt and succeed in expanding her literary technique and writing style. Kim Baldwin is an author who has achieved both." – **Arlene Germain**, reviewer for the *Lambda Book Report* and the *Midwest Book Review*

❧

ROSE BEECHAM

"…her characters seem fully capable of walking away from the particulars of whodunit and engaging the reader in other aspects of their lives." – *Lambda Book Report*

"When Jennifer Fulton writes mysteries, she writes them as Rose Beecham. And since Jennifer Fulton is a very fine writer, you might expect that Rose Beecham is a fine writer too. You're right…On the way to a remarkable, and thoroughly convincing climax, Beecham creates believable characters in compelling situations, with enough humor to provide effective counterpoint to the work of detecting." – *Bay Area Reporter*

❧

Ronica Black

"Black juggles the assorted elements of her first book with assured pacing and estimable panache…[including]…the relative depth—for genre fiction—of the central characters: Erin, the married-but-separated detective who comes to her lesbian senses; loner Patricia, the policewoman-mentor who finds herself falling for Erin; and sultry club owner Elizabeth, the sexually predatory suspect who discards women like Kleenex…until she meets Erin." – **Richard Labonte**, Book Marks, Q Syndicate, 2005

"Black's characterization is skillful, and the sexual chemistry surrounding the three major characters is palpable and definitely hot-hot-hot. If you're looking for a more traditional murder mystery, *In Too Deep* might not be entirely your cup of Earl. On the other hand, if you're looking for a solid read with ample amounts of eroticism and a red herring or two, you're sure to find *In Too Deep* a satisfying read." **Lynne Jamneck**, L-Word.com Literature

❧

Gun Brooke

"*Course of Action* is a romance…populated with a host of captivating and amiable characters. The glimpses into the lifestyles of the rich and beautiful people are rather like guilty pleasures….[A] most satisfying and entertaining reading experience." – **Arlene Germain**, reviewer for the *Lambda Book Report* and the *Midwest Book Review*

"*Protector of the Realm* has it all; sabotage, corruption, erotic love and exhilarating space fights. Gun Brooke's second novel is forceful with a winning combination of solid characters and a brilliant plot." – **Kathi Isserman**, *JustAboutWrite*

❧

Jane Fletcher

"*The Walls of Westernfort* is not only a highly engaging and fast-paced adventure novel, it provides the reader with an interesting framework for examining the same questions of loyalty, faith, family and love that [the characters] must face." – **M. J. Lowe**, *Midwest Book Review*

LEE LYNCH

"There's a heady sense of '60s back-to-the-land communal idealism and '70s woman-power feminism (with hints of lesbian separatism) to this spirited novel—even though it's set in contemporary rural Oregon. Partners Donny (she's black and blue-collar) and Chick (she's plus-sized and motherly) are both in their 50s, owners of the dyke-centric Natural Woman Foods store, a homey nexus for *Sweet Creek*'s expansive cast of characters....Lynch, with a dozen novels to her credit dating back to the early days of Naiad Press, has earned her stripes as a writerly elder; she was contributing stories to the lesbian magazine *The Ladder* four decades ago. But this latest is sublimely in tune with the times. "
– Richard Labonte, Book Marks, Q Syndicate, 2005

RADCLY*f*FE

"...well-honed storytelling skills...solid prose and sure-handedness of the narrative..." – **Elizabeth Flynn**, *Lambda Book Report*

"...well-plotted...lovely romance...I couldn't turn the pages fast enough!" – **Ann Bannon**, author of *The Beebo Brinker Chronicles*

ALI VALI

"Rich in character portrayal, *The Devil Inside* by Ali Vali is an unusual, unpredictable, and thought-provoking love story that will have the reader questioning the definition of right and wrong long after she finishes the book....*The Devil Inside*'s strength is that it is unlike most romance novels. Nothing about the story and its characters is conventional. We do not know what the future holds for Emma and Cain, but Vali tempts us with every word so we want to find out. I am very much looking forward to the sequel *The Devil Unleashed*."
– **Kathi Isserman**, JustAboutWrite

FOREVER
FOUND

Visit us at www.boldstrokesbooks.com

FOREVER FOUND

by

JLEE MEYER

2006

FOREVER FOUND
© 2006 By JLee Meyer. All Rights Reserved.

ISBN 1-933110-37-6

This Trade Paperback Original Is Published By
Bold Strokes Books, Inc.,
New York, USA

First Printing: Bold Strokes Books 2006

Credits
Editors: Jennifer Knight and Shelley Thrasher
Production Design: Stacia Seaman
Cover Design By Sheri (GRAPHICARTIST2020@HOTMAIL.COM)

Acknowledgments

As a first-time author I have many to thank, not the least of which is the amazing staff at Bold Strokes Books.

Jennifer Knight—she once described herself as a craft fitness trainer, but she is so much more. She had to do some major whipping this author into shape and did so with humor and understanding. Although the process was, at times, daunting for me, the finished product and those produced in the future are much improved because of it. Thank you, oh goddess of whip-cracking.

Shelley Thrasher—a fine eye for detail and a steady and, dare I say, relentless way of insisting that details fall into the proper places, you are a wonder.

Stacia Seaman—several years ago Stacia took pity on a fledgling writer and gave her some pointers. After many rewrites, she finally made the comment, "in fact, I kind of like it." There was no turning back after that, and I count Stacia a friend. Thank you.

Radclyffe—for liking the work well enough to take a chance on the possibilities, thank you. For creating a professional organization that nurtures excellence, there are not adequate words.

Cheryl—reading the first draft of a first novel and declaring it terrific kept me writing. Your unshakeable love and faith have completed me.

Dedication

For Cheryl—you are my sun, my moon, my stars,
my love. Only you.

Prologue

The two little girls were deep in concentration, looking through magazines in the family room of the large home. They sat right next to each other, arms and legs touching, Keri turning a page and Dana taking it from her at the midpoint. Their feet didn't come close to reaching the floor.

Keri, the elder by three days of their six years, said, "I like this one. It's not all gooey with that lace stuff. My grandmother wears that and it tickles when I kiss her."

"You'd wear something like that? Can't brides wear pants? That looks stupid." Dana had decided she didn't like dresses at all and hated the few times she'd had to wear one.

"You think I'd look dumb in my wedding dress?" Keri's large blue eyes reflected hurt. "Scooter, that's mean!"

Quickly regrouping, Dana amended, "No! It wouldn't look dumb if *you* wore it. It…it would look dumb if *I* wore it. You know I hate dresses."

They returned to the magazine.

"I know! Let's have a wedding! I'll be the bride and you can be the…the…groom!" Keri's eyes were dancing now. She started bouncing up and down on the couch.

Dana wasn't sure. "Well, I don't know. Aren't boys the only ones who get to be grooms?"

Keri screwed up her face in thought. "Eww. That couldn't be right. You should be able to marry who you want, right?"

"And married people have to kiss and stuff. If I have to kiss a boy, I'll barf." Dana mimicked getting sick on the magazine.

Undaunted, Keri asked, "But you could kiss me, right?"

Dana blushed. "Well, yeah, course I could kiss you. I love you. Silly."

They resumed their page turning, but a moment later Dana grabbed the magazine and threw it on the floor. She seized Keri's hands and the words came out all in a tumble. "MyKeri, will you marry me? Then we could live together and everything forever! I could even stand the kissing part! Please?"

Keri threw her arms around her best friend and yelped, "Yes! That's what we'll do!" She pulled back, looking intently in Dana's green eyes. "Are you sure, Scooter? We have to ask our parents if it's okay, you know."

Dana thought about it. She wasn't looking forward to telling her dad. Solemnly, she pushed back the lock of coal black hair that had fallen over her eyes. "I love you, MyKeri. There couldn't ever be anyone I could love more than you." Her father would just have to understand.

Just then they heard Keri's mother calling from downstairs. "Girls, come on down for chocolate chip cookies. I just got them out of the oven!"

Proposal forgotten, the two took off like a shot out the door, giggling and scuffling as they raced through the large house on their way to the kitchen.

"I get the first cookie!" Keri squealed as she rounded a corner and streaked down the hall, Dana hot on her heels.

"No way! Whoever gets there first, that's the rule!" Dana's longer legs pulled even and started to gain distance.

"Wait! My house!" When that didn't work, Keri squealed, "My Moms!" She immediately regretted her words when Dana stopped short and turned around, an injured look on her face. Hastily, she said, "I'm sorry, Scooter, I didn't mean it. I promise. Moms is yours, too."

A deeper feminine voice behind them said, "Okay, you two." They turned to see Carolyn Flemons smiling at them. She motioned toward the kitchen and put her hands on Dana's shoulders to give her a gentle squeeze. "You'll share the cookies and me. Let's go."

Once they were sitting at the table, each with a chocolate chip cookie and a glass of milk, all seemed forgotten. About halfway through the second cookie, Dana put the delicious treat down and wiped her mouth on her sleeve, neglecting the paper napkin in her lap. She turned to Keri's mother, who was at the table with them, drinking a cup of coffee and reading the paper.

"Mrs. Moms?"

Carolyn Flemons paused between sips of coffee. "Yes, Scooter?"

Sitting up straighter, Dana asked, "Can MyKeri and I get married?"

The cup seemed suspended in air; both Keri and Dana watched in fascination as it dropped to the table, breaking and soaking their cookies. When it hit, everyone jumped to their feet and ran around trying to find paper towels, the garbage can, a whisk broom. The activity kept them all busy for a few minutes, but eventually they returned to the table and Carolyn asked, "I'm sorry, Scooter, what were you asking?"

Decidedly more nervous than when she asked the first time, Dana glanced at Keri for reassurance, then tried again. "Can I get married to MyKeri?"

"Well..." Carolyn talked to the wall above Dana's head, trying not to sound as disconcerted as she felt. "Usually just a man and woman get married. A boy and girl. But you can always be best friends, right?" When she finally lowered her gaze to her daughter and almost-daughter, she saw only disappointment. Trying again, she added, "Besides, you wouldn't want to get married until you were grown up. That's a long time from now."

"But I love MyKeri!" Dana said, "I'll never love anyone else like her, I know it."

"Momma, please?" Keri begged. "We talked about it and that's what we want. Please?"

Carolyn sat back in her chair. "Look, I'll tell you what. If, when you grow up, you still want to get married, then you can." The girls squealed their delight and hugged each other. "But!" They got quiet immediately. "You have to be at least twenty years old and really have thought about it, okay?"

Keri's eyes became very round. "Twenty *years*? That's older than you are! Momma!"

Carolyn kept her face schooled to neutral. "No, Keri, in fact I am *older* than twenty, but that's how old I was when I met your father. You still have to agree, both of you."

Dana asked, "What about Mr. Flemons? Will he say yes?"

With two sets of beseeching eyes on her, Carolyn finally smiled. "I'll take care of him. You two just get to be twenty years old, then we'll talk about it."

Keri exclaimed, "Momma! Where's the Polabear camera? We can take a picture!"

"I'll get it and take two pictures, one for each of you."

Carolyn went to a cupboard and pulled out the instant camera, dutifully taking two pictures of the little girls, chocolate smeared on their joyful faces, arms around each other's shoulders. After they watched the pictures form on the paper, they celebrated by another round of cookies.

The girls were so lost in excitement and sugar buzz they didn't hear the doorbell ring. Their chatter only stopped when they heard voices being raised.

Dana put a hand on Keri to quiet her. "Shh. Listen, that's my dad."

An angry male voice said, "Where is she? We're leaving."

They heard Carolyn Flemons's voice but couldn't make out what she said.

"No! I'm taking her now. Dana? Get in here! We're leaving!"

Dana said, "I gotta go. He sounds mad."

"Why? Are you in trouble?" A look of worry was on Keri's face.

Eyes never leaving the doorway, Dana said, "Dunno. Since my mom left us he's mad all the time."

They heard heavy footfalls coming toward the kitchen. Dana quickly took one of the photographs, carefully placing it in the back pocket of her pants.

Carolyn's voice was angry when she said, "Sean! Let me drop her off in an hour. You've been drinking, it's too dangerous! Stay here if you want, I'll make fresh coffee."

He wheeled on her. "Listen, you bitch! I'm taking *my* daughter and we're leaving. I'm moving us so far away you'll never see us again. You can ask your asshole of a husband all about it." He took Dana roughly by the arm and snarled, "C'mon, and shut up."

As she was forced from the room, Dana called back to Keri, "I'll see you at school tomorrow."

"The hell you will," Sean Ryan growled, and kept dragging her behind him.

Keri screamed, "Scooter! No!" She ran after them and caught Dana's hand. "You can't take her! She's my friend!"

Dana's father raised his arm as if to strike Keri, and Carolyn's voice cut through the chaos. "Don't you dare touch her!" He lowered his arm and waited stiffly as she pried Keri's hand from Dana's and held the screaming, kicking Keri tightly to her. Tears brimmed in her eyes. "You go with your dad, Scooter. It'll be all right. We'll straighten this out. It's okay."

Dana looked up at her father and knew it would not be all right. She refused to walk willingly, so he dragged her out to the car. Keri was hysterical, sobbing and yelling for her to come back.

"I'll call you," Dana yelled as her father threw her in the front seat. "I'll write every day! I promise!"

Sean Ryan told her to shut up, got behind the wheel, and started the engine, cursing the whole time. The tires squealed as he roared down the street.

Breaking away from her mother, Keri ran to the curb to see Dana craning out the window, looking back at her. They disappeared around the corner and out of her life.

CHAPTER ONE

Dana slowly made her way down the carpeted hallway toward the large conference room. Her attorney, the one who'd magically appeared at her hospital bedside when she regained consciousness two weeks earlier, had picked her up at her apartment in Cow Hollow. He hustled into the meeting room ahead of her and was setting out his papers, probably handing out his card to the big guns. *Officious little beast.* He was practically salivating when Mike Flemons's law firm contacted Dana and wanted to meet.

Dana was in pain. She'd only been using crutches for a week, so her hands and armpits were killing her. When she'd discharged herself from the hospital, she'd refused to use metal canes, afraid they looked too permanent. Told she would always have a limp, she was determined to not only walk normally, but play soccer again. Deep inside, the fear of losing her career was festering, and the constant reminder of the crutches and every nerve in her body didn't help her mood. She kept moving.

Her doctor had advised against her leaving the hospital, but after four weeks, Dana couldn't stand it any longer. She'd also been advised not to live by herself, yet she had no choice. She knew she could manage. She'd discussed this meeting with her doctor, who seemed to think it was too soon. It had only been a month since the accident, and Dana was too vulnerable, physically and emotionally. The physician had wanted to refer her to a grief counselor to deal with her losses before she tried to make important decisions about her life.

Dana liked Dr. Showalter, but ignored her. There was one reason she was here: MyKeri. As horrible as the Flemons family had been to her father, as responsible as they were for her family's misery and for her current situation, she still needed to see MyKeri. To meet the woman she had held in her heart since they had drooled over the same toys together as infants. No amount of raving about the horrible Flemons family by her father could erase the secret part of her that still loved MyKeri.

Dana had been ready to let her lawyer handle everything, as he had suggested. She had listlessly thumbed through the thick legal document he sent to her, shock and medication making concentration difficult. But then she had seen a list of who would be at the meeting. If Keri's presence had been held out as a carrot, she was the starving rabbit. It didn't even occur to her to ask why Keri would attend. But, deep down, she hoped Keri would be there because she, too, needed to see her childhood companion.

Pain shot through her leg when she came down on it instead of putting her weight on the crutches. Dana swore under her breath and stilled until she could breathe again. A thin sheen of sweat popped out on her forehead and upper lip. A few more steps and she'd be at the door, then inside, and there would be MyKeri. She had no idea what to expect. Rationally, she knew not to expect anything but an apology and money. Lots of money, according to her lawyer, Jacob Simon of Wells, Jenkins, and Wells.

With each step the accident came vividly to mind. They were returning from one of her soccer matches in San Jose, the first one her father had consented to attend. Someone driving a Flemons-owned vehicle had swerved or drifted—she had no memory of it—into their northbound lane, causing Sean Ryan to overcorrect and slam into a sound wall on Interstate 280. And that was that. All of her hard work to reach the pro level, gone. Along with her father.

Yet here she was, clinging to some idiotic notion that Keri Flemons would still be MyKeri. That she would fly into her arms, never to be separated again. She was embarrassed and ashamed of her own thoughts. *Let's just get this over with.*

The door swung open as she was about to reach for it, and a familiar face registered surprise, quickly screened with a smile.

"Shelley?" Dana vaguely remembered Mike Flemons's secretary from when she was a kid. She'd aged. Dana guessed twenty years would do that.

"Yes. Hello, Dana." Shelley's eyes were filled with compassion and concern.

She had always been nice to her, Dana recalled, and even now she was thoughtful. She showed Dana to a seat and helped her get settled, making sure she had a glass of water. Then, giving her a surreptitious pat on the back, she went to the opposite side of the long table and sat down next to Mike Flemons. The chair on the other side of him was empty.

Dana thought about the quickly concealed shock on Shelley's face. She had seen it before. A few teammates had visited in the hospital. The scrapes, cuts, and bruises that peppered her face were purple and yellow now, but the stitches weren't out in some places, and she'd lost weight. More importantly, she'd lost muscle mass, something that was very depressing to an athlete. She made it a point to avoid mirrors. The full-length cast on her leg was cumbersome, and she hurt everywhere most of the time. But her mind was numb and that was fine.

She focused on one thing: where was MyKeri? Aside from Shelley, the others present were men. She recognized Mike Flemons, but the rest just registered as expensive suits. Flemons looked exactly like she remembered him—not a tall man, but solidly built with thick white hair and dark blue eyes. She'd puzzled over that as a child and had once asked MyKeri why his hair was white when he didn't look like a granddad.

MyKeri had said, "Daddy says he has maturely white hair, because he's so smart."

She adored him, and Dana had always thought he was nice, but over time that had changed. Her father had spent twenty years giving her every reason to hate Mike Flemons. He was the man responsible for all that befell Sean Ryan—the loss of his wife, the countless job changes, his drinking. It was all Mike Flemons's fault. Had he treated her father fairly, their lives would have been very different, her childhood would not have been so hard.

Dana turned her head at the sound of a woman's voice coming from an office connected to the conference room. The speech pattern was rapid and excited, like that of a teenager telling a story about something that happened at school that day.

Mike Flemons cleared his throat and scowled. He rose from his chair and quickly walked to the door and opened it, saying a few short words Dana couldn't hear.

A female voice petulantly replied, "What? Okay! I'll call you back."

Then Flemons stood back to make way for his daughter as she strode into the room and plopped down in a vacant chair next to his. She had yet to acknowledge any of the people present.

Dana stared at her. She was a knockout. Blond hair fell in soft curls around her hunched shoulders. Dressed in tight jeans and cashmere sweater that clung in all the right places, she had a perfect, quite feminine, figure. When she finally looked up, the large blue eyes that matched her father's for color were cool and appraising, but nonetheless stunning, set in an oval face with a flawless complexion and full lips.

Keri's gaze finally settled on Dana and faltered for a moment, then dropped to her lap. She seemed to concentrate on something in her hands.

Hearing her name, Dana turned to Mike Flemons, who said, "I just wanted to express our condolences on your father's death. I know I speak for Keri, too, when I say how sad we are for these tragic circumstances."

"Thanks." It was all Dana could manage. Why was Keri even here? Was she really being used as bait? Suddenly Dana felt foolish and embarrassed.

She heard a theatrical sigh and caught Keri pointedly checking the time on her expensive-looking watch.

A distinguished-looking man with a neatly barbered beard and shining bald head started to talk. "We, meaning the Flemons family, will cover all of your medical expenses, of course. That includes rehabilitation fees and compensation for your salary as a member of the soccer team, plus an additional sum equal to five years of your salary."

Jacob Simon, her attorney, interrupted. "That sounds generous at first blush, but you know that women in pro soccer don't make much money. Ms. Ryan has always had to work another job, too. Then there's pain and suffering. My client lost her father as well as her career."

Dana was only vaguely aware of the dickering that continued around her. She couldn't take her eyes off MyKeri. Her thick blond hair was streaked with white by the sun and surrounded her face. Although Keri hadn't looked up again, Dana saw the same long eyelashes she remembered from childhood. Keri's nose was no longer an upturned child's nose. It was straight, perfectly setting off her full sensuous mouth. Dana wondered if she still had the tiny mole just below her left ear, the one that matched her mother's. The one she always called her "beauty mark." And when Keri unconsciously used her tongue to moisten her lips, Dana reacted as though she had been physically touched.

But Keri had not raised her head since she came into the room except to pointedly stare at her watch. From the subtle movements of her upper arms Dana guessed she was either playing a game on her phone or text messaging. Keri sighed again and gave an eye-roll in the direction of the attorneys, paying no attention to anyone else.

Dana wondered what the hell she was doing that was so important she could not even pretend an interest in the proceedings. Ignoring the pain in her legs, she struggled to sit up taller and asked, "What are you doing?"

Keri appeared oblivious to the question, as did everyone else.

Raising the volume, Dana demanded, "I said what are you doing?" Suddenly the room was silent.

Keri's head jerked up, her expression one of surprise. "Are you talking to me?"

Dana felt her face start to flush. "Yes. What are you doing?"

Keri squirmed slightly, then folded her arms defensively over her chest. "I had to send a message to…someone. I didn't want to interrupt the meeting."

Mike Flemons admonished, "Keri, this is important."

"Yes, well, my cell is so *slow* at sending text, that's why it seemed too long. Guess I'll have to get a new one. Sorry."

Dana didn't think she sounded one bit sorry.

The bald lawyer, the lead dog, smoothly intervened. "Anyway, all we need is your signature on these forms, releasing the Flemons family from any responsibility for further costs, beyond what we've discussed." He pushed the papers in her direction, but her attorney intercepted them.

As he looked them over, Dana couldn't take her eyes off Keri, who was glaring at her, lips set in a thin line, a mocking smile.

"Why are you here?" Dana asked her coldly.

Again, all murmuring ceased. She could almost feel the Flemons contingent closing ranks. Their silence was not about surprise or well-meaning politeness. It was a calculated condemnation of her temerity. Who was she to put Mike Flemons's daughter on the spot—to draw attention to the bad manners of his spoiled darling?

Dana's skin prickled and her belly churned. These people didn't give a damn about her. All they wanted was her silence. They wanted her to disappear. They were paid to make sure that nothing and no one dragged the Flemons name through the mud. If they couldn't do it legally, she wondered what other means they'd be willing to sink to. She had no illusions. Her father had told her exactly how ruthless this family and their hired guns could be.

Keri's eyes widened, and she glanced at her father and the lead attorney. "She doesn't know?"

"Know what?" Dana tried to control her growing frustration. "How many times do I have to ask the same question?"

The lead attorney's deep voice intoned, "Ms. Flemons was behind the wheel on the night of the accident. All of that was in the police report." He couldn't have been more solicitous. He deserved an acting award.

Turning on her own lawyer, Dana rasped, "Why didn't you tell me?"

Simon sputtered, "I thought someone in your fam…I mean…You were sent a copy of everything." Perhaps realizing her confusion, he amended, "I can't see why it's relevant. Do you two know each other?"

"We *used* to know each other." Keri's voice, cold and brittle, cut through the tension. "In fact, when we were *children* we promised to be best friends. But Ms. Ryan seems to have forgotten that."

Dana whirled around in her chair. Staring in disbelief, she roared, "*Forgot?*" She struggled to a standing position and leaned heavily on the conference table. "Just who the hell do you think you are? Have you ever worked for anything in your worthless, insignificant life? Have you ever *wanted* for anything?"

She was vaguely aware of some male voices trying to calm her down, but all she could see was resentment in Keri's eyes. Taunting her. Validating everything her father had said.

Dana stood to her full height, and although she teetered precariously, she silenced those around her. "I get it. You came here with your pack of wolves to take care of a little problem. Some nobody you used to know might cause the Flemons clan some bad publicity. Might want some of your precious money for having her life ruined. I guess you've had the final say, haven't you? Your family turns me out, you kill my father and maim me so that I'll never play professionally again! How inconvenient that I lived. Why don't you ask your daddy for his gun and shoot me—get it over with now."

Keri shrank back in the chair and Mike Flemons was instantly standing behind her, one hand protectively on his daughter's shoulder. "Dana, that's enough! Remember, your father had been drinking. We're being more than generous in giving you this settlement."

Dana couldn't believe what she was hearing. "Giving me? She killed my father! I don't even know where my own mother is! I have nothing! And you're *giving* me?"

Suddenly all the attorneys were on their feet arguing with each other and with Simon. But Dana could only see Keri.

Keri suddenly slammed her hand down on the table, and everyone shut up. She stood and leaned so that she and Dana were inches apart. Dana thought she saw remorse, but it was gone before it was there.

"She's right. I owe her an apology. I'm sorry for the accident, Ms. Ryan. It might have been avoided if your father's reflexes were better, but alcohol slows reflexes." Keri glanced sideways at her father. "Daddy, pay her triple what we offered. That ought to help ease the pain."

With a sweet smile at Dana she sat down, a smug look on her face.

Dana was speechless. Keri was buying her off. Wanting her to go away. She wondered how long she had been using money to take the place of a conscience.

After a moment, she quietly asked, "Where's the release?"

It was immediately in front of her, with pen. Knowing that if she sat down, she might not be able to get up again, Dana leaned awkwardly on the table as she read the agreement. After scratching out a passage or two, she initialed everything and signed on the line provided, then pushed the document across the table to Keri and her father.

"You'll cover my medical and rehab and pay my attorney," she told Mike Flemons, then cutting to Keri, added, "Other than that, you can take your money and shove it."

Grabbing her crutches, she struggled to get situated, aware of everyone's eyes on her. The pain was agonizing but she didn't care. Her attorney started to rise.

"No. Stay and make sure they agree to everything. I'll call a cab." Allowing herself one last look at Keri, she said bitterly, "All these years, I thought maybe you still…remembered…Silly me."

It took a moment to negotiate the door, but she was able to get into the hall without asking for help. She knew that any jostling of her precarious hold on her crutches would cause her to collapse. Panting from the effort of walking, sweat trickling down her back, she vowed to get to her apartment before breaking down.

With each painful step toward the end of the hallway, she felt she was being watched. Awkwardly, she turned and saw the blue eyes of her childhood friend, just before the conference room door closed.

❖

Keri returned to her seat at the conference table after watching the tall, thin woman hobble to the elevators. She'd had to fight the urge to help her. Weird.

Shaking a vague uneasiness from her mind, she picked up her cell and dialed her grad school friend Marci. She had cut off their earlier conversation because of her father and didn't even get to text message her more than a couple of times during the embarrassing meeting.

Turning her back on the men still discussing the settlement, she said, "Marci, hey. Sorry about that. When Daddy calls, I have to perform. Now, tell me more about Ms. Loser from Saturday night."

She guffawed into the phone as Marci continued her tale of dating woe. Marci was always good for a distraction. The truth was, Keri felt uncomfortable about the meeting and was still upset over the accident. She had been saddened to learn that someone had died that night. It had all happened so fast, she hadn't known what to say to the police so she'd told them she couldn't remember anything. Her recollection now was that she had drifted slightly into the lane to her right and quickly corrected back to her own lane. But the older model car next to her new BMW-5 series had suddenly swerved and crashed into the sound wall. It was horrible. She and her friends had pulled to a halt and run back to help. Someone called 911. Then the police and ambulances and fire trucks arrived. Soon after that, her father was there with their attorney.

Her friend Joey wouldn't let her get too close to the crashed car, saying it was leaking gas. She found out later it was really because the people inside were so messed up. A few days after that her father told her who had been in the car. Sean Ryan and his daughter Dana. *Scooter.* Talk about a voice from the past.

Dana's father had alcohol in his blood at the time of the accident, and Keri hated to admit it, but she felt better knowing that. She was sorry for Dana, but Daddy had promised he'd make sure she didn't have to worry about bills. Really, she thought it was handled. Then last week her father had told her the lawyers wanted her to apologize to Dana Ryan and get her to take a settlement and not sue the very deep family pockets. Dana had hired an attorney; didn't they all?

Keri supposed she could have refused, but Daddy was mad enough as it was. She'd totaled her other car two months before the accident and had gotten a reckless driving citation. The truth was that she'd had an argument with her date at a party the night of the accident and decided to leave early. Anyone who needed a ride had to leave with her. She was pissed and maybe driving too fast. Everyone was talking and laughing, and she'd turned up the car stereo to drown them out.

But the details didn't matter; the accident was not her fault. Sean Ryan was a drunk driver, and that was all the police had needed to know. She resented having to even be at the damned meeting, and she certainly wasn't going to play nice just to please her father. She knew he wanted her to talk to his minions like they mattered, but it was obvious they thought she was a spoiled brat so what was the point? They were paid a ton of money to do what they did.

She was still irritated that he'd made her end her call to Marci so abruptly just so she could sit there while the lawyers fought with each other. He always treated her like a child at times like this. She should have just refused, Keri thought, glancing disdainfully over her shoulder at the men. They were so full of themselves now, clapping each other on the shoulder and pouring drinks.

She supposed she'd agreed to show up partly to placate Daddy, and maybe because she had some curiosity about Dana Ryan. She'd also felt a little guilty, which was crazy, because it wasn't her fault Mr. Ryan had lost control of his car, and she resented having to behave like it was.

She'd been so peeved, she hadn't trusted herself to look up when she first came into the meeting room. She knew exactly what they were all thinking. She'd even heard one of those suits saying something about "making that brat come out of this squeaky clean." Jerk. She had tried to avoid looking at Dana as long as she could, and she'd had to force herself to not stare when she finally had to say something to her. Dana's short-cropped dark hair was patchy in places, and her face was a blotch of bruises, scrapes, and cuts. Keri knew she'd suffered a bad leg injury. She'd heard the rescue personnel almost had to amputate to get her out of the car.

Those green eyes were still the same, and Keri had caught herself falling into them momentarily, but she knew better than to be sucked in to some delusion of the past. This wasn't Scooter. This was some money-grubber, just like half of her girlfriends. Hell, just like *all* of her girlfriends. Besides, Scooter had waltzed out the door and never contacted her again. They were twenty-six years old now. No way was she being nice to this person; Keri didn't care how banged up she was.

She could not believe it when she was in the middle of text messaging Marci about how boring the meeting was and Dana started talking to her. The woman had deliberately made her feel uncomfortable. Pinned to her chair by those accusing jade eyes, Keri had no clue how to respond. What did Dana expect from her—wasn't an apology enough? If she'd known how bitter Dana was, she would have told the attorneys to go fuck themselves and not shown up for the meeting at all. Why should she be a punching bag for a woman who obviously needed professional help to deal with her issues?

Maybe she could have handled Dana's bizarre accusations more tactfully, but she wasn't used to being ambushed. All she'd done was react to being unfairly attacked. How was she supposed to know that nobody had told Dana who was driving the car? No one had prepared her for that little bombshell. Keri flinched all over again, thinking about the shouting and the mean things Dana said. It was not her fault things had gotten so ugly. She had no intention of backing down from a woman she didn't even know, except as a childhood playmate. If there was one thing she'd learned from her father, it was that the best defense is a good offense.

Anyway, she'd offered the pitiful woman more money than she would ever see in her life under most circumstances. Even now, she could not believe that Dana Ryan had thrown almost two million dollars back in her face. No one had ever looked at Keri with such undisguised contempt. And her eyes, the raw pain she'd seen in them, almost like Keri had hit her. For some reason that look was the worst part of a really unpleasant afternoon.

Keri had been unable to prevent herself from peeping out the door to watch Dana leave. It was almost as if she'd needed to see her face one more time so she could—what?—substitute that image with something more neutral? Dana must have sensed her presence because suddenly they were looking at each other and time stood still. For a crazy few seconds, Keri had wanted to go after her, then the elevator door opened. The moment disappeared and so did Dana. Just like she did twenty years ago.

"Keri? Are you still there?" Marci sounded put out.

"Yeah. Look, hold on a minute, would you." Keri tried to pay attention to her father's lead attorney. The guy seemed to be congratulating himself, as if the financially positive outcome was his doing.

"Well, that went better than we could have ever hoped for," he said, shaking hands with the other attorneys. He thanked her like it was an afterthought, adding, "Your offer certainly seemed to be the deciding factor, Ms. Flemons. Very intuitive of you to guess how she'd respond. You should study law."

It wasn't even worthy of a reply. Refusing to look at her father, Keri stood and grabbed her backpack, phone to her ear. Mumbling a goodbye to everyone, she escaped out the door.

"Sorry. I had to say good-bye to Daddy," she sighed as she walked down the hall.

"Did you win?" Marci asked.

"Yeah. It was no big deal. Let's go out tonight, okay? I could use some fresh blood."

"Want to go to that new place south of Market? I hear it's hot! I think it's called 'Crush.'"

"Yeah, let's go there. I feel like I've screwed every girl at Cal Berkeley. Maybe graduate school where I went to undergraduate was a bad idea…"

Marci made a rude comment, and Keri laughed harshly and stabbed the button for the elevator. She'd done her good deed for the day; now it was time to party. She was restless and she only knew one cure for it—she was going to fuck her brains out tonight.

As the elevator descended Keri leaned back and closed her eyes. *Fuck my brains out. Always works.* For some reason, it didn't seem appealing today. *Oh, well.* The door opened and she slung her backpack over her shoulder, making her way through the reception lobby.

CHAPTER TWO

Three years later Keri Flemons marched into the boardroom of the administrative offices of the San Francisco PickAxes. The conference table was full and the room stuffy. An uncomfortable silence fell over the people already seated. Keri recognized most of those present, having attended games and team functions with her father all of her life. Some were armchair athletes, several had played ball in college, most had a passion for the sport. One or two were what Keri had overheard some of the players refer to as "jock sniffers," men who tried to grab some reflected glory while hanging out with them. A few were only in it for the prestige.

Thomas Concannon was in several of the latter categories. He had no love for the art of the game, but definitely had a taste for power. Keri sat at one end of the table, Concannon at the other.

The other people gathered for the meeting were the minor partners in the team. "Minor" meaning they were very wealthy and were willing to put up millions to be a part of the organization. Keri was the majority owner, a relatively recent state of affairs and one she suspected was not entirely welcome in some quarters.

She got to the point. "I called this meeting because I have some questions. I want to know why so many of our front office staff are threatening to, or have, quit. I want to know why the stadium vendors, who have been here for years with no complaints, are considering suing this organization. I want to know why two of our best players are making noises in the media about wanting to be traded, at any cost. And I want to know why I had to read about all these problems in the newspaper instead of being kept informed through you, Thomas."

She had rehearsed this speech many times, but actually saying it made her perspire. She kept her eyes firmly locked on the operations manager, clinging to the lessons her father had taught her about confrontation.

Thomas Concannon shifted in his chair. He was short and stocky, with thick white hair and a beard that matched. The beard camouflaged a smallish chin, and his eyes were so tiny she had never been able to tell what color they actually were. Beady and murky blue, she finally decided.

She'd never understood why Daddy kept Concannon on his management team. She didn't like his secretive and conniving ways, and he was unpopular with the other staff. Her dad always said it was good to have a pit bull around, as long as he was on a short chain. He had told her Concannon kept him on his toes, and besides, he was good at the business side of the operation and had negotiated some amazing deals for the team.

Now the pit bull was in the boardroom, and he was patronizing her. "Problems are bound to crop up after a change in management, Keri. These people are just trying to see how much they can get away with. I'll have them whipped into shape or out of here in no time."

"And the reason you didn't forward the personal notes of condolence about my father's death to me?" One way or another, his answers to her questions would dictate her future. She knew the answers already, from people she and Daddy had trusted. But she wanted to see if Concannon would be honest with her.

He hesitated, probably trying to figure out who had told her about the mailbags in the storage room so he could fire them. "You wanted those? I just didn't want to bother you with thousands of cards in your...grief."

You sonofabitch...Strike one. She was silent for perhaps fifteen seconds while all eyes settled on her. She waited until there was some throat clearing and chair squeaking. *Daddy, wish me luck.*

"I appreciate your thoughtfulness, Thomas. But I still want to read them. Please have them delivered to my home. Today."

Concannon's smile was just short of menacing. Keri fought to maintain her steady gaze. "Of course, my dear." Placating the demanding heiress and managing to patronize her at the same time. *Strike two.*

"Now, Thomas, about my questions. I've been told and *have read in the newspapers* that over half of the front office personnel, most of whom have been with the team for an extended period, have resigned or are considering it. This seems an abnormally high number, under any circumstances. Do you have an explanation?"

All eyes shifted to Concannon, who sat in his chair, fingers steepled, eyeing her. "I presume most have personal reasons for resigning. Some had reached retirement age, some are, as I recall, going on to different positions. Several I wanted to replace with employees more loyal to… the owners' interests." He smiled coldly. "We must look out for the investors, Keri. This isn't a welfare system."

Chairs creaked as attention came back to her. Keri fought to not react to the obvious dig at her father. "And the lawsuits that we're being threatened with? Surely you don't think those will be good for investors."

"Totally without merit," Concannon replied dismissively. "Those vendors have been operating without increases in the percentage charged to them for years. Some didn't even have an updated contract. With a new stadium come new expenses and opportunities for revenue. I was only charging what other teams do. The vendors have been spoiled and have moaned about the increases."

Sitting forward, Keri said, "I've been told some of them have been threatened physically, their property has been vandalized, and they're frightened." She was aware that all the men in the room were now straining to hear, seemingly riveted by the exchange. She guessed no one ever challenged Thomas Concannon.

"I don't know anything about that," he said. "I'll investigate it."

Keri gave him a thin smile. She felt a measure of satisfaction seeing his jaw muscles working overtime.

"Now, the matter of Jerry Mercer and Sylvester Williams talking to the media about wanting to be traded. They are two valuable members of the team. Why are they unhappy?"

"It's a ploy for more money. I'm sure their agents staged it."

Strike three. "They still have two years to go on their contracts. Why go to the media instead of talking to you? Or have they been to you?"

She knew the answer to the question, at least AJ's version of the answer. The team photographer of many years, and confidante of most of the players, had been her primary contact. Shelley had also confirmed what he told her. It had taken several months of soul-searching before she'd finally decided to take over management of the team, but here she was. This meeting was the final straw.

"Their demands are unreasonable," Concannon said. "We have solid contracts. They can't break them."

"But they need to be heard. Morale is important to a team. To winning."

He gave her an indulgent smile. "Perhaps you would like to talk to them. I'm sure they would feel *listened* to if a woman was meeting with them. Then send them to me and I'll settle it."

Keri returned his smile and started gathering her tablet and papers. She replied, "I'll do that. Thanks for the suggestion, Thomas. We're already working together as a team. Oh, and I'll need the personnel files and org charts. I want to be prepared by Monday morning."

Concannon looked blank. "Monday morning?"

"Yes. I'll be taking over my father's office. And the managing partner duties. Thank you for filling in while I finished my coursework and worked through some…grief. But as majority owner, it is my duty and privilege to take back the reins."

The room was silent. Concannon stiffened and his face darkened.

Keri decided she'd made her point and now would be a good time to leave. Rising from her chair, she straightened to her full height of five foot seven and, with a bright smile, said, "I've asked Shelley to come back to the organization as my assistant. She's agreed. I'll see you Monday. Good day, gentlemen."

As she walked down the hall she heard loud male voices exploding behind her. *Let them rant. There's nothing they can do about it.* She let out the breath she had been holding and resisted the urge to run down the stairs and out of the building.

Her car was parked about fifteen feet from the elevator in the player and staff garage. Keri had grown up a football fan, coming to games with her father since she was a little girl. When he bought the team they would often discuss strategy and team business. Daddy liked to bounce ideas around with her. Even in college she would fly to training camp when she could. She'd meet the players and their families and attend owner meetings with her father. When AJ contacted her and told her the state of the team, the pieces just fell into place.

Her coursework at Cal was completed. She had only her dissertation to finish and she'd have a PhD in sociology. She could even use the experience of being the operating partner of the team as a topic for her dissertation if she chose. Her professors would love it. They were big football fans. She didn't much care; it was convenient.

Leaving the garage, she drove halfway across the parking lot and stopped, looking back at the new stadium that adjoined the PickAxes administrative building. Daddy would get a kick out of this. His daughter, the apple of his eye, taking over the team. She missed him so much. Her life had been crap since his death. Actually, her life had been crap for a while; she just hadn't realized it until he died.

She shook her head and turned to drive home, feeling like the hole in her heart was the size of the stadium.

The Flemonses' house in Presidio Heights was built shortly after the 1906 earthquake. While Pacific Heights, with its hills and huge mansions, garnered more press and tourists, this quiet area behind and above the former army presidio had its share of breathtaking views and elegant homes. For the most part, the homes were more down-to-earth and rugged, not having been intended for the *nouveau riche* of the gold rush days who wanted to compete with Nob Hill, but rather for officers and well-to-do residents of the city.

The Flemonses' home was large and spacious, having undergone an extensive remodel just ten years before. It was Carolyn Flemons's swan song to domesticity, the project she seemed determined to complete before walking away from her family. She oversaw the construction, retrofitting for the latest building codes to protect against earthquakes as was demanded by the city inspectors, and then made it large and lovely to accommodate Mike's new responsibilities as team principal owner.

They kept the high ceilings, as well as the handcrafted crown molding. Most of the original lighting fixtures were simply rewired and restored. Additional lighting was added, but it was built in to ceilings and walls and very subtle. A number of walls had been removed and the halls widened to get rid of the claustrophobic feel of the early twentieth-century structures. The bathrooms were large and spacious, and the kitchen opened to the family room. The entire house was done with minute attention to detail. Rich fabrics adorned the window coverings and blended with the warm reds, chocolates, and golds the rooms were painted in. A family friend had once remarked it was like being inside a tapestry woven in Europe in the last century.

Keri didn't know the value of the art, but several guests had been mightily impressed over the years. The furniture was functional and designed with comfort and style in mind. In the living room, the pieces had been made by hand to accommodate the larger-than-life athletes who so often were entertained at the house. The five fireplaces were kept clean and in working order, given the climate of San Francisco. Keri could remember stoking fires during every month of the year; when the fog rolled in, the sweaters came out and people did what they needed to do to ward off the chill.

She pulled through the gate and parked in the smallish garage, a converted carriage house, behind the main building. The fit was tight, but there was room for three vehicles. She entered through the back door of the house and threw her briefcase and purse on the pine bench just inside the door, absently resetting the alarm system. Next, she shed her coat and shoes, padding through the kitchen to the back stairs leading to the upper floors. She now slept in the master bedroom. After hanging her designer suit in the walk-in closet, she went to the bathroom to shower off the meeting she'd just come from. Donning her old Cal sweatshirt and a pair of soft worn jeans, she put on some warm socks and went downstairs to the family room to build a fire.

Keri had been home for only a few hours when the mailbags arrived. She recognized one of the men who lugged them in as Frank Owens, the equipment manager who'd been with the PickAxes since she was a kid.

"Bring them in here, please," she said, leading the way to the room where the fire was blazing.

Frank arranged the three bags in the corner farthest from the blazing fire, then asked, "Is it true you're gonna take back the team?"

Keri smiled warmly. "Yes, it is."

"Hah! Mr. Mike would be proud of you."

Touched, Keri stuck out her hand. "I know we've probably been introduced and I've seen you around the clubhouse for years, but I'm Keri."

Frank Owens immediately pulled off his team cap. The hand he held out was big and rough, testifying to years of hard work in the trenches. He wasn't tall but powerfully built, with little of the softness one might expect with age. Keri wondered if he had played football in his youth, but guessed that wasn't the case. His large brown eyes were friendly, and when his cap came off, a tuft of gray hair from a cowlick on the crown of his head stood at attention. He elbowed his workmate, a younger and larger version of himself, who had to be a relative. The young man sported a matching cowlick in his thick, light brown hair.

"Oh, um, I'm Frank Owens. This is Mike, my son. I named him after your dad." He studied his boots. "Mr. Mike was always good to me and my family. It seemed right to name my first son after him. Mike's going to college on a football scholarship next year. He's working with his old man to get some money for that. Right, Mikey?"

Mike grinned back at his father. To Keri, he said, "San Jose State. They won their division last year and this year looks even better. I have a chance to make the team as a freshman. We might even make a bowl game."

Frank looked at his son with obvious pride. "Anyway, I've been with the team since you were little. Your dad was always bringing the latest pictures, bragging how smart you was, what a good athlete. I guess I figured I already knew you. Nice to meet you."

Keri felt a lump form in her throat as she absorbed this man's genuine admiration for her father. "Well, thank you for bringing these over. I guess I've got my work cut out for me." She stuck her hands in the back pockets of her jeans and stared down at the mailbags. So many people had made the effort to reach out. "I should have taken them sooner. I just…couldn't." She fought to keep her voice even.

Frank awkwardly patted her back. "It's all right, ma'am. No one expected you to get right on it. Shelley and the front office girls was all set to start answering them for you, but Mr. Concannon put a stop to it. Said to throw 'em in the old equipment room. Said it was a waste of paid hours. They even told him they'd do it on their own time but—"

"He said that?"

Frank shot a worried look to his son.

She quickly added, "Don't worry. I won't say anything. I appreciate knowing. Maybe I should be doing this myself anyway."

"Mr. Concannon don't, uh, don't understand much about some things," he mumbled, half to himself.

The comment got Keri's attention. "Frank, tell me what you mean. I promise it will just be between the three of us."

He exchanged another look with his son, then said, "Mr. Concannon, he just don't get how a team works inside. It ain't just money. But he don't understand that part."

"Frank, would you mind telling me what you think makes a team work on the inside?" Seeing a look of doubt on his face, she explained, "You know I've taken on a big job. I'm going to need help. I'll be talking to a lot of people in the next few weeks. You've been here for a long time. You'll be helping me and the team. Please."

"Well, all I meant was that a team has to work together to get to win a Super Bowl," Frank said. "They can't be thinking about the money or the ads they'll be in or, um, all the pretty ladies who'll be running after them. And that means *all* the people with the team, you know, not just players. That's all I meant." He stuffed his cap back on his head.

"I see." Keri decided not to put her employee in the position of having to explain much more. It was her job to find out exactly how Thomas Concannon had or had not been running the team. "Thanks again for bringing the cards and letters. And thanks for sticking with the team like you have. I appreciate it."

"You're welcome, ma'am." Frank looked relieved.

Walking them to the front door, she said, "See you around the park, okay?" She added to Mike, "Good luck with your scholarship. I'm sure your dad will keep us up to date, right, Frank?"

Both men pumped her hand vigorously before taking their leave.

"Thomas, you prick," Keri murmured, hitting the code to open the driveway gates, then closing the door after them.

Meandering to the kitchen, Keri chose and opened a good bottle of Zinfandel and poured herself a glass, then continued to the family room where the bags were located. She sat down heavily on the well-used leather couch that always reminded her of her father and stared into the crackling fire.

How had it come to this? Her mother had left to "find" herself just after the house renovation was done. Keri was, what, eighteen? Carolyn Flemons had said she was tired of being a housewife and needed space. But Keri had heard their raised voices, bore witness to her mother's tears and her father slamming out of the house, not to return until the wee hours. Keri tried to ignore the silences between them. She remembered it was just before she left for college. Daddy never said a word, just worked harder. Eventually, Carolyn filed for divorce. She was currently living in Paris.

Keri refused to speak to her. Perhaps she felt guilty. While she and her mother had been close when she was little, they had drifted apart, and for a long time before Carolyn left, it had been Keri and Daddy. She couldn't have been much more than seven or eight when she started taking her father's side in everything. She refused to listen to her mother, although, in truth, her mother never tried to argue her side of it. Maybe because Keri never asked. The rift probably grew worse when her parents started arguing so much, and Keri emotionally divorced her mother when they finalized the end of their marriage.

Carolyn had offered to come back for the funeral, but Keri had been adamantly opposed to the idea. She wasn't going to allow her mother to just waltz back into her life now that Daddy was gone. She couldn't deal with that emotional bombshell and her father's death at the same time. It was too much.

Her mind strayed to that dreary overcast afternoon in January, over a year earlier, and to the cold, hard wooden pew in the front row of that cavernous church sanctuary. She had never felt so lost and alone. Her black suit hung loosely on her already slender frame and, for the first time in her life, she wore a hat with a veil. Tears seeped from her eyes, and she blew her nose now and then to try and stem the tide of emotions that flowed without ending.

She usually wore her hair around her shoulders, but that day it was up and away from her face. It was Shelley, not her mother, who had helped her get ready for the ordeal. Shelley had been there, in the background, as always. She was also there when Keri found out her father had died.

Staying at the family home on her Christmas break, she had just returned from having breakfast with an old high school friend. Daddy had left early in the morning, flying his Cessna 210 to Los Angeles to meet with an agent. He'd planned to have dinner with Keri when he returned that night.

Keri still couldn't think about it without her eyes starting to fill again. They had argued that morning, about Gloria. It was so clear in her mind. Word for word.

"I just don't think she's good for you. She wants to control every move you make."

"Daddy, it's not that bad. Besides, I've been with her longer than any of the others! Didn't you meet Moms when you were twenty-six?"

"Twenty, actually, but she wasn't fifteen years older and divorced. Gloria cares for no one but herself. You're rich, intelligent, and beautiful. She wants to possess you. I don't like it."

"Daddy, men do this all the time. Look at half of the owners. They dress their wives or mistresses up like trophies and parade them around."

Her father had sighed in exasperation. "Honey, you know I think that stuff is stupid. Besides, that's not who you are in any way. I want you to have someone—man or woman—who loves you for the sweet girl and beautiful person you are inside. That isn't Gloria and I think you know that." He stopped and looked at her for a minute. "Do you really love her?"

Keri avoided her father's eyes. "Well, we've been together for two years. That's a long time."

He laughed. "Long for *you*. But sweetie, that's an eyeblink."

"I'll have to decide what's best for me, Daddy. Maybe you just don't want me to be a lesbian."

He'd thrown up his hands in frustration. He went to get his overcoat and briefcase. Standing by the back door, he said, "You're the most stubborn daughter I have ever known. And just for the record? Your mother and I have suspected you were gay since you were little." He left to go to the carriage house.

She ran to the door, feeling like a selfish child, and called to him, "Hey, Daddy! Don't forget, I take after my old man. Besides, I'm the only daughter you have. Moms thought I was gay, too? How old was I?"

He grinned at her. "I think you were in the first grade. Thereabouts. You give it some thought. Now, I'm late, we'll talk about it tonight." He'd hesitated, then put his briefcase down and walked to her, putting his hands on her arms and addressing her directly. "I want you to love someone and have someone love you the way your mom and I loved each other. That's all, but it's everything."

His eyes usually looked sad when he spoke of his former wife. But that day, there was no sadness. He actually winked at her. She never found out what that was about.

She hugged him and said, "I love you, Daddy."

Thank God she had told him she loved him. It was the last time she ever saw him.

Five hours later the doorbell rang, and when she opened it, there were Shelley, AJ, and a stranger. Her eyes fell instantly on the stranger's clerical collar. She looked in Shelley's and AJ's eyes and knew. Her father was dead.

She vaguely remembered sagging and reaching for the door frame. AJ must have guided her to a chair. The rest was a whirlwind of activity around her. It was all surreal. Someone had called her mother, someone had notified the papers. Neighbors brought food over. Several friends heard about it on the news and called. Flowers started arriving. Shelley and her staff and AJ and Eva, his wife, were always there for her. She remembered Shelley drawing a bath for her and making sure she was soaking; it must have been late that night. When she was toweling off, she heard her crying. But as soon as she opened the door, Shelley was there, red eyes the only evidence of her own grief.

Losing Daddy felt like her life had been ripped apart cruelly and without reason. There was no time to say good-bye. Suddenly she was reeling, untethered. She had no relationship with her mother, but at least she was alive. Most of her identity was as Mike Flemons's daughter. Graduate school didn't matter, girlfriends didn't matter, money didn't matter, *nothing* mattered.

Her memories of the funeral ceremony were vague, to say the least. A lot of influential people said nice things. Big deal, they were looking for a photo opportunity.

Zander MacCauley, though, became a friend that day. The all-pro quarterback of the PickAxes was beautiful physically, to say the least. He had stayed at her side for most of the day, even stepping in to save her from having to ride in the limousine with Thomas Concannon. She had insisted on watching the cemetery workers lower the casket into the ground. It was a way for her to deal with the horrible finality of it all. Daddy wasn't coming back.

Zander had held an umbrella over them and waited patiently while the process was completed, then offered his arm and guided her back to the limousine. The ride to the family residence was silent. Keri was only vaguely aware of Zander's presence in the car as she looked out the window, studying the rain running in small rivers down the tinted glass.

Late that day, alone and sleepless in her bed, she'd taken an inventory. Her father gone before her twentieth-eighth birthday. A mother she'd been estranged from for ten years. No one to love. No one who loved her. A lot of money. She'd have traded every cent for another day with her parents together and…a real friend. She hadn't had a real friend since…Scooter. And look what she'd done with that when she had the chance to show real friendship. She'd treated her like dirt.

Coming out of her reverie in front of the fire, Keri got up and went to pour another glass of wine and call her favorite pizza joint to deliver. Ignoring the bags of mail for a little longer, she sat down to wait for her pizza to arrive.

Although she hadn't admitted it to her father that day, she had known she would be breaking up with Gloria. She didn't love her. And now, since Daddy died, she felt even more incapable of loving anyone. More than once lately she had found herself wondering what love was, and if she was just one of those people who would never know. But, somehow, she *did* know. Or at least she knew what it wasn't.

Without her permission, her thoughts drifted back to the funeral once more. The wake had been held at the Presidio Heights home. Shelley had supervised the cleanup, and she and Zander were the last to leave.

❖

Keri had watched out the window as their cars pulled away and the automatic gates closed at last. There were no more tears left. The past few days had taken them all away. Only sure that she was too dry and too warm for how she felt in her heart, she'd shed her black suit and put on jeans and a sweater, a heavy barn jacket and boots, and went to the garage for one of the cars.

It wouldn't be long before the gates would shut, but she needed one last moment, in private, with her father. Dusk was drawing close when she reached the cemetery. Climbing out of the car, she stared across the hill, taking in the rapidly deteriorating weather. The wind and the rain were strong, and she needed to feel it soak her hair and skin, so she set off without the umbrella she kept in her car.

As she neared the gravesite she saw a tall figure with short dark hair standing in the rain, head bowed, next to the mound of freshly turned earth. Dressed in dark clothing, a camera carelessly slung over a shoulder, the stranger seemed to sense her presence and turned to look in her direction. Large eyes made shadows by the poor light regarded her. Then the figure turned and slowly walked—no, limped away.

Keri stood there, unable to move. Whoever it was mirrored her sorrow. Inexplicably, she sensed that the stranger understood every facet of her grief, past and present, and even felt compassion for her. She wanted to follow, but could only manage to make it to the grave before sinking to her knees, grief-stricken, and lying down beside her fallen father.

❖

Keri resigned herself to a difficult evening. After eating some of the pizza she'd ordered, she opened the first mailbag and dumped the contents on the floor. For the next hour she read the notes, separating them into different stacks: fans, business, owners, personal acquaintances. She cried constantly.

When the phone rang, she ignored it, not in the mood to talk to the person she guessed was at the other end.

When the third call came, she sighed and picked it up, not wanting to deal with five or ten more of the same she knew she would receive. A familiar voice purred. "Darling. Why haven't you returned my calls?"

"Because there's nothing to say, Gloria."

The purring continued. "That's not what you said last week when we met for dinner. I thought you rather liked dessert."

Keri rubbed her forehead with her free hand. She had broken it off with Gloria shortly after her father's death and had been in a haze since then. Focusing on her studies had saved her from the crippling depression she felt looming constantly. She didn't date and had no desire for physical intimacy. She attended a few team functions with Zander and thought of him as a friend. He made no demands and they never talked about personal issues.

When Gloria called recently, Keri had suddenly longed for the touch of a woman and had finally agreed to dinner. The results were, in retrospect, disastrous.

"Look, we should never have…done that," she said. "Nothing has changed. We agreed before we even went out that night that it was a one-time deal."

The purring stopped. "We agreed to nothing. I want you back, Keri. You should be with me. You should sell that stupid team and be with me. You know it and so do I."

Keri waited for her ex's temper to cool, searching for the right words. Quietly, she said, "That's not going to happen, Gloria. It's over between us. Last week was just…what it was. I'm sorry if you thought otherwise."

Gloria abruptly said, "I'll call you next week."

The line went dead.

Keri put the receiver back on the base and stared into the fire, remembering Gloria's hot hands and caresses. Gloria had possessed her and driven her to a mindless climax within minutes, smiling smugly when Keri had recovered enough to get up and leave. In hindsight, she could see she'd let loneliness drive her into her ex's arms. As soon as it was over she'd regretted it.

"Why did I *do* that? Am I so pathetic that the promise of sex can make me jump through her hoop one more time? I'd be better off in a women's bar." She smiled at the irony of that. Gloria owned Crush, the best woman's bar in the city.

She took a sip of wine, her gaze on the fire.

"I suppose I should be grateful to her. It's good to know at least I'm not dead from the neck down anymore. Oh, Keri, use better judgment next time, 'kay?"

A loud snap of the dry wood burning in the fireplace brought her back to the stacks of envelopes spread before her. She decided to give it one more hour and then quit for the day. Most of the cards were, predictably, from fans. The notes were sweet and sincere. She kept sorting, quickly separating those written by someone's secretary and those that came from the heart. She realized she would need Shelley's help answering the first group. But the ones from the heart were hers.

After a few moments she came across a handwritten note, addressed to her personally, not just to "The Family of Mike Flemons." A sense of anticipation ran through her. She opened it and read, then reread the brief lines.

> *I'm so sorry about your father's death. It must be unbearable for you. I know he loved you dearly. Hope you didn't catch cold from the rain that evening.*

Keri was stunned. The mention of the rain…She searched around for the envelope. No return address. *Damn.* It was postmarked a few days after the funeral. The woman at Daddy's grave. It had to be.

She stared at the note, seeing that mysterious figure again. Tall. A limp. Keri couldn't be sure about the color of the stranger's eyes because the light was too poor. Age was impossible to judge, but Keri knew. The person at the graveside was exactly three days younger than she. It was Dana Ryan.

A headache started behind her eyes. She placed the note in the "personal stack," too tired to think anymore about the woman to whom she had felt such a strong connection as a child. Why on earth she had been so kind after what had happened two years before, Keri couldn't even begin to fathom, and she didn't want to start down that particular track again now. Sighing, she turned out the lights and armed the security system. Right now she had bigger fish to fry. She fell into an exhausted sleep.

CHAPTER THREE

K eri arrived in the office at six a.m., armed only with a jumbo latte and an overstuffed briefcase. By the time Shelley peered around her door at seven, she was busily plowing through the myriad of legal documents associated with the team.

Shelley Douglas was in her late fifties, plump and short, with hair that looked like a wig from the War of 1812, no chin, false teeth, and a mind like a steel trap. Busy every minute, she had been Mike Flemons's executive assistant and a family friend since Keri was two years old. She had tried to work with Concannon for about six months, but finally quit. When Keri contacted her and asked her to come back, she'd readily agreed.

They worked well together. Shelley had always been a rock. Stoic, never ruffled. Keri had been surprised to see her tears at the funeral. Since her father's death, Shelley had shown her a hundred kindnesses. Whether it was dropping off food for her occasionally or helping her deal with the mountains of paperwork associated with a sudden death of a wealthy man, she had always been there for her. She never judged, only gave opinions when asked.

Keri felt they had grown into friends as adults, and she was grateful for it. Her father's will had left Shelley taken care of; she didn't have to work. So when Shelley agreed to come back and help, Keri was enormously relieved.

Today, as in most for the past few weeks, they sorted and organized without much conversation for hours. Finally, Shelley suggested a cup of tea and a walk. Keri tossed her pen on the desk, stood, and stretched. The idea of some fresh air was immensely appealing.

As they strolled around the stadium, maintenance workers would often come up, introduce themselves, and welcome Keri, saying it was good to have a Flemons back with the team.

"Wow, this is a bit overwhelming," Keri said. "I'll never remember all of their names. Are they glad to see me because my dad was so good or because Concannon is so bad?"

Shelley grinned and looked out at the field. "Probably both. People loved and respected your dad. Thomas is so heavy-handed, he's alienated just about everyone in the organization that he controls."

Keri eyed her. "And those he doesn't control?"

"Well, Thomas sucks up to the owners," Shelley said after a moment. "He tells them what they want to hear to keep them on his side. That's where his efforts are focused. I think anyone else is expendable. He probably just doesn't care."

"Why do you think Dad kept him on? I asked him, and it seemed like he thought Thomas was really good with contracts. I think he just turned a blind eye to the rest."

Shelley said, "You know, there were a few years there, when your dad first bought the franchise, when he was scrambling for money and got taken by some pretty wily agents for contracts he shouldn't have signed. One of the other owners recommended Thomas. He was able to bring in a few investors when they were needed, and he had been around football contract negotiations long enough to really help out. Personally, I think the other owner wanted to get rid of him without having to sack him. And I think your dad was contemplating how to do that, too, just before he died."

Keri looked away from Shelley quickly, not wanting to lose control of her emotions in so public a place. Shelley had finally answered a question that had been bothering her for a long time. Daddy had never explained his plans like that, perhaps because he wanted to handle things his way. He'd known how Keri felt about Concannon. *Probably the last thing he needed was his spoiled daughter whining at him to dump the guy because she didn't like him. Oh, Daddy, I'm so sorry.*

But she was encouraged by one thing. If her father was considering getting rid of him, she was going to follow through. It gave her permission, in a way, to make it happen. She knew she had a lot to learn about running a football team, and she was determined to do it, but Thomas Concannon was not going to be her teacher.

"Your dad cared," Shelley said. "He was fair and just. That's why everyone is so happy to see you. They know how close you two were. I'm sure they're hoping some of him has rubbed off on you."

Smiling sadly, Keri said, "I hope so, too."

Shelley seemed to choose her words. "But, you know, I did always wonder why he didn't fire him. There were several opportunities. This behavior of Concannon's is not new. Your dad would be furious, have to go and soothe ruffled feathers, but he didn't say anything to Concannon. At least not that I know of. I never really understood why."

Keri turned as she heard her name called.

AJ Harden walked through one of the entrances to the stadium, waving. He was a tall, thin man with a talent for taking stunning sports photos.

Beaming, he strode up to them and said, "I came by see how Keri's first few weeks are going, and to check on how you two are working together. How are you, Shelley?"

"Good to see you, AJ," Shelley replied. "I think we're doing pretty well together. What do you think, Keri?"

Keri smiled at Shelley. "Better than I could have hoped, given what we're trying to do."

Shelley said, "How's your family, AJ? I owe Eva a call, so please tell her I'm being whipped back into shape but will talk to her soon. Do me a favor and take a walk with Keri. I've got to get back, but I think she still needs some fresh air. This morning has been enough to put anyone in a stupor."

AJ grinned. His black hair was shot with gray, but his ebony complexion was without wrinkles and his deep brown eyes danced with warmth. To Keri he said, "My pleasure. I have an idea to discuss anyway. Just in case you're feeling like you're taking too much time on your break." As Shelley started walking away he called after her, "I'll pass the message to Eva. You give our love to Hal, okay?"

"Will do." Shelley waved as she disappeared down the ramp to the exit door.

Keri smiled at her old friend. She had known AJ most of her life. He'd been the team photographer since her father took over the PickAxes. He was trusted by the players and had taken some award-winning photos over the years. He suffered from arthritis now, but that hadn't seemed to slow him down.

"What can I do for you, AJ?" she asked as they started walking. "Aren't the boys cooperating?"

"Well, I have a request. I need another photographer."

"Why? Are you okay?" Keri tried to sound casual but the fear was there. She couldn't take another part of her past leaving her.

AJ quickly reassured her. "I'm fine. I can do the job."

He took her elbow as they continued their stroll. She remembered the many walks they had when she was a child and smiled. She also remembered that there were usually three on those walks. Scooter was always there. She forced her thoughts away from those memories. Dana Ryan had weighed increasingly on her mind since she had found the note of condolence.

Keri had thought about her often in the past three years. She hadn't wanted to admit it then, but no one else had ever refused Flemons money. As bitter as the words were that they exchanged, at least Dana had been honest. She hadn't been willing to sell out her principles, however misguided.

That was another thing. Keri found herself replaying the accusations of that day regularly. They had each accused the other of abandoning the friendship. Keri hadn't seen or heard of Scooter until she found out who had been in the car that day. Yet Dana had acted like it was Keri who had abandoned them. Then, the graveside. She found herself suddenly desperate to know more, to talk to Dana Ryan. She just didn't know how.

"Here's what I'm thinking," AJ said. "I want to…um…I want to record this year in a special way. You are the first woman to come in and take such an important position in such a large franchise. Add to that your youth and beauty. This is a very macho world. You're going to run into obstacles that a man wouldn't. Period."

Keri nodded. "I know. I'm sure the cannons are being loaded as we speak."

"Well, what if we announce that we're going to make a book out of your first year? We say it's historic, and we hire another photographer to help because I can't be in two places at once. I'll take care of the team, and the other one takes care of the book and maybe helps out with some of the more athletic assignments, such as climbing up on the scaffolding to get those difficult shots during the games."

Folding her arms, Keri said, "I get it. If there's a photographer present at meetings, even those that are normally private, there's less chance of an ugly confrontation. Interesting. On the other hand, we might get some pretty good grandstanding too."

Keri wondered if AJ was trying to let her down easily about retiring from the team. If he brought in another photographer, then everyone could adjust to him and AJ could reduce his own involvement. Maybe he, too, didn't like the idea of a female operating partner. A part of her didn't believe it, but a part was suspicious. She hadn't realized how cynical she'd become. In her life, Daddy was the only person who was always honest with her. Wait, not the only one. Hadn't Dana Ryan told her what a spoiled bitch she was? Make that two.

AJ smiled. "That's why I think it should be still photography. They'll be more likely to allow a photographer if there's no sound involved. They can't be heard being jerks. And most have no appreciation for how one picture can tell the whole story. They think everything is video and sound bites. Plus, we'll have a witness. One on our side."

Keri hesitated, then asked, "You're on our side, aren't you? Why don't you come with me and hire someone else for the team shots?" She knew she might be shooting herself in the foot, letting a new photographer get close to the team, but she trusted AJ. Oh, make that three. Anyway, someone new was a crapshoot. He would take time and energy. She had enough on her plate as it was.

Shaking his head, AJ said, "Yes, I'm completely on our side, Keri. But to tell the truth, I think I'll be a bigger help keeping the players and coaches in line. They have their share of chauvinists."

The wisdom of his reasoning was solid, and Keri felt a weight lift from her shoulders for more than one reason. AJ was committed to the team and to her running it.

"Agreed, but I don't know, AJ. How will we know if we're hiring a photographer who supports us? Do you have someone in mind?"

AJ looked out at the scoreboard. "Well, I think we should advertise, then narrow it down to a short list. And I think you should consider a woman for the job."

Keri looked hard at him. "You want a woman to handle this? I thought you were talking about a guy who'll look like an enforcer with a camera around his neck."

AJ chuckled. "No. There are some excellent women photographers out there. Besides, do you want some guy following you around for a year? You might be able to find someone nice and quiet, someone whose work you like. At least interview some women, okay?"

"I don't know, AJ. Follow me around? All of a sudden this isn't feeling that good. I have my moods, you know."

"I know, honey." AJ's voice was gentle. "Just find someone you click with, maybe someone who knows what it's like to lose something precious, too. You'll be able to demand space when you need it."

Keri felt her eyes start to prick, and the familiar chime of her cell phone provided a welcome distraction. Pulling it from her pocket she saw Zander's number. "I've got to take this. Um, I'll have Shelley get the HR person to post an ad. Maybe we could go over the list of applicants together, to help narrow it down. Would that be okay?"

He saluted and grinned. Keri leaned up to kiss him on the cheek and flipped open her cell to take the call. They waved good-bye as she walked back to her office.

❖

Keri was addressing a new stack of contracts when she heard a soft knock on the door and Shelley popped her head in, then came in with a fresh pot of tea and several thick files.

"You know, you don't need to knock," Keri said, not for the first time.

"I know."

Keri smiled. Shelley had her standards, and Keri knew that knocking on the boss's door was one way she showed respect. She'd come to appreciate the gesture.

"So, what charming new project did you bring me?" she asked, taking the cup Shelley passed her. "Garbage contracts? I've never seen so many, right down to toilet paper. The paper in this office alone probably amounts to a small grove of trees." Under her breath she muttered, "Something else to feel guilty about."

The past month had gone by in a blur of meetings and research. She read contracts, personnel folders, tax returns, letters, government regulations. The meetings went on forever. She hadn't gotten home before ten or eleven every night since taking over. Weekends were just more of the same, only at home, dressed in her sweats in front of the fire in the family room. Now Shelley was bringing fresh problems for her to address. *Oh, Daddy, life was so much easier when you were here.*

She had a profound new respect for her father and how he had managed the team seemingly without effort. She also suspected that Thomas Concannon was trying to bury her under a mountain of paperwork to get her to quit. That thought kept her going on those lonely nights when all she had for company was another vendor contract.

Grinning, Shelley plopped two thick files in front of her new boss. She had developed a sense of admiration for this beautiful young woman. Keri hadn't complained, had come in prepared every day, asked intelligent questions, and was always patient and understanding with the employees. A far cry from the Keri Flemons before Mike Flemons's death.

She was frustrating the hell out of Concannon, too. It was all good. Shelley worried about her, though. The circles under her eyes were telling. When Keri didn't know she was being observed, Shelley often caught a sad expression on her face. She wondered how Keri would handle this next situation.

"Applicants for the photographer position and sample portfolio photos," she said. "Some are pretty impressive. I set it up for you the way AJ requested. The photos are in the first file, no names—they're numbered on the back and each number relates to a resume. And I shuffled the photos so you won't be looking at consecutive ones from the same person."

Absently staring out the window, Keri replied, "Good idea. That way I can narrow it down to the work I like the most, then see if one photographer stands out. If we're going to do this it needs to be fast. I'm tired of getting hammered in every board and vendor meeting. Maybe if it's being documented, they'll think twice about some of their language, at least. I mean, I swear, but not every other word. I think some of them do it just to get a rise out of me."

Shelley laughed. "I know what you mean."

"A few of those guys use the f-word as a noun, verb, adjective, adverb, and conjunction, all in the same sentence."

Tapping the files, Shelley said, "Get to work. The sooner we have someone, the better."

Keri grinned and sat up straighter. "Yes, ma'am! Yeah. A witness. That's what we need."

As Shelley closed the door, Keri felt a little bit of hope. She had just realized that she trusted Shelley. That made four people she could count on to be honest with her. And two of them she actually got to work with.

Hours later found her again staring out the window. She'd been through the photo file many times. Still, one set kept drawing her in. She could easily pick out each photo taken by number nine. The way the photographer captured emotion was uncanny. Even the ones of athletes at full speed. But the shots of their faces during quiet moments, those were what sold her. Number nine was number one on her list until she pulled the resume. Reading the name at the top of the page sent her mind careening in a million directions at once. Eventually, she reached for the phone and dialed.

"AJ? Hi, it's Keri. Well, I've made my choice about the photographer, and it's a woman. But I think I'm going to need your help convincing her. It…well, it's Dana Ryan."

AJ said, "I see." A pause. "Yes, I knew she'd applied. Why do you think she'll need convincing?"

Letting out a sigh, Keri said, "Come on, AJ. She hates me. She probably has no idea I'm managing the team. It's not like we've made any formal announcements."

She'd wanted to delay that announcement until she had dealt with the internal politics behind closed doors. The last thing she needed was an exhibition of public backstabbing that would make fans, agents, and team members nervous.

"Maybe you should choose someone else," AJ suggested blandly.

Like she hadn't tried. "I don't want to hire any of the others. Hers were the only photographs that worked. She's exactly what we're looking for."

"What would you like me to do?"

"Talk to her. See if she's at least willing to meet with me."

If there was one thing Keri could be certain of, it was that Dana Ryan would walk if she was ambushed. Given the PickAxes' connection with the Flemons family, she couldn't fathom why Dana had applied for the job. No doubt she'd assumed that with Mike Flemons dead, the team was under Concannon's management, just as the newspapers had implied. Keri dug out the ad that personnel had posted. It didn't mention her name at all. It was a basic ad for a sports photographer. They hadn't told personnel any more than that on purpose. The new appointment was supposed to be a surprise Keri could present at the next board meeting, along with some of her new plans for the team. Well, surprise!

She slumped back in her chair, suddenly bone tired. She'd been working eighteen-hour days for weeks, dealing with one crisis after another. She was looking forward to at least having someone else around for conversation, maybe even having a friend. Now, suddenly her regrets about Dana Ryan were rearing their ugly heads again. Would it never end? Her throat felt constricted and she resisted the tears that were threatening.

She realized AJ had said something about speaking to Dana, but she was only half listening. Already, she was preoccupied with the problem of how she would convince Dana to work for her. Obviously throwing money at her one-time friend was not going to cut it. Dana Ryan had to be one of the few people on earth whose sense of honor outweighed financial considerations. If she agreed to take the job it would only be because she was truly interested in it. Keri wanted that kind of commitment. She wanted the kind of woman who would see the job as an artistic challenge and deliver her very best work. This would have to be her approach with Dana. She would have to sell the job as the career-making assignment it could be. Somehow she would have to draw Dana into her vision.

"Do whatever you need to, AJ," she said, suddenly more confident. "I just want her to come to the interview with an open mind."

AJ said, "Okay. I'll let you know how it goes."

Keri thanked him, sent her love to his wife, and hung up. She sat for a few minutes, watching the rain that had started to fall, her feelings a tangle of disquiet and anticipation. *Well, Keri, be careful what you wish for. You might just get it.* Hadn't Daddy always said that? Now she knew what he meant.

Addressing the favorite photograph she kept behind her desk, she said, "Daddy, I'm stumped. I've thought about apologizing to her, telling her what an ass I was about her father and the accident. I know what it's like to lose a father now. I didn't like Mr. Ryan because he took her away from me, but that doesn't mean she didn't love him. And you know what? Scooter was at your graveside. Someone got me home that night. It had to be her."

Keri doubted she would have been that forgiving herself, at least not then. Perhaps not ever. Maybe she should just forget about interviewing her. But she knew she wouldn't. She knew, even if Dana

Ryan threw a camera at her or, worse, refused the interview, she was going to try. Try to…she didn't know what. She slowly got up, turned off her desk lamp, and made her way to her car and home.

CHAPTER FOUR

Dana switched the red light on and the overhead light off, then placed the paper in the solution and started the timer. Leaning back and folding her arms in front of her, she watched the photo come to life.

"Photography, the old-fashioned way. Ya gotta love it."

Her darkroom, set up for black and white and color, was her refuge. She had all of the digital cameras and paraphernalia she needed, but this was where her art took form. Hand developing from 35 mm film, using her trusty old Nikon cameras and lenses.

She could capture the images, and most of the time that's what she did. She was beginning to make a living doing it, too. In here, she could take any photograph and make it better. One of her favorite memories was of Sarah, an old friend and teammate, bringing a disposable camera shot of her and her boyfriend and begging her to do something with it. The picture had captured the two of them well, but the cheap development process had made the image fuzzy and half was in shadow.

Dana had cut, cropped, changed the exposure, and brought out the best colors, then blew up the final product as a gift for her friend's engagement party. It was Sarah's favorite present, bringing tears to her eyes.

Yeah, this was definitely where she was happiest.

After watching the current picture appear in the fluid, she picked it up with wooden tongs and hung it to dry. She made some further adjustments to the exposure and put another piece of paper in to develop. But before the image could emerge, the front door intercom buzzed. Dana quickly set the timer, pulled off her protective gloves, and exited behind a blackout curtain in her tiny darkroom. She wasn't expecting anyone and was tempted not to answer. But she would feel bad if it was an emergency, so she hastened through her flat, intending to send whoever it was on their way and be back in time to rescue the photo.

Reaching the front door, she pressed the intercom button. "Who is it?"

A male cleared his throat and said, "Dana? It's AJ Harden. Can I come in?"

Dana stared at the speaker. "AJ? Oh, sure! Come on up." She buzzed him in and opened the door, only slightly aware of the old jeans and ratty sweater she was wearing. She had seen AJ from a distance as she watched Mike Flemons's funeral, but she hadn't talked to him since six months after the accident that killed her own father.

There was only one reason he could be here—her application for the PickAxes' team photographer position. Her first thought was that he wanted to let her down easy. She'd only been a professional for two years, and most of her experience was with women in sports. But she'd won a few small awards, and *Sports Illustrated* had published an article for which she'd done the photography.

When she'd seen the job advertised in a sports photography magazine, her instinct was to tear out the page and burn it. Lousy luck that the perfect opportunity to take her career to the next level was with the PickAxes. The Flemons family yet again. But as she thought about it, she began to wonder what was stopping her from applying. Why should she allow that family to impede her career choices? So what if they owned the team; she'd probably never have to even see Keri Flemons.

Besides, it was AJ who'd first suggested that she go into sports photography and loaned her enough money to get the initial equipment. She'd been an amateur photographer for years, and she was able to use her pro soccer connections to get a few meager assignments. One thing led to another, and she now had a small foothold she could build on. This was the perfect opportunity.

And here was AJ, knocking at her door. Maybe he thought she was ready. Maybe that was it.

He was so happy and chatty as she let him in that she almost laughed. He actually seemed nervous, like *she* was interviewing *him*.

She managed to exchange a few meaningless comments before curiosity got the better of her.

"AJ? Is this about my application?"

He grinned and said, "Yes, yes it is. By the way, your portfolio is very impressive. I'm proud of how well you're doing."

Dana was thrilled at the compliment. AJ Harden was one of the best sports photographers in the country, and any words of encouragement from him carried a lot of weight.

AJ studied his large hands. "This job is a special project, Dana. It will last for about a year. It's going to be a book. About the new managing partner's first year in the business of running a football team."

Dana's stomach started to churn and she wasn't sure why. She was a little disappointed, because she'd hoped to study with AJ. This would be much more tame, but probably interesting. "Oh. Well, are you still considering me?"

He smiled again. "Yes. Of all of the applicants, your work made you the best qualified."

She was pleased and relieved at the same time. "Thanks! A year's assignment would be good. Get some bills paid, learn the team from a different perspective. Are you saying I'm hired?"

"That depends. I think you should talk with the managing partner and then decide."

Tentatively, Dana asked, "Thomas Concannon? To be honest I haven't heard great things about him, but I'm flexible. As long as he doesn't want a date." The joke seemed to fall flat. "Sorry, I didn't mean to offend. I'm sure he's a nice guy."

AJ seemed slightly awkward. "The new managing partner of the San Francisco PickAxes is Keri Flemons. That would be who you need to interview with and who you would be working with for the next year."

Dana sat motionless. She couldn't make sense of what AJ was saying. Keri Flemons wanted her to work with her for a year. Impossible. "You're joking."

His warm brown eyes held hers. "No. She told me that your photographs were the only ones that would do. She asked me to talk to you to make sure you knew the interview would be with her. She didn't want to blindside you."

Suddenly Dana was on her feet, pacing. Her leg felt like it was on fire as the memories of that day in the attorney's office came flooding back. "Blindside me? Like she's done all my life? *She's* being thoughtful?"

"It's not like that. She's changed."

Dana growled, "*Changed?* From a snotty bitch to a more powerful bitch? Does she want to start me in the job and then fire me? That might be good for a few laughs." Her pacing picked up speed. "You know I can't do this and you know why. I shouldn't have applied for the job."

AJ was quiet, then asked, "Why *did* you apply, Dana?"

Dana stopped pacing. "I thought I'd be working with you. I didn't know Keri was the managing partner. I wanted to learn from the master, about *sports* photography, not taking glamour shots of the beautiful owner of the team who thought she'd come in and make a splash by dabbling at running it. And a book to immortalize her efforts. Perfect!" She raised her voice. "That's not what I do! She can't make me her little lapdog! No!"

"Dana, sit down and listen to me for a minute!"

It was an order and Dana sat. Her face felt red and she was sweating, her heart hammering in her chest.

AJ spoke very calmly. "Look, the book was my suggestion. And, I regret to say, so was the idea of her running the team."

Dana snorted. "Yeah, I'll bet you regret having to work for such a self-centered snot." The look he gave her told her she'd gone too far. She sniffed and said, "Go on."

Sighing, he continued. "Look, this is all in confidence. Do I need to make you sign a confidentiality agreement? Because I brought one, and you would have to sign one anyway to work on this project."

"No, of course not," she said quickly, embarrassed that she'd been so outspoken in her dislike. "I mean, I'll sign the agreement, but you know I'll hold anything you say now in confidence."

That seemed good enough for him. "You may or may not have heard rumors about Thomas Concannon and the way he's been running the team. He's been very high-handed, fired longtime employees, tried to force others to quit, messed with their pensions. He's also trying to force longtime vendors out of the stadium so he can replace them with people handpicked by him. Anyway, I finally decided to tell Keri about it. That was my mistake."

He shook his head and leaned closer, his eyes reflecting his concern. "I told her about the vendors and staff, but I think what really tipped it over the edge was something Concannon did with the letters of condolence about Mike's death. He had them shoved in bags in the back of the equipment room. She was livid when I told her. Two weeks later she started talking about taking over the team, like her dad had done. A week after that she told the board."

Dana was amazed that Keri would take on that large a responsibility. "Why didn't she just use her controlling percentage of the team to hire someone else and get rid of him?"

"I'll be damned if I know." AJ raised his hands and let them drop in frustration. "But she hired Shelley back, and it looks like she's been working day and night trying to get up to speed. And, Dana, I'll tell you something else. Shelley told me on the phone last night that she hasn't complained once and she's avoided publicity. I came up with the idea for the book as a measure of protection for her."

Dana focused anew on AJ. "Why would she need protection? Is she being threatened?"

"Not overtly. But you know this business. It's a good ol' boys' club. They're doing everything they can to test her. Most of it is just bullshit, but Concannon is fuming. Power is quite an aphrodisiac and he has a taste for it. He's not going to give it up easily."

"Are you trying to make me feel sorry for her?" Dana almost laughed at the mere idea.

"No. Just filling you in on the politics so you can see why you'll play a key role. Keri needs someone on her side to at least make them think about some of the things they say. And to head off some of the uglier confrontations, or at least record them on film. People tend to behave better when there's a camera in the vicinity."

"AJ, you said 'someone on her side.' I hardly think I qualify for that role. I hate her."

"Do you?"

Unable to meet his eyes, Dana looked at the floor and said, "You know what happened."

"I know some of what happened. But here's what I know for sure. That's in the past, and Keri Flemons wants to interview you for a job that is all about the future. Will you go in and at least talk to her?"

"I don't know, AJ. This seems crazy."

"Maybe it's time you cleared the air. If nothing else, you can tell her to take her request for help somewhere else. Maybe that will make you feel better."

Dana knew it would definitely not make her feel better, and that puzzled her. For all the times when she'd thought about really telling off Keri Flemons, now, for some reason, she felt protective of her. She studied AJ for a long moment. "Old man, you sure know all the buttons to push."

Her wary indecision must have been evident on her face, because AJ leaned forward and took her hand. "Just do the interview. Maybe you'll both decide this is a bad idea."

"Entirely possible." Dana still couldn't imagine what made Keri think they could be in the same room for an interview, let alone work together. There had to be some other agenda. She almost wanted to meet with her just to find out what it was.

AJ seemed to read her lapse into silence as a good sign. "Can you be there Wednesday at two in the afternoon?"

"Okay. But I don't know why I'm doing this."

Her companion grinned widely. "Because you can't resist a challenge."

When Dana shrugged distractedly, he got up, gave her a warm hug, and was out the door within thirty seconds.

To the closed door, she mumbled, "Wait. I hate her." But she didn't go after him to turn the opportunity down flat. Instead, she wandered back in the direction of her darkroom.

The bell signaling the end of the development process for her photo had long since sounded. Dana pulled it out of the solution and inspected the ruined picture. Absently, she tossed it in the trash and closed the darkroom down.

Her stomach was growling so she went in search of a can of soup to open. All she found in her near-empty cupboard were some old cans of green beans and a jar of hot cocktail sauce. The refrigerator yielded some film packets and moldy cheese and several bottles of beer. She gave up and rambled through her apartment, looking around for the last place she had left her slippers.

Like many rentals in San Francisco, hers was the first floor of an old Victorian. Her landlord and friend, Jim Miller, occupied the top floor of the three-story building and had lovingly restored the outside elegance and remodeled the inside to the current century. He even kept the rent reasonable for her. The apartment on the second floor was now empty, the renter having transferred to the East Coast.

Instead of the small narrow rooms with high ceilings that marked the architecture of the Victorian era, Dana's living room was large and light and led into a compact but well-appointed kitchen. There were two bedrooms, a half bath for guests, and a large full master bathroom with a claw-foot tub and separate glass-enclosed shower. Central heating was a blessing and a rarity in this town that was rarely too hot, but sometimes bone-chillingly cold with fog and rain. The smaller bedroom served as her office, complete with another bathroom that had become her darkroom.

She wandered back to the bedroom in search of the missing slippers. There she changed out of her jeans and sweater into some thick sweats. The surroundings were Spartan, to say the least. Except for a decent living room sofa, a comfortable chair, and the expensive bed her injuries had forced upon her, the rest was stuff she'd assembled herself. Finally looking under the bed, she groaned as her leg made itself known. But at least she had her fuzzies. She chose to ignore the dust motes.

She limped slightly as she went to the tub and started the water. After pouring half of the container of mustard salts into the steaming bath, she watched as the water turned golden. Usually this treatment helped ease the aches and pains that had been her constant companions since the accident.

"Now, a cup of hot tea." She was unconsciously assembling her thinking package: a hot mustard bath and a cup of tea. She returned to the kitchen and put on water to boil, selecting a ginger tea from the several boxes she had. A few minutes later, steaming cup of tea in hand, she remembered the running bath water and quickly headed for the bathroom. The phone started ringing.

Hoping that it might be Shelley rescheduling or canceling her meeting with Keri, she picked up.

A deep masculine voice said, "Hey, Dana, what are you up to?"

Laughing, Dana said, "I'm about to let my tub overflow all over your beautiful Italian tile floors, Jimmy. Hold on a sec."

She hurried toward the bathroom as she heard her landlord squawking through the receiver. Cranking the faucets closed, she looked longingly at the steaming tub and growled into the phone, "This had better be good. I really need this bath."

Not at all intimidated, Jimmy said, "Why did you answer? Expecting a hot date to call?" Jimmy could be such a bitch.

"No, my dear. I have a job interview Wednesday and thought maybe the call was about that. I do so want to pay my rent this month, you know?"

"Ohh. Nice. A job interview? As in a nine-to-fiver? You? What about *Sports Illustrated*?"

"That's still pending. Who knows when they'll get around to it?"

"Yeah, but the piece you did on women in soccer was well received, by both the women and the men who like to ogle the women."

Dana grinned. "Everyone did seem to enjoy it."

Chuckling, Jimmy said, "You walked a pretty fine line there. The pictures managed to make them look sexy *and* athletic. The girls must have loved it. And loved you for doing it, eh, Dana?" The unmistakable subtext in his voice made Dana roll her eyes.

"Now, Jimmy. You know I never kiss and tell. Naughty boy. Hey, why did you call? I really want to get in the tub before the water is tepid."

Jimmy's voice went from teasing to serious. "What's up? You sound a million miles away."

Dana smiled at the concern in her friend's voice. "I just need some time to think."

"How about you think for an hour and then I come down with pizza and wine?"

"Make it an hour and a half and you have a deal."

"Great! I need a favor and I want to soften you up."

Dana groaned. "You want me to be your date *again*? Your firm is going to think we're serious!"

Jim was an incredibly handsome and successful attorney. He stood about six three, lean and muscular from hours at the gym, and his blond hair and blue eyes had women *and* men swooning. Around her and his friends he really let his feminine side show, but at his firm, he was positively macho. He wasn't out at work and had no plans to be.

Dana went with him to formal parties and company affairs as his date. She didn't mind, and she knew they looked good together. At five ten with almost black hair and a creamy complexion, not to mention her large, emerald green eyes, she was the perfect foil for him. Black Irish and Scandinavian genes made for a handsome couple. He even bought her new clothes when the occasion called for it, since she had neither the money nor the inclination to add to her wardrobe.

Jim said, "Yes, I do and no, they won't. It's a charity thingy, the usual. But some important clients will be there, and we're expected to make a showing. Can you be straight for a few hours with me?"

Dana frowned into the receiver. "Jimmy, you know I hate that shit. I get stuck with all the wives and they can be sooo boring. And the ones that aren't…well, hell, they're *straight*." She knew she was yanking his chain but it was fun to tease him.

"I know, I know. But I'll bring a really good bottle of wine tonight. See you soon. Go think!"

Placing the phone and cup on the stand next to the tub, Dana shed her clothes and sank into the still-hot water with a groan of relief. Her thoughts immediately returned to AJ and their conversation. She could call the PickAxes' office in the morning and cancel the interview. She didn't owe Keri Flemons anything. And she didn't *want* to owe her anything, either.

She'd never seen a bill for her hospitalization or rehabilitation. Both had been long and arduous. She'd also never seen a bill from her attorney or the one she'd been expecting for her father's funeral. Other than that, the Flemons family had faded into her past until AJ had contacted her with his idea of pursuing sports photography. Every dollar of the money he'd loaned her she paid back as soon as possible, afraid somehow the money came from Mike Flemons. She went without everything but food and rent to clear the debt, and sometimes food was scarce.

Now, the possibility that she might be risking dependence on the Flemonses yet again rankled.

"Get over it, Ryan. You can quit any time you want. She can't make you do anything you don't want to do. As long as you make it clear to her from the beginning that you're in it strictly for the money. And it will look good on your resume. You don't give a shit what happens to her or the damned team."

Feeling better, she ran some additional hot water in the tub and grabbed some soap. She could go to the interview and find out what the bitch was offering, then decide what she wanted to do. She'd keep it strictly business. Any offer of friendship would be easy to deflect.

Unfortunately for her resolve, she kept seeing Keri the day of her father's funeral, collapsing on his grave in the fog and rain. She had gone to her, carried her sobbing to her car, and driven her home. Keri barely seemed to know she was there. She mumbled the code for the gates, and Dana had walked her to the front door, making sure she was safely inside before she left. The next day, she'd called the PickAxes' office and left a message that a Flemons vehicle needed to be collected from the cemetery.

AJ's comment about the notes of condolence had just confirmed again how devastating Mike Flemons's death had been for Keri. And, somehow, it had touched her heart. No matter what, Keri had always touched her heart.

Shaking herself, she muttered, "Doesn't matter. It's just business." She'd go and check it out, and she would turn it down if she even sniffed the manipulation she suspected was just under the surface.

❖

Keri checked her watch again, waiting for Marci to show up. It had been months since she'd seen her, and they had agreed to meet at one of their favorite haunts, The Buttery Nipple. Many a night in graduate school Keri had picked up a woman there and gone home with her for sex. Sometimes she'd even return to the bar and pick up a second liaison.

Marci was her customary half hour late, and they hugged their hellos.

"Hey, you look tired, girlfriend. Too many women, too little time?" Marci gave the familiar wink that used to amuse Keri, but this time only served to annoy her.

"Too many late nights reviewing contracts and putting out personnel fires."

Marci smirked. "I can't believe my friend, Keri Flemons, is harnessed up to the working world. After all the years we spent avoiding Droidland, here you are. Can't you just pay someone else to do all this shit? You do own the team."

Keri shook her head. She didn't want to get into it with Marci. It had been a while since she'd had any fun; in truth she hadn't had sex since that wretched encounter with Gloria. And sex was always her antidote for stress.

"Maybe I will hire someone eventually, but for now I'm stuck with doing it myself." Seeing the look of disbelief on Marci's face, she added, "I have to know how bad the damage is before I can bring someone in. It's a huge investment."

Marci folded her arms and cocked a knowing eye at her.

Feeling defensive, Keri said, "What?"

"Oh, you are a sly one. Of course, the bigger the executive, the more women flock to your doorstep. I'm on to you, my friend. Hell, I'm even jealous."

Keri tried to keep the irritation out of her voice. "Jealous of eighteen-hour days?"

With a smug chuckle, Marci said, "For what, six months? Then you can hire someone and take all the credit. Poof! Instant sports genius! You always were attracted to sports jocks."

Marci continued to tell Keri what Keri was thinking as Keri stared at her. There was no way she'd believe the real reasons Keri had for taking over the team. In fact, maybe Keri was just kidding herself. Maybe she'd tire of this as she tired of everything, eventually. Maybe she would suddenly wake up bored and go on to other, more pleasurable, ways to spend her time. Marci seemed so sure.

Marci never tired of playing. A trust-fund baby and proud of it, she prided herself on never working a day in her life. She played tennis, skied, sailed, and fucked with equal enthusiasm. She kept a personal trainer and wasn't shy about the occasional need for some plastic surgery to enhance her California Girl appearance. In fact, she still sounded like they both did in high school and college. When they ended every sentence like a question? And talked so fast no one could understand them?

And she seemed sure that Keri was a kindred spirit. Maybe she was.

When Marci elbowed her, head tilted toward the door, Keri turned to welcome anything that could possibly shut her companion up. She didn't have to look far.

A vaguely familiar and strikingly attractive blonde sidled up and planted a sloppy kiss on Keri's lips. "Hi, sugar! Long time no… anything. Where have you been?"

Keri resisted the urge to wipe her mouth with her hand and smiled at the woman. "Oh, I've been out of town. Working. How have you been, um…"

"Charlotte. That's okay. I can't remember your name, either. But I do remember some other very important things about you. Much more important than your name. You busy later?"

Keri turned to an ogling Marci, raised an eyebrow, then smiled at Charlotte again. "Why, no, I'm not. What's wrong with right now? Come on, let's go."

The blonde made a noise that sounded like excited agreement and followed Keri's lead through the crowded bar and out to the back alley. Without preamble Keri pinned her to the wall and set about devouring her with her mouth and hands. Within minutes she had brought her to a noisy climax that had them both leaning against the filthy brick wall, panting.

The blonde caught her breath and said, "Oh, sugar, you're just as good as I remember. Now it's my turn. You want it here or at my place? I've got some great toys back there."

Oh, that Charlotte. Keri straightened herself up and leaned in to kiss the woman on the cheek. "No, thanks, I have to be up early. But, hey, can I have a rain check?"

The blonde smiled and closed her eyes halfway. "Anytime, sugar, anytime."

They parted in the alley and Keri made her way to her car, carefully avoiding the front of the bar or anyone that resembled Marci.

Driving home she said to herself, "Ker, you are definitely getting old. And you aren't even thirty yet."

She didn't want to have to explain her sudden departure to Marci. The thought of the coarse remarks her friend was sure to make turned her off. Marci cared about nothing and no one but herself. Charlotte seemed like a nice woman; there was no reason to make her the butt of a joke. These reservations surprised Keri, and the irony that Marci's behavior resembled her own, in the not distant past, wasn't lost on her.

She really did have a long day tomorrow. She really was tired and needed to get some sleep. Keri dwelt on these justifications for a moment, aggravated that she didn't feel as relaxed as she'd expected. Uneasily, she recalled being in the alley, her body reacting as she aroused her companion. She had enjoyed Charlotte, enjoyed pleasuring her, but she hadn't wanted the pleasure returned, and it wasn't Charlotte's face she'd seen when she closed her eyes. That fact was even more disconcerting than her lack of satisfaction.

The face she'd seen was none other than Dana Ryan's. Even though Dana's face was a patchwork of bruises and cuts the last time she saw her childhood friend, it was still Dana's face, but she was healed. And her eyes spoke only love. Even though she knew how Dana felt about her, that face had haunted her on and off since that angry meeting.

Despite her attempts to steer her mind elsewhere, her thoughts drifted to that day. She'd met Marci after that meeting and gone out for some fun. After more than enough drinks at a new women's bar named Crush, she'd proclaimed herself bored with college coeds and hit on the owner of the bar. And guess what? The owner hit back, luring her to her office and having her on the desk. Mindless fun.

It was the beginning of her ill-fated relationship with Gloria. She was older and so different from the kids Keri had been playing with. Everyone at the bar wanted the small and fiery woman. She was demanding in bed and had a voracious appetite for Keri. She made Keri feel dangerous and daring and very grown up. Daddy didn't care for her, but somehow that made the sex even better.

After a few months, though, she had grown weary of Gloria's demands on her time and her constant nattering about how spoiled she was. The sex wasn't as inviting knowing what came before and after.

The one thing she had never said out loud, and preferred not to think about, is that the first night she'd been with Gloria, the night they'd gone to her bar and Keri had gotten dead drunk and made it with her on the desk—that night when she closed her eyes and felt the orgasm begin to rise from her core—she'd seen only the green eyes of Dana in her mind. She'd cried that first time. Gloria thought it was because of her prowess as a lover, and Keri did nothing to dissuade her.

The truth scared her. The tears hadn't been about passion, they'd been tears of guilt and regret. Keri had blotted that moment out of her mind, afraid to take a closer look. But it was always there, and as she drove home from her alley encounter with Charlotte, away from the mindless banter of Marci, she felt afraid.

In the years since that horrific meeting, she had changed, and, in hindsight, she realized that somehow it had been a defining moment, a catalyst for the changes. Dana's words stung and they had stuck. When she'd turned down the money, Keri couldn't understand her thinking. Daddy had called it foolish pride, something a person in her position could not afford. But even then, Keri had sensed there was more to it than that; she'd had an inkling of the disillusion that had driven Dana's decision, and it made her very uncomfortable.

As time passed, Dana's contempt began to make more and more

sense to her, and she felt shame at her behavior. It seemed a long time ago, now, but Keri was afraid it probably felt like yesterday to Dana. It was not the kind of experience easily forgotten or forgiven.

She had no way of knowing how the interview would turn out tomorrow, but AJ had at least gotten Dana to agree to come. Maybe she'd be stood up. Maybe Dana would throw the offer in her face. At least she would know, because the possibilities were driving her crazy.

CHAPTER FIVE

Dana walked down the hall, trying to control the butterflies that were threatening to become much larger in her stomach. She was going to be talking alone with Keri for the first time since they were children. She had no idea what to expect. She'd been on an emotional roller coaster since agreeing to the interview. One moment she wanted to tell the bitch where to get off, the next she wanted to ask a million questions. She cycled between plotting some plan of revenge like selling her photos to the tabloids, and the completely irrational urge to protect Keri from the same tabloids. Confusion didn't even begin to describe it.

Still, her feet kept moving. One way or another, she and Keri Flemons needed to resolve some things. Needed to put their emotional houses in order when it came to each other. At least Dana did. Even if she told Keri off finally and forever, at least that would be some kind of resolution. Then she could move on. Because somehow, she wasn't moving on, at least not emotionally. She'd been with some great women, and she'd wanted to be in love, but it had never happened. She knew that resolution with Keri Flemons was the only way that could happen. She'd given her heart to MyKeri and never gotten it back, and despite herself she was still drawn inexorably toward the one person in the world she had truly loved. If she was ever going to find a way to free herself, the time was now.

Her hand was trembling slightly when she opened the door and saw the receptionist, a young man. He was big and beefy, perfect for a football organization. He could easily stop anyone who didn't have an appointment. He looked up from his seat behind the large desk. The team logo was emblazoned on the wall behind him.

The California PickAxes had a long and vibrant history of success. But with salary cap restrictions and then Mike's death, the last season was less than the fans had come to expect.

The young man smiled at her. "May I help you?"

"I have an appointment with Ms. Flemons. Dana Ryan."

Tapping a few keystrokes into his computer to check for her name, he smiled again and turned away to pick up a visitor badge that was printing.

"Here you go. Please sign in. The badge allows you to go anywhere on this floor by yourself for the day. If accompanied by Ms. Flemons, of course, anywhere else. Have a good meeting, and please return the badge and sign out when you leave."

The young man handed her the temporary badge, and she peeled it off the paper and slapped it on her jacket lapel. She thanked him for his directions. Keri had mentioned it was Mike's old office so she had a vague recollection of where she was going.

Walking down the halls, she found herself slowing to see all of the famous photographs lining the walls from past glories of the team, many of them taken by AJ Harden. She imagined one of her shots up there someday and smiled. But the closer she got to the executive suite, the more impossible the task seemed. Her gut was turning to water, and no amount of logical reasoning was going to change that.

"Oh, Lordy." Looking furtively around, she spotted a women's restroom. She quickly pulled open the door and ran smack into Keri Flemons, exiting at the same moment.

Keri jumped back. "Oh!"

They looked at each other for a long moment, then Dana stammered out, "I, um, was just..." She tried to say something normal but was unable to find her voice.

Keri started for the door again, sliding past Dana in the doorway. "Excuse me. I should watch where I'm going." She hurried down the hall.

Dana stood in the doorway, staring at the retreating figure. Her understated suit revealed a beautiful figure, with shapely calves and ankles. The subtle sway of her hips was hypnotic, even with a quickened pace. She registered a hint of Keri's perfume in the air. *Well,*

Dana, guess you can't leave. You've been spotted. My God, she's grown more beautiful than I remember. This is probably one of the worst ideas you've ever been talked into.

She quickly used the facilities, grateful that no one else was around, washed her hands, then rummaged in her bag to find a brush. To waste even more time, she reapplied lip gloss, wryly noting that normally once she left her flat in the morning, she usually forgot about such things. But this was not a normal morning. Keri's eyes were different than those she remembered three years before. She wasn't sure what it was, perhaps just maturity. Somehow they had more depth. She closed her eyes and took a deep breath to try to refocus on her purpose.

"Come on, D," she chided the pale, dark-haired woman in the mirror. "Let's get it over. You applied for the job and you agreed to the interview." Her green eyes looked frightened to her, and she noted the shadows beneath them, a testimony to her sleepless nights. Her hair was back to its almost-black and thick luster, and it was longer now that she wasn't playing ball anymore.

"Well, at least you're taller than her, and in decent shape. All the bruises are gone and the scars...what are you doing? Preening for a meeting with the woman who wrecked your life?" The rebuke was cut short by the sound of someone coming into the bathroom. She put her lip gloss in her pocket, picked up her black leather backpack, and limped out. Funny, she hadn't been limping when she came in. Maybe she needed a reminder.

Feeling like a condemned woman, she trudged down the hall and opened the door to the suite. Shelley Douglas looked up and broke into a huge grin. Glancing over her shoulder at the closed door of Keri's office, she stood and opened her arms to give Dana a big hug.

"You look wonderful! My God, you've become such a beautiful woman. I followed your career, honey, but the pictures in the magazines were usually of you covered in mud. And I saw the portfolio, you are very talented! It's so good to see you!"

Just then the door to the inner office started to open and Shelley moved away from Dana, giving her a sly wink of encouragement.

"Um, Keri? Your ten o'clock appointment just arrived."

Keri stood in the doorway and smiled tentatively. "Hello again." Her dark blue eyes were soft and inviting, and every part of Dana felt magnetized to the vision of her beauty.

A look of surprise on Shelley's face vaguely registered, and Dana managed to explain, "We kind of ran into each other in the bathroom."

Shelley nodded slowly.

Keri seemed to be having a hard time finding words, and it frustrated her. "Why don't you...why don't we start?" She turned on her heel and strode back into her office.

Uneasy, Dana caught a final reassuring glance from Shelley, then followed Keri into the office. She sat down in a chair in front of the large cherrywood desk and looked around the impressive room while she waited for Keri to settle in. It hadn't changed a whole lot. She could still feel Mike's presence. Beyond the desk, which had more than a few file folders neatly stacked on its corners, a narrow table stood in front of a picture window that looked out onto the stadium.

A vase of fresh flowers and several pictures were arranged on the polished wood surface. Dana stared at the pictures. One was an official photo of Mike as the managing partner of the team. Next was a candid shot of Mike and the commissioner of football with Zander MacCauley and the coach, all four men soaked in champagne and holding up the Super Bowl trophy. Beside that was a candid shot of Mike and Keri. Father and daughter shared the same mischievous grin, but Keri's beautiful blue eyes and blond hair were all from her mother.

Dana loved that photo. She had taken it through a telephoto lens on a winter day at one of the games and sent it to Mike anonymously. It was before the accident that killed her father, when she was an amateur and still clung to the possibility that Flemons and his family were not the scoundrels her father believed. No sense wasting a good photograph. It captured the love and closeness father and daughter obviously shared. Mike had evidently thought so too.

The last frame contained an old picture of Mike, Keri, and Moms. Keri, held in her mother's arms, was giving the camera a toothless grin. Mike was on the other side of Keri with a protective arm around them both. It made Dana smile.

"I guess as a photographer you must always be interested in photos, right?

The sound of Keri's voice made Dana's eyes jump to her. "Uh, yeah, I guess." She tried to make conversation. "Which one is your favorite? The Super Bowl shot?"

"No. The one of my dad and me. A fan sent it to him. I don't remember it being taken, and Dad always said he wished he knew who it was so he could thank him. Now that he's gone...I treasure it even more." She finished the sentence almost in a whisper and looked away as tears flooded her eyes.

Dana tried to help Keri through the moment. "You wouldn't remember it being taken because the photographer probably used a telephoto lens. It often captures special moments better."

Keri cocked her head slightly and Dana's breath caught in her throat. The mannerism was so familiar and so comforting it sent her back in time, making it hard to relate to Keri as anyone but the girl she'd once loved. Making a conscious effort to force herself present, she busied herself with the portfolio she had pulled from her backpack.

"I brought some additional photographs," she said, hoping she didn't sound as shaken as she felt.

"Thanks." Keri had collected herself, but Dana could sense the tension in her. "This morning I looked through the folder you submitted again. You do amazing work. The action shots are terrific, but you capture the emotions of the games so well. You're very good."

Dana blushed and swallowed, then tried to clear a very dry throat. "Well, thanks for the compliment."

Keri lifted her gaze, and Dana fell into the incredible color that had always been her refuge as a child. She could drown in those eyes. She watched as their color darkened and she saw something more. Was it sorrow? Apology? She forced her gaze to her lap, away from what she knew couldn't be true. Keri Flemons never apologized and meant it. Like all of the Flemons family.

A knock on the door ended their silent regard, and Shelley stuck her head in. She seemed to sense their unease and made a fuss out of coming in with two cups of coffee and handing one to each woman.

"You both look like you need some caffeine," she said, offering cream and sugar.

Everyone laughed, and by the time she was through, the atmosphere in the room was more relaxed.

"So, do we have a new photographer?" Shelley blurted out. "I mean photojournalist?"

Keri's mouth fell open, and she juggled the coffee cup as a little spilled. Taking a napkin from the tray Shelley had left on the desk, she said, "Well, we haven't discussed it yet. I think that's what we're here for. Is that okay with you, Shelley?"

Shelley beamed. "Oh, sure. Just checking. Good to see you, Dana." She hustled out of the office and closed the door behind her.

Dana took a sip of coffee, aware of Keri shifting uncomfortably in her chair. Now was the time. "You asked AJ to come and talk to me. Why?"

Keri turned pink and sat her coffee down on the desk, seeming to gather her thoughts. "Look, let's be honest. I know you have some very negative feelings about this family, me in particular. But this has nothing to do with our past. The reason I asked you here is strictly business. I went through every applicant and their photos without knowing any names. Yours were the ones I kept coming back to. It's as simple as that."

Dana was stunned. "That's it? You liked my portfolio and so we should just move on and work together like our personal history doesn't exist? AJ said the assignment was for a year. I would be assigned to you for a *year*. And we ignore what's happened?"

"No. That…we need to talk at some point. I just thought…"

Leaning toward Keri, Dana repeated slowly. "Just ignore it? Pretend it never happened because that would make you feel more comfortable? And *your* comfort should be my main concern, naturally?"

Keri bristled. "Look, I wanted to apologize for my behavior three years ago. It was rude and arrogant. I'm sorry, and I know it must have hurt you."

Dana almost laughed at this transparent manipulation. Keri had always been good at saying what people wanted to hear in order to get her own way. Dana had watched her do it with her mother on countless occasions. "Do you really think a grudging apology from you is worth a dime to me?" she said with quiet control. "I'm not one of your family's yes-men, and I'm not one your suck-up friends."

"I don't know what you want from me." Keri's face was dull red, and her chest rose and fell unevenly.

Dana figured she'd probably never been spoken to so bluntly or called on her behavior in her adult life. And now she was running a football team. How was she going to stay in her bubble and make that work? It would almost be worth doing the job just to watch her fall flat on her face.

An uneasy silence stretched between them as Dana contemplated her companion's adolescent statement. Finally, without anger, she said, "I don't expect you to know what I want from you, Keri. That would require empathy."

She watched the barb register and wondered if she'd gone too far. Fully expecting Keri to ask her to leave, she placed her coffee cup on the desk and returned her portfolio to her backpack.

"Wait," Keri said sharply. "Please don't go. I know I screwed up. I know we can't pretend it never happened. But this is business. This is something that could work for both of us, and I have a feeling your career matters more than the past or you wouldn't be here."

Dana let her hands rest in her lap. Keri's perceptiveness surprised her. So did her determination to persuade her to take the job. As a child, Keri had always gone after what she wanted, often heedless of risks or alternatives, and her father was famous for his stubbornness. Dana guessed this was a trait Keri had inherited.

"You're right," she conceded. "My career is the only thing that would make me set foot in your office."

Did she imagine the quick flash of pain that darkened Keri's eyes? She looked again, but there was no trace of anything but the same single-minded determination Dana knew from long ago. It had spelled trouble then and it probably did now. All the same, she'd found it hard to resist as a child and that, apparently, hadn't changed.

As if sensing her hesitation, Keri said, "I respect that. You're a true professional, and I want the kind of person who'll see this job as an artistic challenge and deliver her very best work. Done well, this could be a career-making assignment in sports photography. We both know that."

"Point taken. So, tell me more about the job."

Keri looked relieved. Her words rushed out. "The team's important to me. I don't want to throw all my father's hard work down the drain because he died. I...owe it to him."

"You want a tribute book?"

"No." Keri seemed frustrated with herself. "I'm not explaining this very well. I guess what I'm trying to say is that this isn't about me grandstanding and *pretending* to be the managing partner. I know AJ wants someone else in the room to protect me, and God knows that would be nice, but that's not why I want you. I'm not looking for one of those reverential books that only include the flattering stuff. I want an honest account, and I think you're the right person to deliver that."

Dana smiled faintly. She certainly wouldn't pull any punches, and if Keri remembered anything of them as children, she would know that. "I think it's an interesting project, but I'm still not sure why you want a book at all."

Keri let out a frustrated sigh and leaned her elbows on the desk. The play of emotions on her face was too rapid to interpret, but determination was definitely one of them.

"Dana, I'm planning to turn the team around and win another Super Bowl." The look of disbelief on Dana's face must have been obvious. Keri's eyes narrowed, and in a tone just short of anger she said, "You might think it's ego and maybe you're right, but this is a key period in the history of the team. This project could be an important record, maybe even an inspiration to other women who end up working in very nontraditional situations."

Keri hurried on. She looked at the photos in front of her. "I'll pay you well, but I know money won't sell you on this. And, although I know you probably won't believe me, that's reassuring. So, I'm asking you to give it a chance. If, after a month, we can't stand each other, or you can't stand me, you walk, with a two-month bonus and a glowing recommendation from me and AJ. If you want to continue, well, there it is."

She sat back in her chair, folding her arms over her chest, staring at Dana with an unmistakable challenge in her eyes. Despite herself, Dana was impressed that Keri seemed to be thinking about something other than having a good time. She wasn't taking for granted her inheritance—she actually wanted to prove herself worthy of it. Was that the real reason she wanted the book—an unconscious insecurity about her place in the world her father had built and dominated? Did she need to see images of herself running the team to make her believe she was capable of filling her father's shoes?

It made sense, but it also raised the stakes for the project. Keri might think she wanted the truth recorded, but Dana suspected she would be less enthusiastic once she saw how exposed she would be. Cautiously, she said, "What happens if, after a year, you've made a mess of it? The team is in worse shape than when you started? Will you own up to that? Or will the book just die because you failed?"

Keri seemed taken aback, as though she'd never considered failure an option. "The book will go forward regardless. If I fail, maybe it will turn into a case study at Stanford—'How Not to Run a Football Team.'" Her mouth quirked at a corner.

Dana started to reply but Keri interrupted her. "I have to warn you, there are people out there who don't like the idea of me taking over for my dad. Because I'm a novice, because I'm a woman, you name it. Some will try to intimidate me, manipulate, seduce, whatever will get them what they want. It has been ugly and will probably continue to be."

Dana felt her stomach and jaw tighten. "Then those people will have to be willing to do it in front of a witness with a camera." She saw the change in Keri's face and realized that she had just practically accepted the job. Holding up a hand, she forced out the words she had rehearsed so often at home. "You and I have a past that can't be erased. We might not be able to get beyond that. You should know that if I take this job, nothing changes between us." When Keri nodded, she added, "There's something else. You have to be willing to take an honest opinion from me. I don't tend to hold back."

After a moment, Keri said, "I know that about you and I don't want you to hold back. Ever."

Dana stopped breathing. Her grasp on the cup was so tight she hoped it didn't shatter. This wasn't part of the plan.

The intercom sounded. Keri hit the button. "Yes?" Her voice cracked and she coughed.

Shelley said, "Jameson Brown is here for his ten-thirty appointment."

"Oh. Ask him to wait just a moment, please."

She leveled her eyes at Dana. "Are you accepting the job? It means we'll have to be together a lot. The hours will be erratic, but I'll try to give you comp time to make up for it. The terms are as I mentioned. Do you want to get back to me?"

The words popped out of her mouth. "I accept. One month. When do I start?"

Keri broke into a broad grin that lit up her beautiful face. Dana's heart skipped.

"Do you have a camera with you?"

Dana's hand automatically went to the bag that was sitting on the floor beside her chair. "Always."

"Then let's get started. I have a difficult appointment waiting right outside the door. By the way, you will be held to a strict confidentiality agreement. Do we need to sign that first?"

"AJ mentioned that. You have my word. I won't betray you."

Keri studied her, then dropped her eyes to her desk. When she looked up the pain in her eyes was unmistakable. "You mean like I betrayed you? Nice shot."

Dana felt the color rise to her cheeks. "I didn't mean—"

"Yes, you did," Keri said brusquely. "Now, what about compensation? We haven't really..."

Dana fiddled with her camera, head down. She hadn't meant to be so transparent and found herself feeling bad for hurting Keri. "Yes, we have. You'll pay what I'm worth." She looked up, concerned suddenly. "One thing, though. I'm a photographer. I'm not that strong a journalist. As far as the commentary for the book, I wouldn't be the best choice. You should know that, up front."

Keri seemed to recover quickly and her eyes sparkled. "Good. Because that's my strong suit. If we need more help, we'll get it."

Dana found herself wondering if the hurt she'd seen in Keri's eyes was just one more manipulation to get what she wanted. In a split second, she was hot all over. Instead of telling Keri to go to hell, she was going to be working with her on a daily basis. She had schooled herself to take time to consider the job, but she had agreed with barely a second thought! Keri could *always* do that to her. Dana could never refuse her anything. But it wasn't too late. She could throw the job in her face, having the last laugh on Keri Flemons. That's what she would do.

Keri stood and came around the desk, offering her hand to Dana to shake. She smiled and asked, "Shall we get to work?"

Dana looked at the slim delicate fingers, only able to nod. As she shook Keri's hand she saw the light blue of her eyes turn a shade darker and was entranced.

Keri seemed reluctant to let go of her hand, but released her after a long moment, then turned to open her office door.

Dana stared after her and resisted the urge to smack herself in the head. Keri's voice held a note of unmistakable satisfaction.

"Shelley? Get employment papers ready for Ms. Ryan, with a start date of today. And send Mr. Brown in. Ms. Ryan will be staying for the appointment."

❖

Jameson Brown was five foot ten and built like a fireplug. For all of his bulk he possessed amazing agility and had been a very productive running back for the team, gaining over a thousand yards per season for several years. He was sitting in the outer office of the managing partner because of some remarks he had made to a print journalist a few weeks before. He glowered at the team pictures surrounding him in the waiting room.

When he entered Keri's office, she thought he seemed surprised to see someone else at the meeting. Keri guessed that a woman with a camera would only make his mood darker, but it would also throw him off for a bit. Already having someone else in the room was having its desired effect. Since she was still trying to recover from her meeting with Dana and the handshake that was nothing if not distracting, she tried to give him her undivided attention.

Keri smiled a polite greeting and motioned for him to take the chair directly in front of the desk. Dana stood off to the side, closer to Keri, sighting through the lens of her camera. Keri felt every millimeter of the distance.

Slouching in his chair, Jameson glared across the desk. "What's this? We gonna record the meeting or something?"

"Pardon me, Jameson. I should have introduced you. This is Dana Ryan. She'll be on a special team assignment for the next year, and this is part of the assignment."

"To take pictures of me?" He brightened a bit, giving Dana a more appraising look.

Diplomacy was new to Keri but she knew it was needed. "Well, yes, in a way. Look, you can ignore her for the purposes of this meeting. She's under a confidentiality agreement so nothing we say leaves this office. Okay?"

He looked a bit suspicious, then shrugged noncommittally.

Keri steeled herself and started. This was the first major personnel problem in which a player was involved. It was also the first one in which she felt compelled to intervene. The coach had distanced himself, claiming ignorance. Thomas had done the same thing, saying it was no big deal. But it *was* a big deal. To her and many fans, it was a very big deal.

"Do you know why I asked you to come here today?"

He shifted uncomfortably in the chair and looked down. "Yeah. It's about that 'faggot' remark I made to the newspaper guy. Look, I apologized for that. What's the big deal? I meant it. I don't want no faggots in my locker room."

Keri was quiet, letting him settle down. Dana didn't move, but Keri heard the shutter clicking.

"In the eyes of a lot of fans, that remark took you from being a terrific football player on their team to being just another bigot. You have disappointed many, many people. Our switchboard and email system have been deluged. And, for the record? That apology was halfhearted at best."

He folded his arms over his muscular chest and slouched farther in the chair. He was digging in.

Keri leaned forward and put her forearms on the desk. "Jameson, you're African-American. Have you ever been called the 'N' word? And I don't mean by your friends, kidding around. Maybe not recently, but ever?"

"Yeah, of course I have."

"How did it feel? To have all that hate and misunderstanding in one word, tearing you down just because of the color of your skin?"

He hesitated momentarily but shook his head. "I've been over that. It felt bad but this is different. I don't care what people do as long as it ain't in front of me or aimed at me. That's what I'm saying."

Keri spread her fingers out as though handing him something. The unconscious mannerism made her catch her breath. She'd seen her father use the same gesture a thousand times. "Okay, that's a place to begin. And I'll help you. If there's one thing I won't tolerate, it's sexual harassment." Both Dana and Jameson shot her a look. She pulled a pad of paper over and picked up her pen, poised to write. "Now, which guys have been making out in front of you?"

Jameson looked confused. "What? No one!"

Keri tapped her pen a few times. "Oh. Okay, who made a pass at you?"

He sat up straight in the chair. "Nobody!"

"Touched you inappropriately?"

"No!"

"Tried something in the shower?"

"*No*! What are you talking about?"

She put the pen down and folded her hands in front of her. "Bigotry is what I'm talking about. Your bigotry."

Keri waited. So did Jameson and Dana. Finally, Jameson nodded slightly and the tension in the room eased.

Jameson tried to sound conciliatory. "Look, all that means is we don't have any fag...er...gay guys on the team. I was just saying that's the way I like it. That's all. I didn't want to upset our gay fans. You know?"

Keri looked at him. "Except for one thing. We pretty much *know* how many African-Americans are on the team by their skin color. We don't know how many homosexuals are on the team because it is forbidden to tell. So we probably do have some gay guys on the team, but they have to hide. They have to sound just as bigoted, just as bawdy, and just as intolerant as the next guy. They have to put up with fag jokes in the locker room that I dare say you don't have to tolerate about blacks. At least your color proclaims your difference. You can't hide it. Hiding an essential part of yourself can be very damaging and hurtful."

Jameson shifted again. "Okay, I can see that. But it's not like I'm the only one who feels this way."

"Well, unfortunately, you're the only one who chose to speak his views publicly. By the way, did you ever play against Bill Millard when he was with the Cowboys?" She was referring to the retired all-pro defensive lineman who had recently announced he was gay.

Jameson smiled. "Yeah, he was super good. I almost never got any yards on his side of the field. And he didn't do cheap shots. I respected him."

"And now?"

He was silent for a few seconds. "Now I still respect him. I'll make the apology again and mean it this time. Sorry for the hassle, Ms. Flemons."

"Thank you, Jameson. I only want you to consider the man, not his sexual orientation or his religion or his color. I'm sure not saying that there aren't homosexuals who are jerks. There are. But their sexual orientation is just a part of them, like your skin color is part of who you are." She tilted her head slightly and grinned. "Sorry if that sounded like a sermon. You are such an important part of this team, I felt I had to say something."

They both stood and shook hands. The camera was clicking in the background.

Keri said, "Thanks so much for your time, Jameson. Good luck this year."

"Um, no problem." He hesitated, as if trying to decide what to say. The internal argument was brief, and he gave her a small smile that reached his eyes. "I really liked your dad. He was a fair man. I think you must be like him." He then seemed to remember Dana, who had dropped her camera to her side a few seconds before, after capturing the handshake. "Nice to meet you, uh, Ryan is it? You ever play pro sports?"

Dana blushed and grinned. "Yeah. Pro soccer for a few years."

"Why'd you quit? You look like you could play right now."

Keri tensed. But Dana smoothly said, "Oh, I cracked up my leg in a car accident a few years back. Let's just say that if you saw my speed you'd know the answer."

"Oh, I know that one. Too bad. Well, I guess I'll see you around then."

After he left, both women let out a collective sigh.

Keri met Dana's eyes and said, "Thanks for not mentioning the accident…in a way you could have." She didn't know what else to say.

Dana softly said, "You handled that meeting very well. That took courage the men running the team don't seem to have."

Keri ran a hand tiredly through her hair. "Yeah. They could care less about anything like this. They just want it to go away."

"Why did you take it on?"

Keri looked into the emerald eyes studying her. "Because it matters to me. I've been in and around the professional sports world most of my life, and I get tired of it. Every time a man shows compassion he's a fag. A woman excels in sports and doesn't sleep with every man in sight so she's a dyke. And nobody does anything about it. We're all so afraid of the hatred behind the remarks." She caught herself and laughed a bit. "Listen to me, Little Miss Self-Righteous. That must sound weird coming from me, eh?"

Dana was quiet. But her eyes never wavered from Keri's.

Her intercom sounded and Keri absently hit the button. "Yes, Shelley?"

"Sorry to interrupt, but Ms. Steeple is insisting on talking to you. I've put her off three times this morning."

"Damn. I forgot. I'm supposed to meet her for lunch. Ask her to hold for a minute, would you? Oh, and call Zander and tell him yes for next weekend."

"Got it."

"Thanks, Shel." Shifting her attention back to Dana she said, "Well, I guess you'd better get started with your paperwork. That and what you just witnessed ought to be enough for one day. Right?"

Dana noted that the air seemed to have gone out of her sails and wondered if it had anything to do with the caller. Keri looked downright miserable. "Okay. Should I see Shelley about the paperwork?"

"Yes. Thanks."

Dana shoved her camera in her pack and asked, "What time do you want me tomorrow?"

"Anytime. I'm usually in early. We'll figure out the day when you get here. My first meeting isn't until," she checked her calendar, "noon."

Keri seemed distracted, and Dana moved to the door to let herself out of the office.

"Oh. Dana?"

"Yes?" Dana turned to look at the stunning woman that was Keri Flemons. Sky blue eyes took her breath away.

"I'm glad, I mean, good to have you aboard."

Dana nodded and left the room. She felt slightly dazed. None of her rehearsals had prepared her to meet the woman with whom she had just spent two hours. Walking to Shelley's desk, she noticed that the light that had been blinking on the phone console was steady. Evidently Keri was talking to Ms. Steeple.

"We're going to try it for a month and see how it goes," she told Shelley. "I guess I need directions to personnel."

Shelley gave her a warm smile. "I have to call AJ. I promised to let him know. Oh, hon, I'm so glad! She needs an ally around here. So far, there aren't that many."

Dana almost said something about hardly considering herself an ally but stopped, knowing now was not the time. "Well, if Ms. Steeple has called so often, she must be an ally, right?" It was shameless prying but she was curious.

"Gloria Steeple." Shelley pronounced in a disgusted tone. "She's awful to anyone she isn't trying to schmooze. That means me and anyone who gets between her and Keri. So watch your back, sweetie."

The comment about watching her back was disconcerting. Shelley obviously had some wrong assumptions about what was happening here. Dana had no intention of becoming Keri Flemons's ally or friend. She would make her reputation on this woman's back and be gone. As a matter of fact, Keri's failure in the new job that seemed so important to her could be quite a nice payback, in and of itself. She'd have to think about that.

❖

Ten minutes later Dana took the stack of papers she was to fill out and headed down to personnel, then over to security to get a permanent badge. After three hours she emerged, glad it was over, and limped to her car. *I hate paperwork.* A moment after settling behind the steering wheel, she heard tires squealing behind her, and a black Mercedes zoomed past and jerked to a halt beside a smaller, silver sports car.

Keri had barely exited the 420SE before it tore out of the lot. Keri leaned heavily on the door of her Audi, staring after the departing taillights.

Dana reflexively ducked a bit to make sure Keri didn't see her, sensing both of them would be embarrassed at her witnessing the private moment. She stayed until Keri was safely inside the office complex before starting her car.

As she drove home she thought about the day. Being that close to Keri had been unsettling, and rather than confirming how despicable Keri was, the hours they'd spent together seemed to show a woman who had changed. Just how much, Dana couldn't tell. Most unsettling of all was her attraction to that woman. Dana had heard rumors that Keri was a lesbian, but celebrity gossip was notoriously unreliable. Still, Keri's comments about sports homophobia certainly could have had a personal basis. Keri was rich enough she could fuck a woman in the owners' box and people wouldn't say a word. She really seemed to care.

Each week the newspapers had at least one or two stories linking Zander MacCauley and Keri Flemons. They made a beautiful couple and the media ate it up, the society pages and gossip columns treating them like an item. Dana wondered who Gloria Steeple was. Shelley certainly didn't like the woman, and Keri had looked unhappy in the parking lot.

"It doesn't matter, so drop it," Dana chided herself. "You are her employee, a ghost from her past, and she's someone you can't stand. You agreed to take this job for the money and the prestige, and so you could give her some payback for all the shit she's put you through."

But her words rang hollow as she spoke them. She'd had everything firmly set in her mind before the interview, but watching Keri speak with Jameson Brown had shaken her. The Keri she saw in that difficult meeting wasn't quite as monochromatic as the one she'd imagined since the accident.

Fog was settling in, and mist was developing. Perfect. She drove to the beach. Over the years, the cold wind of the North Pacific and the heavy fog had been her only companions when her mood matched the weather. She would walk for as long as her now-aching leg could take it, then put a towel in the driver's seat and go home. She had done it so often she kept towels in the back of her car just in case.

She replayed the interview as she plodded through the sand and surf, careful to keep a watchful eye on the waves. The meeting with Jameson, the phone call. All of it was intercut with Keri as a child and Keri as the selfish woman who ruined her life. Her thoughts swirled to the lonely child she had become the day everything in her life had changed. Crying, writing long letters and asking her father to mail them. And never a word in return. But that wasn't Keri's fault, now was it? Tears seeped from her eyes and were quickly dried by the wind. She was soaked by the fog.

After a long time her leg could take no more, and she slowly made her way back to her car.

Chapter Six

Tiffany Murphy winced. Having her tongue pierced last night had seemed like a good idea at the time. Now, she couldn't talk, and the pole and stud kept clanging against her teeth. The idea of going on the wagon had never been more appealing.

She put the finishing touches on polishing the bar, threw the bar rag over her shoulder, and dawdled toward the back door of Crush, lighting a cigarette. Before the nicotine had time to hit her system, the black Mercedes her boss drove roared into a parking spot behind the run-down building and jerked to a halt.

The car was still rocking from the sudden stop when a small, attractive redhead with medium length hair and large, calculating hazel eyes jumped out. Tiffany groaned. It looked like the boss was not in a good mood. Gloria Steeple swept past her with a stony expression and marched through the kitchen into her office, slamming the door.

Tiffany took a couple of hasty puffs, crushed the cigarette beneath the heel of her Tony Lamas, and followed her into Crush. It wasn't rocket science to guess what today's drama was about. Gloria had spent half the morning preening before she went out to meet with her ex, going on about having her back by the time she returned that afternoon.

"Guess things didn't go as planned," Tiffany lisped to herself and headed for the storage room to get more beer for the coolers. "You must have asked Keri for *her* opinion. Good for you, Keri. Stick to it. Ow."

Gloria chose that moment to yank her door open. Shooting Tiffany a murderous glare, she said, "What did you say?"

Tiffany smiled innocently and shrugged her shoulders. "That front door is…stuck…not opening right. You have any oil around here?" She winced and covered her mouth.

Narrowing her eyes Gloria said, "Is it me or are you mumbling like the village idiot? If you're looking for oil, try the storage room. And hurry up. I have a meeting here in a few minutes, and I want you available in case I need something."

Nodding, Tiffany scuttled to the storage room before any more talking was called for. Fifteen minutes later a short, stocky man with tiny eyes and a white beard bustled through the back door. Tiffany was surprised to see him use that entrance.

"May I help you?" Her tongue was throbbing.

He looked at her intently. "I have a meeting with Ms. Steeple. Where is she?"

Figuring anyone that rude had to be an invited guest, Tiffany pointed in the direction of the office.

A few minutes later two more people came in the back way. One was way old, a man dressed in a three-piece suit that looked like something from the retro store. The other, a very tall, beefy woman with long dark hair and flat black eyes, held the door for him. She was wearing a dark, well-tailored pantsuit.

She gave Tiffany a once-over and said, "Steeple."

Again Tiffany pointed. As they walked past, she couldn't help but notice the old man's thick eyeglasses and full, almost purple lips. His eyes were everywhere, reptilian, but rheumy. She imagined that if she were to see his tongue, it would be forked. She could identify.

Involuntarily shuddering, she muttered, "Gloria, what are you up to now?" and went to find some ice to suck on.

❖

Inside the small, dimly lit office the air was stuffy. The tall woman pulled a standard bar chair around for the old man to sit in. She stepped aside and stood with her back against the door, watching.

The silence in the room became uncomfortable. Gloria was sure that it wasn't her meeting to start so she put off saying anything, instead smoothing her moss green come-fuck-me dress with the generous amount of cleavage revealed. She had expected to have more positive news to report. A lot was riding on this. She looked to Thomas Concannon to take the lead. He cast around the office and spotted the only other chair, close to the beefy woman. He chose to stand and when he spoke, Gloria thought she'd never heard him sound so nervous.

"Uhm…I was expecting Artie. Mr. Terrell. I've always placed my bets with…"

The old man's gravelly voice interrupted. "Artie ain't coming. He sold your marker to me." His smile revealed disconcertingly bright white and, certainly, false teeth.

Thomas sputtered, "*Sold* the marker? What are you talking about? I owe Mr. Terrell a small amount of money and I am going to—"

"He *owed* me." The old man coughed tubercularly. Gloria wasn't the only one who reflexively leaned away. "Now *you* owe me. So cut the shit, Concannon. You lost a truckload of money and I bought the debt. I want to know about Mike Flemons's kid. And I want to know why I had to read it in the papers. And why I'm here and who this broad is." He kept his eyes on Thomas but used his thumb to indicate Gloria.

She leaned forward to protest being talked about like she wasn't there, but at the same time the tall woman who had been standing by the door appeared at the old man's side. The words died on Gloria's lips. The woman looked lethal.

Thomas visibly tried to regroup. His forehead was glistening with perspiration. Addressing the old man he said, "I don't believe we've met. My name is Thomas Concannon. And this is my associate, Gloria Steeple." Hesitantly, he offered his hand.

It was ignored, but the blindingly white teeth again appeared in the center of the wizened face. "Allow me to introduce *myself.* I'm Rolo Bongiavanni and this is *my* associate, Gina Pescetti. From Napoli. She's my right-hand man." He cackled at his joke. He had established the pecking order of the meeting without much effort.

Gloria fought to keep her lunch down as the head of the largest crime syndicate on the West Coast stared at her.

"What do you have to do with this?" he asked.

"I own this bar."

He looked around. "So what?" Thomas started to interject, but the old man held up his hand and silenced him, keeping his eyes trained on Gloria.

She swallowed. "Uh…I used to have a relationship…I was Keri Flemons's lover. For two years." Well, that was stretching it, but he didn't need to know that.

The old man stared at her a moment, then laughed and coughed, dislodging the dazzling teeth. They clacked dangerously in his mouth as the purple lips reached around them, pulling them back in place before they escaped.

Gloria could feel the blood draining from her face.

"So the great Mike Flemons's only kid is a dyke? Huh. Kids these days. Can't control 'em. That don't tell me why you're here." He waited for her to answer.

"Well...Thomas came to me and I..."

Thomas cut in by raising his hand for permission to speak. Bongiavanni, known as Bongi everywhere but to his face, nodded in his direction.

"Look, Rolo..." A slight movement from Gina Pescetti caused him to reconsider. "I mean, Mr. Bongiavanni. The reason you didn't know sooner was because I didn't know. Flemons marches in after a year and announces she's taking over her father's position. Because she inherited the controlling interest, she can do that. Believe me when I say, most people aren't happy."

Bongi smiled again—truly a frightening sight—and Thomas fell silent. "I don't care about *most* people. Artie said the deal was control of the concessions in trade for your marker. Now I find out everything's been put on hold until the new managing partner reviews the contracts. You promised it within a year. What are you gonna do about it?"

"Well, that's why I brought in Ms. Steeple here. She says she can get Flemons back into a relationship and convince her to sell her part of the team."

Bongi shifted his focus to Gloria. His eyes flicked up and down, settling on her ample chest for a few seconds before creeping up to her face. Suddenly Gloria fervently wished she'd had time to change before the meeting. Her skin crawled under the scrutiny.

Talking to Thomas, Bongiavanni said, "Okay, she's a nice piece of ass. If she gets the broad to sell, who's buying?"

"I am," Thomas said. "I'm putting together a consortium of interested investors so that when she decides to sell, we can close the deal immediately. Then you will have all the concessions. That will more than cancel my debt."

Casting his eyes back to Gloria, he asked, "What makes you think you can get the Flemons kid to sell? What do you get out of it?"

Gloria was tired of being talked around. She tried to make the most of her turn. "I get a one percent finder's fee, and I'll have a beautiful, really wealthy girlfriend. What's not to like?"

Bongi's snake eyes glittered. "And that's the reason? What else?"

"I own paper on this bar," Thomas said. "She gets to keep it if she succeeds. Otherwise…"

The silence in the room could have been sliced. Suddenly the Day-Glo dentures showed themselves again, coupled with drowning laughter. "Okay, it's a deal. You got two months to make something happen. If it don't, we'll talk again." Bongi ticked his head toward the woman behind him. "Gina will be keeping an eye on things. You got anything to report, talk to her. She'll be around. Right, Gina?"

Gina Pescetti's head jerked, evidently agreeing. She then helped her boss up and held the door for him to hobble through. Just before she moved to follow, she looked long and hard at Gloria.

As frightened as Gloria was, her gaydar sounded off the chart. After the door swung shut, she sat back heavily in her chair and gasped out, "Jesus, that was scary. You never said anything about the mob. What the hell is going on?"

Thomas took out a handkerchief and mopped his face. He was flushed and didn't answer for a moment. "None of your concern, Steeple. Just keep your eyes on the prize and get Keri Flemons to sell me her interest in the team. I don't care how, but you'd better deliver."

Gloria felt her own temperature rise. "Hey! You. Never. Mentioned. The Mob. The deal's off."

When Thomas stood, she could see sweat stains in the armpits of his very expensive suit. "You'll do it or you'll be out on the street, and I'll bulldoze this piece-of-shit place you call your business." He stuffed the handkerchief in his pocket and was gone.

Gloria pushed back from her desk and bellowed, "Tiffany! Get me cup of coffee, and stick some whiskey in it. Now!"

When the young bartender appeared with the ordered drink, Gloria gulped down a few swallows.

"Who were those people?" Tiffany lisped. "They looked like they belonged on *The Sopranos*." The way she spoke, it sounded like "Thopranoth."

Aggravated, Gloria put the mug down and stared at her. "What the hell is wrong with you today? I can't understand a word you're saying!"

Tiffany grinned and opened her mouth to display her red and swollen, newly pierced tongue.

This day was not going well for Gloria. "Now, why on earth did you go and do that? Ears, okay. Eyebrows, whatever. But why the tongue? You sound like Elmer Fudd and Yosemite Sam combined!"

Giving her a conspiratorial look, Tiffany leaned in and said, "My girlfriend says it will make sex better. They said my speech will clear up soon."

Gloria could tell she was trying her best not to use her tongue too much. It took a moment to figure out what she'd said. She asked, "Make what better? Sex? Ooohh. I get it. So, did she get her tongue pierced at the same time?"

Tiffany looked confused.

Gloria continued, "Does she already have it pierced?"

"No. But she might."

"Uh-*huh*. Because she wants you to be satisfied, right?"

"Yeah."

"Right after you get her off a few thousand times. Shit, Tiff, when are you going to learn? You always bend over backwards for these women, and they never bend for you! Now you're unintelligible. Get out. I need to think." She plopped her face in her hands, trying for a coherent thought.

Clearly crestfallen, Tiffany started to leave.

Eyeing the woman through her fingers, Gloria said, "Wait, wait. Let me see again."

Tiffany opened her mouth to reveal the skewered body part.

Resisting another shudder, Gloria managed, "Well, it's kind of sexy, really. I mean, if your girlfriend doesn't appreciate it I'm sure *some* girl out there will. Keep ice or something on it, okay? And for God's sake practice talking so you don't sound like some escapee from a cartoon. Now, go."

Tiffany beamed. "Thanks, Gloria. You're the best!"

Gloria looked at the closed door after she had left. Lowering her head back into her hands, she muttered, "Crap."

CHAPTER SEVEN

K eri? It's Moms. This is my third attempt. Honey, how long do you want to keep this up? Don't you think it's time to at least talk about this? I love you. Please call."

Carolyn Flemons left her number, as always, before disconnecting. She sighed and walked into her kitchen to make some tea. Mike's daughter was just as pigheaded as he was.

She took the tea and wandered through the beautiful 4000-square-foot home she'd created. The condominium was situated on top of the Four Seasons Hotel. She'd been living in San Francisco for the past six months. Although she stayed in the background at Mike's funeral, she'd flown in from Paris to attend, then flown back and started getting her affairs in order to leave. There wasn't that much to do; the wheels had been in motion before Mike died.

Carolyn paused at a window and soaked up spectacular views of San Francisco, the waterfront, the Bay Bridge, and even the baseball park. Mike would have loved it. He could have walked to the baseball games. He loved baseball and had always tried to make a few games during the season. He said he liked it because he wasn't responsible for them winning or losing. He could just enjoy the game.

Fighting the tears that were trying to form, she sat down in an overstuffed chair and stared out at the water. A huge container ship made its way slowly over to the Oakland Shipyard, probably for repairs. A tanker full of crude oil had lumbered by before, turning toward the Refinery in Richmond. Beyond its dour bulk, a sleek cruise liner was gliding toward the piers of San Francisco. In their midst the tugboats,

Coast Guard craft, and sailboats danced around them. The harbor was always busy.

Now in her early fifties, Carolyn was often told she looked a good ten years younger. She exercised and ate to maintain a healthy life. When she gazed in the mirror, she saw her blond hair dusted with snow white, creating a highlighted effect. She had never passed through a graying stage, just white. She idly wondered whether or not she'd have it colored once the white overtook the blond. Mike had never minded his white hair. *Such an important decision.* Her face was that of an older Keri. But Keri had her dad's smile. Carolyn had always been glad of that. He had a great smile.

She closed her eyes. She'd cried so much over the loss of her husband and child. Twelve years ago, the arguments had started. Mike Flemons was a wonderful man, but he was no saint and he loved the ladies. She'd refused to face it for a long time, but when that horrible incident with Scooter and Sean Ryan happened, she couldn't bury her head any longer.

She had confronted Mike and he'd adamantly denied messing around with Dana's mother. Carolyn had accepted that at first, but she'd started paying more attention to the teasing from the board members when they were at games. How cute the cheerleaders were. The charming conversations he would have at cocktail parties with half the good-looking women there. The late-night "meetings." She wasn't sure exactly when she stopped trusting, but it was the beginning of the end.

Eventually Mike admitted that he'd had a few "liaisons" with other women, but he said they were always one-night stands and insisted that he loved only her. In her anger and pain, she'd made a fatal mistake: she'd had an affair of her own. It was meaningless retaliation, but Mike was livid and very vocal about it in front of Keri.

Carolyn had never brought up his philandering in front of their daughter, and Keri immediately jumped on Mike's side and wouldn't give an inch. She'd closed her ears to any thought of her father being less than perfect and had thrown herself into being with Mike for a few years. Carolyn wondered if Keri somehow blamed her for losing Scooter, because the strong attachment to Mike had started shortly thereafter. And no amount of cajoling on her part could get Keri to talk about that fateful day. Neither Mike nor Keri had ever stopped to consider that perhaps Carolyn missed Scooter, too. That child was one of the sweetest little beings she had ever known, and she often played peacemaker between her headstrong best friend and Carolyn. It broke Carolyn's heart to know that Scooter was left alone with Sean Ryan. Mike said Sean was fired for drinking on the job and his terrible temper. She feared for the child's safety and had even called a social worker friend of hers to see if there was something she could do, perhaps call Child Protective Services. But the sad news was that unless there was ample evidence of abuse or neglect, Dana would stay where she was.

Feeling excluded from her own family and alone in her own home, Carolyn had finally left. The one thing she'd never expected was that Keri would shut her out of her life completely, that she would refuse to consider that there might be two sides to the story. She had made her father into Saint Mike and would not allow anything, even the truth, to tarnish his image. Carolyn's attempts to reach out to her from Paris were met with stony silence.

Life had been so different since the divorce. She was so different. Mike had ignored his attorney's advice and split everything right down the middle. She was a wealthy woman. She'd moved to Paris and started working for an interior designer, eventually developing quite a portfolio and her own clientele. She'd dated a bit, but never anyone seriously. The truth was, she was a one-man woman. She'd fallen in love with Mike when she was twenty, and that was it.

She and Mike had been talking on the phone, emailing each other for some time before his death. He bluntly told her he'd been a fool and wanted to try again. At first, she'd refused to even consider it. But he sounded like he meant it this time. And she missed him so much. She had agreed to move back to San Francisco and give it a try. She yearned for the States and desperately wanted to reconnect with her daughter. Mike wanted that too. He said Keri needed her Moms. He'd spoiled her and she seemed an angry young woman. He confessed he didn't know what to do with her.

Actually, it was his concern about Keri that had prompted their reconnection. After Mike told her about the accident with Dana and Sean Ryan, Carolyn's heart went out to Scooter. Sean Ryan was a mean drunk and vindictive beyond measure. He had gone out of his way to keep the two little girls apart, ignoring every attempt Carolyn made to patch things over for the sake of their daughters. In the end, she'd given up, convinced her pleas only gave him satisfaction. He had actually seemed pleased to hear about Keri crying herself to sleep every night. Carolyn could only imagine how harshly he would have treated his own daughter.

Carolyn was deeply upset when Mike told her about the way Keri treated Scooter when they'd met, and about Keri's dismissal of the whole situation. She seemed to be in a state of complete denial about her own role in the accident, and Mike had wondered if he'd made a mistake protecting her from the consequences as thoroughly as he had.

Carolyn would always be glad that he'd turned to her for help. His willingness to admit mistakes and listen to her perspective transformed their relationship, and before long they started talking about the possibility of a new beginning. Carolyn had been devastated when Shelley called to tell her about Mike's death.

Reflecting on that conversation brought the tears. It still made her feel like her world was crumbling around her. The sound of the phone ringing came as a blessing, and hope forced her to her feet. *Keri.* She raced to the nearest extension, only to see the number of a client displayed on the caller ID screen. During a remodeling project someone had driven a forklift through a very expensive chandelier in Mr. and Mrs. Bichon's home, and they wanted someone's blood. She let the machine take the call and returned to the living room and her favorite chair, picking up the newspaper.

Following Keri's life through numerous articles in both the sports and society sections of the *Chronicle* was as close as she could get to sharing it. She wondered how her daughter was doing after taking over Mike's position with the PickAxes and was fascinated by the decision. The Keri that Mike and she had talked about would not have dreamt of taking on such a mammoth responsibility.

She devoured a gushy piece about Keri and Zander MacCauley with a mixture of amusement and sorrow. She doubted her daughter was romantically involved with the handsome young man and wished she were there to see who really made Keri blush. According to Mike, their daughter was lesbian. Carolyn wasn't surprised. She and Mike had long suspected it, and Keri was experimenting when Carolyn left. By now, she was probably with someone she cared about.

Carolyn sighed. Keri might think she could erase her mother from her life, but Carolyn was certain about one thing. She would not allow that to happen. She was going to keep trying to reunite with her daughter. Keri was all she had left, and she knew Mike would want them to be reconciled too.

❖

At ten o'clock in the evening Keri finally made it through the back door and shed her briefcase, coat, and shoes. It had been a grueling day. After weeks of phone messages, she had finally talked to Gloria and met her for lunch. What had started out pleasantly enough had turned acrimonious when Gloria suggested they steal away to Gloria's place for some time alone and Keri had politely turned her down.

Gloria acted like Keri had committed a crime. Then she backpedaled and tried to seduce her again. Keri had to admit that Gloria could be tempting, but she just didn't have time for the distraction.

Keri was confused about the whole thing. She and Gloria had parted mutually, perhaps a little more on Keri's part, but Gloria didn't put up much of a fuss. Now, over a year later, she suddenly wanted to get together and talk about reestablishing their relationship. Keri knew she shouldn't have weakened that one time and slept with her. It had sent the wrong signal. She had tried to clear that up, yet Gloria behaved like the deal was sealed.

And the phone calls: to the office, her home, two or three a day. She was sure Shelley had noticed and God knows who else. When they had been together, Keri did all the pursuing, or so she thought. Gloria held sex back just enough to make Keri want it all the time. She was older and so different from the college girls Keri had been with before. Gloria wasn't shy about demanding presents, either, the more expensive the better.

Keri never knew if Gloria was screwing others, too, but she suspected as much. Daddy had said she was bad news, and that made her more exciting and glamorous to Keri. His death, though, ended any excitement that was left. Keri had grown weary of the games, the demands. Besides, Gloria wasn't into supporting someone through a hard time. It really was all about Gloria.

By the time Keri got back to the office, she was late for two unpleasant meetings: one with Thomas Concannon and one with the new head of security for the park, a man whose macho attitude set her teeth on edge. Of course, Thomas had hired him.

Keri couldn't wait for Dana to start attending meetings with her, so at least she'd have some female energy in the room besides her own. She didn't want to think about any other reasons for her excitement. Seeing Dana, for the first time, as a woman who had healed from the damage the accident had caused had taken her aback. She was stunning. The ebony hair, longer now and thick and lustrous around her neck, her pale complexion with those glorious green eyes framed by long eyelashes. She took Keri's breath away.

Literally running into her in the bathroom the day of their meeting had tilted Keri's body temperature up several notches. Dana was tall and slender, without excess body fat, athletic but also feminine. Keri vividly remembered every minute of their time together. Even the tough talk during the interview hadn't compromised her appreciation for the woman Dana had become. It hadn't been easy, but they at least came to an understanding, and they'd been cautiously building on their delicate truce ever since.

During the past few weeks they'd formed a friendship of sorts. At least they were working well together. Dana had a wonderful sense of composition in her photos and captured emotions well. As hoped, she had become a buffer for some of the harshness of the meetings. Rarely speaking, she somehow managed to make her presence felt if the discussions got heated. Although she pointed out Keri's anger as well as the others', seeing the photographs was instructional for Keri, and she enjoyed hashing over the meeting afterward with Dana. It had been a relief for Keri to have Dana in the room.

Her contentment evaporated the moment she hit the playback key on her answering machine. She felt her face heat at the sound of her mother's voice, and she picked up her message pad and threw it against the wall.

"What do you *want* from me? Why can't you just leave me *alone*?"

She stormed up the stairs and tore off her suit, leaving it in a heap on the floor. Roughly shoving her body into some jeans, socks, and an old sweatshirt, she tried to calm her breathing. Damn her mother. Just when everything seemed to be getting a little better. Keri stomped downstairs and marched to the bar. She poured a stiff drink—single malt Scotch, Daddy's favorite—and took a healthy swallow, shuddering as it burned a path down her throat.

She was raw. First Gloria, now her mother. Her past was right here in her face. The only one who could help her was dead, leaving her to fend for herself. It was all so unfair! She forced herself to take a few more steadying breaths, built a fire in the fireplace, and warmed some leftover pasta. Not that she was hungry.

Plopping down on the sofa afterwards, she took another sip of her Scotch and tried to pull out of the pity party she knew she was in. Gloria was over. At least she'd managed to extricate herself from that sticky situation. And she could look forward to working with Dana tomorrow, also good. She could almost hear her father say, "Hey, two outta three ain't bad, sweet cheeks," and grin at her. But her mother. Keri was so torn.

She remembered the days when her parents were fighting. She'd be in bed and hear their voices. Moms crying and Daddy storming out of the house. When she'd found out why, she couldn't believe it. Her mother was having an affair. How could she break Daddy's heart like that? It was unforgivable. And so she didn't forgive. She wouldn't listen to her mother's excuses, and she wouldn't say a word when her mother tried to get her to talk about her feelings. Only once had she asked for an explanation, and all her mother would say is that she'd been stupid, but that there were always two sides to every story.

Keri wouldn't have any of it. There was only one side to betrayal. When her mother left, Keri refused to have any contact. Daddy even tried to get her to write or talk to Moms on the phone, but she wouldn't. She threw herself into being with him, taking over hostess duties for team functions, going to all the games, you name it. Although she wouldn't admit it at the time, she probably went to Cal Berkeley instead of farther away, to be there for him. She felt driven to make up for her mother's infidelity. And she plowed through woman after woman to make sure she was never alone, never had time to think too much.

Daddy seemed to be fine with the arrangement and did much the same thing. Team functions he took Keri to, but he also dated quite a bit. But before he died, he'd really stopped dating and seemed much more content to either stay at home or be with Keri.

And he had started talking more about Moms, reminding Keri about the good times they'd had together. He even told her once that he wasn't quite as perfect as she thought he was. Keri recalled exactly what he said. "You know, honey, no one could be as perfect as you think I am. I was just as responsible for the divorce as your mother, maybe more."

She hadn't wanted to hear it. Now she wished she'd asked a few more questions, because here was Moms wanting to meet, to talk. She didn't know what to think. A part of her longed for her mother. But another part of her needed to be right.

❖

Keri quickly walked down the hall from the boardroom to her office, Dana hot on her heels. Once there, they closed the door, dropped into the nearest chairs and grinned at each other, then broke out in laughter. Keri stood to her full height and bowed to an imaginary audience.

"Gentlemen, I'd like to introduce Dana Ryan. She is an accomplished sports photographer and has accepted a one-year assignment with the team. She'll be recording my progress as the managing owner of the team. I plan to make it into a book."

Dana watched in delight as Keri held up both hands and said, "Now, now, Thomas, don't worry. She has signed a strict confidentiality agreement. And I'll be writing the text and have the final say on all content. Dana's actually already been hard at work. You'll forget she's here in no time."

Smirking, Dana said, "I don't think Concannon will forget. And I don't think he felt better when you said you'd be writing the text. He was purple by the time the meeting was over. The slide show was ingenius."

Keri watched Dana's eyes sparkle as she talked and felt content to just listen to her smooth alto. Dana had spent the past week taking surreptitious pictures of each member of the board, and they had put together a show that was gratifying to all. Keri's plan was to spend time mollifying each man. She would give her spiel and then assure them their opinions would be considered and there would be no surprises.

It had worked like a charm. The slide show included candid shots of each of the board members taken during a special party formally introducing the new players signed in the off-season. Keri and Dana selected the most flattering ones to show. The idea of having their faces immortalized brought the men around quickly. Although a few shots would have definitely caused embarrassment if some of the wives got a look, with Dana's careful editing and touch-up, they all looked terrific.

By the time the meeting was over, the men were coming up to

Dana and welcoming her aboard, even making suggestions about shots. All except Concannon. He left the room as soon as the meeting adjourned. Dana smiled and acted as though each suggestion was a new and wonderful idea.

Keri bowed to her audience of one. "And you, Mr. Harris, this picture takes ten years off of your face and ten pounds off of your gut." Turning to the lamp, she said, "Perry? If you'll notice, your mistress is nowhere to be seen, yet she was sitting beside you." She turned to Dana. "How did you get Jack to look like he had more hair?"

Dana rolled her eyes. "All I can tell you is that for projects like this, digital photography was sent by the gods. Was it subtle enough?"

Laughing as she sat down, Keri said, "He would have loved it if you'd given him an Afro, but I think the others might have drawn the line. Actually, it was perfect. Any more and they probably would have caught on to the shameless pandering."

Keri hadn't enjoyed any project so much in years. She suspected the reason was Dana. They had colluded to allow Dana to basically sneak the photos of the board members. Keri would distract one into a certain light or away from his current girlfriend. It was such fun to have a fellow conspirator, to feel not so alone. Then, sitting beside her as she edited the show, watching her long fingers fly over the computer as she manipulated the photos into what they needed, had not only caused her to respect her beautiful friend's skill even more, it had sent her hormones into overdrive. She slammed that door quickly.

"Who would have thought those guys were such peacocks? I mean, a couple of them, yeah. But they were all loving it by the end." She looked into Dana's eyes. And looked. This woman made her playful, excited about coming to work. Excited to wake up in the morning. Hell, just excited. It had only been a month! That realization thumped her in the heart, and she sat up and started straightening papers.

"Mission accomplished. That was the biggest hurdle for the project."

"They were a pushover," Dana said.

Wanting to sound businesslike, Keri asked, "How are you settling in around here?"

Dana had been lost in the sound of Keri's voice. She had to work to figure out what was being asked of her. "Oh, just fine. Shelley managed to create an office on this floor close to yours. It's small but it's all I need. I can store equipment and supplies, but I'll keep my laptop with me. I'll do a lot of the work in my darkroom at home. Then bring copies in to show you."

Keri leaned forward. "You have a home darkroom? I thought everything was digital these days." She couldn't get enough information about Dana. She hung on every word.

Swallowing to hide her anxiety at talking about herself, Dana said, "Most is. But I like to drag out my old SLRs and use film and spend hours making it just so. Some of my fellow photogs consider me a dinosaur for not switching completely over. But I..." She stopped, coloring slightly and looking down.

"But you what? Dana?" Keri gently prodded. "Please?"

Dana looked at the beautiful creature across from her. She was uncomfortable talking about herself. In her world it always came back to be used against her. But Keri had said "please." "It's where I find peace. I can't explain it any more than that. In the darkroom and walking on the beach. Peace." Her voice had trailed off so that the last word was barely audible.

Keri knew that Dana had just shared something important. Her heart broke for the lovely woman who needed to seek such solitary places to find solace. And her guilt at having caused much of Dana's pain fell heavily on her shoulders. She struggled to keep her composure.

Dana, changing the subject, said, "Say, did you know that Jameson invited me to work out with him? He has a martial arts trainer and another man who helped his rehab from that bad break a few years ago. He's introduced me to a lot of the players, too. So has AJ. Between the two of them, I've met quite a few."

Keri was grateful for the change of subject and delighted with the news. Dana was fitting in effortlessly, and now that the board had agreed to the project, she felt a huge lift.

"Do you think he wants to date you?" Keri's hand almost flew to her mouth in surprise. She had no idea why she asked that question. Feeling the heat in her cheeks, she said, "I mean..."

Dana tried to act like she didn't notice but seemed pleased. "No. I've watched. He's attracted to African-American women. And beautiful ones at that. I think he likes me because I'm an athlete and he feels a connection through the injury. He almost had to retire because of his. I think he wants to get me in playing shape again." She was grinning.

"I think you're in terrific shape. Uh, I mean, if you want to train with him, the team will cover any additional expense." She saw Dana tense.

"Why? As part of the rehab deal? That's over. I can pay my own way."

Desperate to not have this turn nasty, Keri quickly said, "No, not at all. Confidentially, AJ told me that he'd like to have a backup. You know, someone who could climb on up a flagpole for that perfect shot. I think he's eyeballing you for that job."

When Dana smiled, obviously intrigued by the idea of helping AJ with an assignment for the team, Keri let out a breath. Maybe she was catching on to this diplomacy thing faster than she thought. She couldn't deny she enjoyed talking with Dana. She was smart and astute, and she noticed things that Keri couldn't because she was usually embroiled in solving a dilemma. Dana was good at subtext. Her photographs reflected that.

There were a few shots Keri had purposefully kept out of the show. Shots of her. She didn't withhold them because they were unflattering, but because they went beyond flattery. They captured her in a personal, almost intimate way. She felt a blush start to creep up her face and quickly glanced at her watch.

"We'd better get going or we'll miss the practice and interview."

At Keri's insistence, Dana had gone shopping, looking for a smaller camera than the industrial type she usually used. Keri thought she'd get more spontaneous shots that way. She tried to assure Keri that most people forgot about the camera after a while, but Keri was firm in her request. *Everyone's a photographer.*

As a longtime customer of one of the best camera stores in San Francisco, she was allowed to "test-drive" the various models. She was playing with the latest and smallest of the digitals, and the most recent one fit nicely in a pocket. It had great optics for its size. The only concern she had was the built-in flash. It was so bright that it sometimes overwhelmed the subjects and distracted them, thereby messing up that shot and any future ones.

Watching Dana, Keri said, "Well, it's certainly convenient for size. But I see what you mean about the flash. I thought Bob was going to have a coronary in the meeting the other day. He couldn't concentrate after you took the picture."

Studying the small camera, Dana said, "Yeah. I really lost the candid element from then on."

Dana finally looked up. "I'm not sure I can use it. It's too much of an attention grabber. The purpose of getting it was to be in the background. I must admit, though, I've never seen this small a device produce such a huge flash. And it recycles almost immediately." She turned it over in her hands again.

"Translation?"

"Huh? Oh, I mean the flash is ready to take another shot right away."

As Dana started to gather her equipment for the shoot, Keri said, "Maybe there's a way to adjust it. Somehow I think you like your new toy."

Dana just nodded and pocketed the camera. After she'd slung several Digiflex cameras with Nikon F lenses around her neck and pocketed several more lenses in her equipment vest, they walked to the elevator. Once at field level, they went through a tunnel and onto the field. Reporters were already there, interviewing coaches and players, but immediately turned their attention to Keri as soon as someone spotted her.

Dana faded into the background and started taking candid shots of the event. Having gotten what she needed from the interview, she scanned the field and stands for anything that might be of interest.

Few people were there, but two women, up halfway and to the left of the center hash mark, caught her eye. One was tall and dark, dressed completely in black. The other was shorter, skirt showing nice legs and red hair that seemed to have a life of its own.

The redhead was waving, big movements, as though trying to attract the attention of someone on the field. Dana snapped off a few shots. Zooming in and focusing, she realized the tall woman was looking directly at her. She quickly held the shutter down to take a few more in succession, then turned back to the interview.

She walked around to the other side of the group as she switched to a wide-angle lens. Aiming the camera at the interview, she tried to see at whom the red head was waving. When Keri's speech faltered and then resumed, Dana thought she knew.

Holding the larger camera in one hand, she pulled out the little digital and turned it on. She used the cover of the crowd milling around to snap off a few more shots of the women before sliding it back in her vest.

The interview ended a few moments later. As the reporters dispersed, Dana noticed the redhead start down the steps toward the field. Glancing to her left she saw Keri walking toward the stands, a determined look on her face. Dana didn't move until the tall, dark woman began to follow the redhead. A warning sounded inside of Dana and propelled her toward Keri.

She had almost caught up when Keri and the redhead met on the steps. She kept a discreet distance but made sure she was within earshot.

"What are you doing here, Gloria? I thought we'd said what we needed to say."

Standing up one step, the woman locked eyes with Keri. "Darling, I just dropped by to say hello. And to see if you wanted to get together later. We haven't seen each other in so long." Her voice was syrupy sweet.

Dana hesitated. This was obviously a private conversation. But sensing the redhead's companion moving in, she, too, took a few steps to be closer to Keri. It felt like she was evening the playing field.

The redhead didn't look happy to see Dana. "Aren't you going to introduce me to your...friend?" she asked Keri, then without waiting for a response, said, "I'm Gloria Steeple. With a double 'e.'"

Dana lowered her camera. "I'll make a note. I'm Dana Ryan. Nice to meet you, I'm sure."

The two silently glared at each other. Dana wasn't sure what was going on, but she had recognized the name from the first day she met with Keri. Up close, she didn't like her.

Just then the woman in the black pants and long leather coat arrived. She stared intently at Dana's camera. "You took pictures?"

Although the hairs on the back of her neck were at full attention, Dana casually said, "Sure. The interview, and the stands and players. That's my job. I work for Ms. Flemons."

"Give me the film. No pictures."

She reached to grab the camera, but Dana held it away. "Wait a minute! I don't even know if I took any of you, but I have a whole disk of shots here. I need them."

The woman took off her sunglasses to reveal disconcertingly dark eyes. "No pictures."

Keri had watched the scene with Gloria and Dana unfold in

amazement. Dana was actually protecting her. Now the woman with Gloria was practically threatening Dana. She stepped in. "None of the pictures will be used without your written permission. I'll make sure that any of you are deleted. Right, Dana?"

"Oh, sure. I didn't mean to upset you. I'll get rid of any with you in them. Sorry."

The woman was silent for a moment, then replaced her sunglasses, folded her arms, and stood back. Dana blew out a breath, matching the retreat distance.

Keri said, "You didn't introduce *me* to *your* new friend, Gloria."

Fidgeting slightly, Gloria said, "Um, this is Gina. She's...an associate. Gina, this is Keri Flemons." The two nodded to each other, then Gina looked away disinterestedly.

Keri took Gloria's elbow and walked her a few steps away from Gina and Dana. She demanded, "Why are you here? How did you even know I'd be here?"

Gloria ignored the question and said, "Well, are you going to join me later? I've picked out a new restaurant, very good and very private." She flashed a seductive smile. Keri knew the look.

"I can't. I have meetings all day. And I thought we decided this was not a good idea." Keri's kept her voice businesslike. "I really don't want to play these games, Gloria. I have to get back to work."

As she turned to go, Gloria grabbed her arm and spun Keri back to face her. Glancing at Dana who had taken a step toward them, she lowered her voice and said, "Some other time, then. Soon, Keri. We have a lot to talk about. And I won't take 'no' for an answer."

Gloria motioned for the taller woman to follow and left through a stadium door. Keri stood looking after her. She was trembling slightly and started when Dana put a hand on her back.

Dana withdrew her hand and quietly asked, "Are you okay? I can go after them and give that woman the disk, if you want."

Hunching her shoulders, Keri started walking to the exit. "No. Let's go." She was embarrassed to have had that conversation in front of Dana.

Dana was curious and tried for more information. Walking beside her, she mused, "Well, you've attracted a lot of attention in the media recently. Maybe she...likes you." Keri's shoulder's hunched even further, and Dana sensed the topic was closed.

"Anyway, there's something about the tall edgy one. I think I've seen her before. I have a friend at the *News,* and sometimes I help him edit articles and photos for stories. I would swear that's the connection. And he has the crime beat."

Keri glanced at her with surprise. "Really? I mean, she was weird in a very creepy way, but I don't think associating with criminals is Gloria's style."

"I'm sure you're right. But I'll check my file at home, just in case."

Keri kept walking and said, "Are you hungry? Because I was thinking of driving over to the Chalet Inn and Spa. Maybe we can get massages at their spa and go and have something to eat. My shoulders and back could use some attention."

Visualizing volunteering for that duty, Dana stumbled and caught herself. "Oops! That's a...a great idea! Sure."

Keri and Dana took the elevator to the executive floor of the administration building, and Dana hurriedly stashed her camera and lenses in a cubby, intending to pick them up before heading home that evening. Keri went to her office and asked Shelley to cancel an afternoon meeting.

Keri wanted to put some distance between herself and Gloria. She was glad to have someone to have fun with. They had been working twelve-hour days, and although she enjoyed every minute with Dana, it might be nice to just have some downtime.

She realized she didn't know much about the woman who was able to take such intimate photographs of her. She had known her as a child and knew about the accident. But she didn't know Dana the adult at all. They never talked about anything personal.

CHAPTER EIGHT

O nce in the car Dana flexed her fingers. "Phew! I'm grateful you're driving. I don't think I could grip the steering wheel. When that *woman* made a try for my camera I must have started clutching it like it would disappear. Even after they left." Dana was smiling but looking out the window as she made the comment. Keri had noticed that Dana did that a lot—made friendly, even joking comments but without eye contact.

She wanted more. "What's the matter, Ryan? You could take her!"

Turning at last to face her, Dana said, "Yeah, right. Just don't tell Jameson about it. He'll have me doing fingertip pushups and lifting weights for days. What would help more is if I improved running sprints."

She laughed and leaned back in the seat, and Keri relaxed. She started the engine and resolved to enjoy the moment.

Dana watched Keri as she concentrated on maneuvering her Audi TT two-seater through traffic. Her hair was down and she wore little makeup. But her straight nose and perfect full lips and perfect chin had all been there since childhood. She was a vision.

Another thought intruded. "Don't you have to see Zander later?" She knew that Keri had returned his call and they'd talked about a date. It had made her uncomfortable to hear her friendly banter with Zander. And she was uncomfortable that she was uncomfortable.

"No, He's probably working out." She had her cell phone and was dialing information for the spa number. "I don't see him that often. I spend more time with you than I do with him."

Now Dana was really irritated. Keri's comment had made her warm all over. The same feeling she'd had when Keri turned down that redhead and then asked Dana out. Well, of course she hadn't asked her out, but she'd said she wanted to have some fun and she wanted to be with Dana, not the redhead. Dana reminded herself exactly who Keri Flemons was, since she seemed to be forgetting lately: a spoiled, egocentric, manipulating bitch, one that she'd better keep her distance from.

After hanging up, Keri said, "I can't get us into the spa until later. How about going to the restaurant for an early dinner?"

Dana was noncommittal. "Sure. Okay."

Keri sensed a wall had just been raised. Over the past weeks she'd learned to recognize the signs. Just when they started to relax around each other, Dana would pull back. She was always polite and often friendly. But she kept the conversation on business, nothing personal. Except for that one comment about peace, and Keri wondered if she'd regretted revealing that much. They seemed to have a truce and nothing more. It was frustrating.

After a few minutes of stony silence, Keri said, "Why did you think I had a date with Zander?"

Blushing and hoping Keri kept her eyes on the road, Dana managed, "Oh, no reason. He's such a nice guy." That was true. He was a doll. *But she did say she spent more time with me. And then there's Gloria. Stop it! It doesn't matter.*

They *had* spent a lot of time together. Dana had to admit that she enjoyed every moment with Keri. She couldn't help looking forward to seeing her. It was all so confusing.

They drove across the Bay Bridge with windows up, even though the top was down. Dana had to fight the urge to put her hands over her head to protect herself from falling objects. The roadway was always under construction or retrofit against earthquakes. The lower deck they were on was infamous for occasionally having a worker drop tools on hapless motorists, even though there was protective netting to avoid it. Driving unscathed into the sunshine seemed like a miracle to Dana.

They arrived at the inn and a handsome, collegiate-looking valet took Keri's keys after helping her from the car. Dana opened the door herself and almost glared at him for the appreciative stare he was giving Keri.

The old hotel was just right for a leisurely stroll around the extensive rose gardens and then into the restaurant. They shared a light meal and a split of wine. Everything was delicious.

Keri leaned back in the booth after signing the bill. "That was perfect. Why don't we go to the spa and get our lockers and robes. We'll have time to steam and get in the whirlpool before the masseuses come for us. They have separate facilities for men and women so you can be naked. And I plan on looking like hell by the time I'm through."

"I have a hard time thinking of you looking like hell, Keri." Dana just let the words come out. *Maybe it's the wine. Nah. I have a hard time thinking of you as anything but beautiful.* Which was true, but at least she hadn't said it out loud.

Keri smiled warmly. "Likewise, Dana. Likewise." She had the urge to reach over and take Dana's hand but worried that Dana's reaction to the gesture could destroy the pleasant evening they were sharing. Instead she stood and said, "Let's go."

They walked to the spa building still feeling the glow of the wine. Once there, they signed in and were each given oversized terry-cloth robes, flip-flops, and keys to lockers. The lockers were close together in the same section.

Suddenly Dana realized that Keri and she were going to be disrobing in front of each other. She blushed intensely. *Don't panic. Treat it like any other locker room. No attention on nudity. You've done this all your life! Buck up, you big chicken.*

They went to their lockers and stripped out of their clothes. Dana managed to not look in Keri's direction, and they were soon in their robes heading for the steam room. Keri picked up two huge white towels from one of the stacks nearby and handed one to Dana. *Hey, this isn't so hard.*

Just outside of the steam room, Keri took off her robe, hung it on a hook, and shook out the towel to wrap around her torso. Dana stopped breathing. Keri was well-toned and had small but beautifully shaped breasts, a slim waist, and lovely long legs. And she was so blond. Dana tore her eyes away but her senses went into overdrive. She quickly busied herself with her own robe and towel, hoping to hide the rush of heat that had probably turned her entire body fuchsia. When she finally stole a glance at Keri, she thought she saw a bit of a flush on her cheeks.

The steam room was thankfully fogged up and empty. Keri stripped off the towel and folded it to sit on. Dana mechanically followed suit and sat beside her about a foot away, eyes forward. They both let out big sighs as the steam hit them, and Dana relaxed into the moment.

Keri said, "Ahh. Between the food and wine and the board meeting this morning, this day is just about perfect. Except for seeing Gloria. How's your day been?"

Dana closed her eyes and said what she was thinking. "I don't recall such a nice day. Not since...I was a child."

Keri didn't respond. Dana kept her eyes closed until she felt a hand gently touch her bad leg. Her eyes flew open to see Keri leaning over and examining the scars, and she reflexively flinched away. Her reaction was both protective of her leg and protective of herself. She would not allow anyone near it.

"My God." Keri looked into Dana's green eyes and whispered, "The accident."

Dana turned away and slammed her eyes shut, fighting to keep her composure.

Keri whispered, "I'm sorry. I'm so sorry."

"Don't! Just...don't." The silence was deafening. Finally, Dana found her voice again, "I don't usually talk about it. With anyone."

The door to the steam room opened. A big woman with a thick accent and a friendly face, wearing a spa T-shirt, stuck her head in and said, "Donna?"

Dana gave her a small smile. "Close enough. I'll be right there." Standing, she said, "I guess that's my cue. See you in a bit." She quickly got up, pulled on her robe, and followed the masseuse. Keri had to sit for a moment to absorb what had just happened. Her mind and body were at war with each other. Her heart ached for Dana's suffering. She had wanted nothing more than to hold Dana in her arms and tell her the scars didn't matter. But she had *no right*. She was the cause of Dana's pain. She was surprised by her reaction to the scars. She was horrified and ashamed. She found herself wishing she had been there for Dana. She couldn't remember ever experiencing feelings like that for someone. She would give anything not to have been the source of such hurt for Dana.

Feeling a little overwhelmed, Keri forced herself up and out of the room and settled into the whirlpool to wait for the masseuse to call her name. Thankfully she didn't wait long.

Once on the massage table, she thought about Dana again. She couldn't deny her visceral reaction to seeing her naked; it was completely sexual. She'd felt her nipples harden just from the glimpse she'd had when they took off their robes, and again as Dana left the steam room. She was amazing. Her full breasts and caramel nipples caused Keri to lick her lips and swallow. She was a vision of grace and power, regardless of her damaged leg.

As the masseuse worked on her shoulders and back, she thought about the past few weeks spent with Dana. She had to admit that she was happy whenever Dana was around. She couldn't even rationalize it by reasoning that things were going well with the team. It was more than that. It felt like *home* to her. Home in a way she hadn't felt since childhood. She knew she shouldn't be attracted to Dana. She didn't even know if Dana was gay. Keri wondered if Dana realized that *she* was gay. *Well, if she didn't before, today's confrontation with Gloria should have opened her eyes.* But she had asked about Zander. Keri thought it was obvious they weren't romantically involved. She even wondered if Zander were gay himself.

Dana was always available. They were spending a lot of time together, which only made Keri want more. She missed Dana when she wasn't around. But Dana never asked for more, never initiated seeing her outside of work. Her mind kept circling until she dozed on the table.

After the massage she returned to the dressing room to see a freshly showered Dana just getting dressed. Keri felt suddenly awkward and unsure. She asked, "Did you enjoy the massage?"

Not looking at her, Dana mumbled, "Yeah, it was great."

Keri immediately made a decision. Heart hammering in her chest, she said, "Um, I'm going to shower. I feel like a greased pig. Want to stay at the Chalet?"

There, she threw herself at her. She knew the answer might hurt, but she had to get some idea of what Dana was feeling.

Dana knew she should decline the unexpected invitation and get away from Keri, but more than anything else she did *not* want the evening to end. Smiling, she said, "That's a great idea. I'd love a drink. I think they play live music in the lounge. We could go there."

Dana was surprised to see a wry smile appear on Keri's face. Had she misunderstood what Keri was saying? Then Keri dropped the robe and wandered to the showers. The image of Keri, the robe gathered around her feet, was tattooed on her retinas.

It took a few minutes to get herself together, then she noticed that Keri hadn't taken a towel. Picking up one from a nearby stack she arrived at the shower stall just as Keri pulled the door open. They were face to face with only the towel between them.

"I…uh…you forgot…" Dana looked into her eyes and found a tender and vulnerable soul looking back at her.

Keri suddenly swayed, as if she would faint. Dana dropped the towel and grabbed Keri's shoulders to steady her. Unable to stop, she pulled her into an embrace, one that was returned.

She whispered, "Are you okay?"

Several boisterous women burst into the locker room. Dana released Keri and quickly retrieved a dry towel, protectively wrapping it around her shoulders.

Keri managed to stammer, "I, um, I'm fine. But, but I've gotten you wet." She was looking at Dana's shirt and pants, which were now mottled with water. Her nipples were plainly visible through the shirt. Her own were painfully hard.

Dana's eyes went wide. *How could she tell?* Suddenly realizing what was meant, she glanced down at her clothes and registered her nipples. *Damn.*

"Oh! Um, not a problem. I haven't put on my sweater yet. That'll take care of it. Here, let me get you another towel." She kept her eyes averted until she had pulled a second one and handed it to Keri.

"Thanks," Keri croaked.

"I'll meet you out front," Dana said, and hastened to her locker to finish dressing.

In the reception area Dana paid for the massages and sat down to wait. Her mind kept issuing warnings, but her body overwhelmed anything else. She concentrated on breathing to calm down and return some circulation to her extremities. She tried to tell herself that this was MyKeri, her childhood friend. But, as much as she loved and wanted to marry MyKeri when they were children, the intervening years had stolen that resolve from her. She absolutely could *not* be attracted to the adult Keri.

But Dana had never felt what she was feeling now. "I am in such trouble," she muttered.

The spa clerk glanced up at her, then returned to her book.

Keri dressed in a haze. What was it about Dana? Maybe it was the challenge, the fact that Dana wouldn't succumb to her charms. Maybe this was just another game, the kind Keri had played for so long it had become automatic. But somehow she knew that wasn't true. Dana was different, she always had been. When Keri had walked out of the shower and looked into Dana's eyes, she saw Scooter. She'd come just short of passing out. She didn't know whether to laugh or cry when they were interrupted.

Finally dressed, Keri joined Dana in the reception area and, when she tried to pay, found it had been covered. She looked over at Dana to thank her and saw she was sitting bolt upright on a bench by the stairs going up to ground level. Dana hadn't noticed her.

When Keri called her name, Dana blushed as she stood. Keri noticed that her slacks were still damp, and she couldn't resist a smile at the memory of the embrace.

They walked over to the lounge and settled into a small table. After ordering hot brandy Dana checked the bar menu and also ordered a snack, cayenne fries. She seemed completely preoccupied, and Keri wondered if it was because of what had just happened in the shower or whether she was dwelling on the accident. She was afraid to ask.

The drinks came and so did the fries. They were crisp and quite spicy. There were a lot of them, too. Keri had a few but noticed that Dana was practically inhaling them.

Catching movement in her peripheral vision, Keri looked up to see a couple from her Presidio Heights neighborhood, waving. She smiled and excused herself to say hello. Dana watched her go and felt panic rising inside of her. She tried to swallow the fear with the fries. *God, I almost kissed her. What was I thinking?* When Keri returned to the table the fries were gone, and Dana was staring in the direction of the band.

"Oh, my. You really like spicy food." Keri sat down at the table, next to Dana. Dana seemed completely distracted.

"What?" Dana stared at the empty dish. "Oh! Yeah. Would you like another drink?"

"No, I have to drive. Unless…would you like one?"

"Me? No, no, I don't drink much."

Feeling a stab of guilt at the mention of drinking, Keri knew the evening was over. Dana seemed unreachable. "Well, I guess we'd better go then. Are you sure you don't want…anything else?"

She watched as Dana's mouth tried to form words. "N…no…I'm fine."

Before driving back to the city, Keri suggested that they put the top up on the Audi because crossing the Bay Bridge would be cold at that hour. Dana numbly agreed.

As they entered the parking garage at the stadium Keri quietly said, "I had a wonderful day. I'm sorry to see it end. I lo…enjoy being with you, Dana."

Dana stared straight ahead. After a few seconds, she said, "I liked it, too."

They pulled up beside Dana's car and Keri turned off the engine. She dared to explore Dana's eyes. They were charcoal in the dim light of the garage. There was a fire there, smoldering. Unable to stop herself she took Dana's hand and brought it to her lips, lightly kissing the back of it.

Dana shivered. She wanted to say something, but before she could translate what she felt into words, a light swept over the car and the roar of a large engine approaching made Keri release her hand.

"You all right in there, Ms. Flemons?" A gravelly male voice sounded over a loudspeaker.

Keri closed her eyes and sighed. She placed a smile on her face and hit the button to roll her window down. "We're fine, John. Ms. Ryan and I were at a meeting and stopped to grab a bite. I'm just returning her to her car. Thanks for checking! You're the best!"

The security guard chuckled, obviously pleased with himself. "No problem. You and Ms. Ryan drive careful on the way home." He turned off the light and pulled the large SUV away, continuing on his rounds.

Keri turned back to Dana and could see by the lights in the garage that she was perspiring. "Are you okay?"

"I…um…no. I don't feel very well. I've got to go. See you tomorrow." Her hand worked the door handle unsuccessfully. She looked slightly panicked.

Keri hit the central lock to open her door. "Can I help you?"

"No! I mean, I think those fries were a little too spicy and I…I have to get home."

"Dana, if you can't make it we could run into the stadium. You look…a little stressed."

Dana shook her head. "No. I'll see you tomorrow! I mean Monday! Thanks!"

She ripped out of the car, fumbling for her keys. Within seconds her car roared to life and tore out of the garage and across the parking lot, bouncing and squealing as it disappeared into the night.

Keri sat for a moment, wondering. She had seen desire in those eyes, she was sure of it. But she was beginning to realize that her emotions involved more than lust, and that those feelings were hers alone. She wished that guard hadn't galloped onto the scene when he did. Dana was…probably about to blow her off. She still held her and the entire Flemons family responsible for her father's death. She would never allow herself to care about Keri that way, and Keri was deluding herself if she even imagined it.

She ran a hand through her hair. "*Cripes*! Why does everything have to be so *complicated*? Can't a girl just fall in love anymore?" She stopped. "Oh no! I'm falling in love. Am I? I can't wait to see her, I miss her when she's not there, I think she's beautiful. Well, she is. Oh, Lord, this must be what if feels like. And she'll never return it. What the hell am I going to do?"

She started the car and slowly drove home, tears rolling down her face. She had to face the whole weekend knowing how empty her life was, and would remain.

❖

Dana stirred. The incessant ringing must be the machines she was hooked up to, she thought. She could smell that curious mix of medicine, human waste, and antiseptic that signaled "hospital." She kept her eyes closed, unwilling to open them to the devastation she knew awaited her. But the ringing persisted, pulling her further into consciousness.

One…two…three…four. Click. Jim was yelling for her. Then it started all over again. Lots of times. What was Jim doing here? She didn't know him when her father died. One…two…three…four. Click.

"Dana? Dana! Get up! I know you're there! I can see your car out front. Dana? Answer the phone or I'll be banging on your door in five minutes. I mean it! Dana?"

She opened her eyes and the hospital smell receded. Searching for the shrill voice to silence it, she heaved out of bed and limped to the phone on the dresser.

Groggily, she answered, "Hello? Jim?"

"Dana! Thank heaven. I was getting ready to break your door down. Do you know what time it is?"

Clearing her throat, she croaked, "Jim? What's wrong?"

He sounded exasperated. "It's two in the afternoon! Saturday! The charity function? Remember? You, my dear, are my *beard*! Did you forget?"

"Oh. Saturday? Two p.m.?" She dimly remembered seeing her clock before her eyes finally closed the night before. Four a.m. She'd been up all night, sick from the cayenne fries and whatever poison she'd drunk. Her mouth tasted like she'd been licking ashtrays.

Undaunted, Jim said, "I'm picking you up in one hour so you'd better get cracking. I left your outfit in a box outside your door. You are going to be *sexy* today! You can thank me later." He hung up.

"Bitch." She scratched and tried to think, finally making her way to the front door and opening it. A large box labeled Saks Fifth Avenue was leaning against the wall. Jim had been shopping for her again. Dana groaned as she bent to retrieve it.

Fifty minutes later, showered and made-up, she was examining herself in the mirror. She had to admit she looked good in this Sylvia Rykiel stuff. The forest green gabardine suit reflected her eyes and fit her shoulders perfectly. The sleeves were the right length for her arms, and the evening pants flowed across the boots just so. She rarely wore anything that didn't need tailoring. But she needed to have a talk with Jim about the amount of cleavage she was now showing. The pale oyster jersey shell she wore under the suit had a scoop neck that was more scoop than she was comfortable with. Jim knocked on the door and she went to answer. At least he had picked out a great pair of black leather boots for her. Soft and comfortable, easily putting her over six feet. He did love to tower over the straight people.

Opening the door, she held out her arms for inspection. Jim, wearing an impeccable complement to her clothes, came in, circled her, fussed with her hair, told her she needed more lipstick, and escorted her to his new Porsche Carrera.

As they drove north across the Golden Gate Bridge a short while later, he said, "Hon, I've never known you to sleep in. Hot date last night?"

Careful not to move her head, Dana said, "I was with my boss. Long day and I made the mistake of ordering cayenne fries at the end of it. The fries were on top of one or two drinks, I can't remember. I don't want to talk about it. Ugh."

He made commiserating noises. "Well, you cleaned up good, sweetie, and you'll be the hottest woman there. Does that make you feel better?"

"Not even a little."

Jim seemed to read her reluctance. "Just a few hours, then let's escape and go to the Castro and have some fun."

She smiled at her friend. Soon he would be hypermasculine, sharing war stories with colleagues and schmoozing clients. She would be his date. She sighed. She should probably be grateful she wasn't at home morosely dissecting last night. There was time enough for that.

Keri had kissed her hand. She was starting to feel the effects of the fries, and her mind was whirling from the embrace they had briefly shared, then Keri had kissed her hand. She stared down to her lap, where that hand lay. She had spent the night doing the same thing, when she wasn't indisposed. In the shower she had stared at it until the water was tepid. Keri had kissed her hand.

They exited the freeway and wound up the narrow roads of Mill Valley, the views getting more spectacular with each hairpin turn. Shortly they arrived at the Mountain Home Inn, perched on Mt. Tamalpais. Jim insisted on parking the Porsche himself, grousing about Rent-A-Valets being pubescent boys who wouldn't mind taking it for a spin. That meant they had to park on one side of the narrow road and race across to the restaurant before a tourist driving too fast came around a curve and ran over them.

Jim said that the entire inn was reserved for the event. It looked like a Swiss chalet, all wood and windows, and the food was good, but the views were why people came. Beautiful valleys and hills of Mt. Tamalpais and the Pacific Ocean and San Francisco beyond. It all depended on which window you chose for your viewing. They entered and signed in, and he steered them in the direction of colleagues from his firm he'd spotted. She recognized them and set her mind on being stuck for the afternoon and evening. The distraction would do her good. She deliberately held her Kir Royale in the hand that *hadn't* been kissed. Kissed.

After a few moments of small talk, she felt her stomach rumble and realized that she hadn't eaten since the night before. She made a lame joke about Jim starving her. It had enough double entendre in it to get an approving smile from him, and she excused herself to the appetizer table. She left her drink untouched on a bus tray and picked up a small plate, intending to dive into the food. She was so absorbed filling her plate, she didn't notice the person who now stood next to her.

"Excuse me, are you Dana Ryan?"

Mouth full of a miniquiche, Dana silently cursed what little celebrity she had left. She was still occasionally recognized from her Olympic soccer-team days. She quickly swallowed and turned to politely greet the fan.

As she smiled and met the woman's eyes, time seemed to stand perfectly still, then move in reverse. "Moms?"

Warm blue eyes shining with tears gazed lovingly back at hers. "Scooter." Then Dana felt her plate slip from her hands and they were hugging each other tightly and both of them were crying. The room fell silent and witnessed the obviously joyous reunion.

Keri and Zander had just arrived when they heard the commotion. Smiling at a comment Zander had made, Keri glanced over to where the noise was coming from and stopped in her tracks. Her shock at seeing Dana hugging another woman was only eclipsed by realizing who the other woman was. Her mother.

Zander innocently commented, "Wow, looks like old friends have found each other."

"So I see." Her tone must have made Zander stare in her direction, but by that time she was on her way to the reunion. She was furious.

She stopped beside the two women who drew back, holding hands and gazing at her like they did when she was a child and they were inviting her to take a walk. Scooter had always been a sucker for Moms.

"What are you doing here?" Keri addressed her mother.

Carolyn Flemons's eyes went from joy to caution. She seemed to steel herself and dropped Dana's hand. "I came to try and talk to you, Keri. Finding Scooter here was just a stroke of unbelievable good luck."

Keri's face was flushed with fury. She started to open her mouth but Carolyn quickly injected, smiling, "Keri, you aren't a child any longer. You can't just have a tantrum and not expect consequences. People are watching you. We can either take this into another room or you can make a fool out of yourself. Your choice."

Clamping her mouth shut, Keri knew she was right. A lot of important people were here, including the press. She had to pull it together. But she didn't know how.

Under her breath Carolyn said, "Smile and give me a hug. Exclaim about not knowing I was coming to this affair. I'll take care of the rest."

Keri followed directions, and Carolyn took both women in tow and led them out of the door and to another room that was vacant for the time being. She thanked the hostess who had pointed it out and closed the doors.

Once they were alone she folded her arms and gave her daughter a wry look. "Okay, let me have it."

Keri didn't need an invitation. "How *dare* you come to this without asking me! How dare you try to make friends with Scooter!" Whirling on Dana she said, "And you, what are you doing here? Why are you hugging my mother?" She had the vague feeling she wasn't making sense, but the words just came out.

Chagrined, Dana started to answer when Carolyn interrupted. "Keri, calm down. None of this is Scooter's fault. I read in the paper that you might be here. I came with Al Phillips. And it's a fund-raiser for abused children, a cause I am happy to support. It's open to whoever has the money to get in."

"You stalked me? Oh, that's low. I won't see you, and you force the issue in front of witnesses. And you came here with Al Phillips? He was Daddy's dear friend. You've got your nerve. Are you offering to screw him too?" Keri immediately regretted her words, seeing the look of hurt in her mother's eyes. But her mother didn't rise to the bait.

"I didn't stalk you. I was simply trying to see you in person. Is that so much to ask after ten years and your father's death?"

Keri was on a roll. "You left us! You had an affair and you left us! Should I just forget that?"

"I *retaliated*!" Carolyn stopped, then. "It was stupid and I apologized, but you refused to see me. You cut me out of your life like I never existed. Your father never went that far."

Keri was momentarily speechless. Then, "Don't you talk about Daddy! Leave. Just leave this party and get out of my sight. Go back to Paris. And leave Dana alone, too."

At that moment, Carolyn seemed to snap. "That's it. You are

behaving like an idiot, Keri Flemons. Number one, I will go where I please and with whom I please and when I please. I don't need your permission. Number two, for your information I live in San Francisco now. Number three, you may not have had time to really examine just who the minority owners of the team are, but my name is there. I might just decide to sit in on the board meetings from now on. And, *finally*, if Scooter wants to see me, as far as I'm concerned, I would treasure every moment with her. It is her decision, not yours. You aren't six years old anymore. Although you certainly are acting like it."

Straightening her jacket, Carolyn looked at both women. "Now I'm going back out there and having a good time if it kills me. Keri, if you want to leave, fine."

Addressing Dana, she said, "Scooter, I live in the condominiums above the Four Seasons. On Market between Third and Fourth. I'm in the book under C. Flemons. I would love to get together with you and catch up. I've thought about you so often these past years. You've grown into a beautiful young woman. Good evening, ladies."

They watched her leave. Dana was in awe. "Wow. She looks great."

Absently, Keri said, "Yes, she does."

Stealing a sidelong glance at Keri, Dana ventured, "You haven't seen her in ten years?"

Nodding slightly, Keri amended, "Eleven."

Dana tried to hide her shock. "Phew! She can still whip us into shape."

Cocking an eyebrow at her friend, Keri grinned. "You always did take half the blame for the trouble I usually got us into. Actually, she was whipping me into shape. I'm sorry you had to witness that. And I apologize for being so possessive of you."

Keri registered the pleased look on Dana's face, then noticed *her* for really the first time. Taking in the whole of Dana, she could barely breathe. Her mouth started watering when she got to the top that revealed Dana's breasts so enticingly. Forcing her eyes up, she managed, "Uh, I didn't know you would be here. You look really nice."

Dana didn't miss Keri's reaction to what she was wearing. She'd have to thank Jim instead of lecturing him. She normally despised being ogled by men or women. She felt safer hiding her feminine figure. But

Keri's attention was different. It was pleasurable to have Keri react to her.

"I didn't know either. I mean, I knew I was going with my friend Jim to something but didn't connect the dots that it was the same 'something' you and Zander were coming to. I guess we should find them. We've been missing awhile."

Dana had noticed the beautiful dress Keri was wearing when Moms was dragging them to the room. The folds of it caressed Keri's figure and ended above her knees. The color, a deep plum, complemented her blond hair and blue eyes. Keri's high heels were the sexy kind that Dana could never wear. She was entranced.

Keri hesitated. She was firmly rooted in place, only a step away from Dana. She wanted nothing more than to reach for her. She searched for something to keep them alone instead of with others. "I'm sorry if I was rude. I was surprised, that's all. I mean, I didn't realize my mother was in town. I thought she was still in Paris." She thought she sounded like an idiot but didn't know what else to say.

Dana's eyes widened. "I...didn't even know they were divorced."

Keri looked away, embarrassed and hurt. It was clear that Dana hadn't even cared enough to find out what was happening in Keri's life. But, she was there at the cemetery after Daddy died. She had cared enough then. Keri didn't want to talk about her mother.

"Listen, about last night," Keri said. "I was worried about you. Are you okay?"

Dana understood that Keri was uncomfortable talking about Moms, but the topic of last night was something that made *her* uncomfortable. She didn't know what to make of the kiss on the back of her hand and couldn't stop thinking about it.

"Okay?" Dana leaned toward Keri, drawn like a magnet.

Closer now, Keri said, "Yes. You left so quickly and you looked like you were ill." Her lips were moist, so full of promise; her eyes seemed to reflect concern for Dana.

Dana rasped, "I was...I shouldn't have eaten all those fries. I...got sick." Dana was lost and didn't pay attention to the alarms her brain was sounding. All she wanted was to taste those lips. Those pink, full lips.

Keri reached for Dana and was only vaguely aware of the door opening. Her peripheral vision registered a body that somehow sent a message loud and clear to not be caught with a woman in her arms. She squeezed Dana's arms and pushed her away to arm's length, trying to get her breathing under control.

"Oh, you're sick, Dana?" She made a show of friendly concern. "Do you have a fever?"

Keri thought she must be as flushed as Dana appeared at that moment. She had to tear her eyes away from Dana's to see who had intruded.

The small man with odd hair who was watching them intently was none other than Herb Kronerberg, the society columnist from the *San Francisco News*. He was also infamous for feeding more than one gossip rag tidbits of information and writing them himself. For Keri to be seen in the arms of a woman at this point in her nascent career could spell disaster.

Beside her, she heard Dana. "Yes, yes, I think I do have a fever. I'm sorry. Thanks for helping me. I believe I almost made a fool out of myself. I need to leave before that happens."

She brushed past Keri and then past Kronerberg.

He stared after her. "Poor dear, she looked on the verge of tears. You say she has a fever?" His rat-like brown eyes glittered like he had just found a fresh meal.

Keri schooled her features to hide her disappointment. She'd be damned if she'd give him one thing to make innuendos about. "I think so. She almost fainted, as you saw."

He gave her an oily grin, revealing expensively capped teeth. "Yes, I did see that."

"You must excuse me. I'll go check on her." Keri fled the room as fast as she could without breaking into a run.

When she got back to the main reception room she couldn't find Dana, her date, Zander, or even her mother. A minute later Zander and Moms came in the front entrance, both looking concerned.

Keri briskly walked up to them. "Where's Dana? Is she okay?"

Moms gave her a hard look and demanded, "What did you say to her? She had to have Jim take her home. She looked positively devastated."

Keri felt defensive. "Nothing! We were talking and Herb

Kronerberg burst into the room. Dana suddenly became ill and had to leave."

An inkling of comprehension seemed to cross Zander's and Carolyn's face at the same moment. Both had been in the limelight often enough to fear and loathe the name Herb Kronerberg. But Dana probably had no idea who he was or what havoc he could wreak.

Carolyn spat out, "'Plugs.' That son of a bitch!"

Zander looked confused. "'Plugs'?"

Staring at the little weasel when he reappeared with a smug look on his face, Carolyn muttered, "In honor of a hair-plug job gone terribly wrong."

Zander smiled and gazed at Kronerberg. "Couldn't happen to a nicer guy."

Keri paid no attention. She felt sick. She had just destroyed the fragile bond that was growing between them. How could Dana understand the need to protect both of them and the team from Kronerberg's poison pen? She'd probably thought Keri was just looking for an excuse to reject her. She felt her mother move to one side and pat her reassuringly on the back.

"Talk to her and explain," Carolyn said. "She'll understand."

But Keri wasn't so sure.

CHAPTER NINE

Dana came in to work later than usual and walked right past Shelley's office without stopping to say hello. Keri wasn't entirely surprised. She'd wondered if Dana would show up at all.

Catching a puzzled look from Shelley, she said, "I'll check on her," and followed Dana down the hall.

To her astonishment, before she could catch up, Dana turned and said, "There's no need to follow me."

Keri gently reached to touch her arm, uncertain what to say. "Listen. About what happened Saturday—"

"Nothing happened Saturday." Dana had just closed the subject. Her tone was expressionless and her face was impossible to read.

Keri felt queasy. The walls that had been coming down between them seemed to be back up, even thicker than ever. Taking Dana's cue and trying to act as if this were just another day at the office, she said, "Okay. So, let me get you some coffee. No, tea. Mild tea. I think I could use some too. Go to your office, sit down and relax. We have a vendors' meeting coming up, but we can talk about that later."

"Fine. Please don't trouble yourself about the tea. I'd like some time to myself this morning." Dana reached for her door handle.

Accepting the rebuff and the hurt that went with it, Keri turned to leave. She heard a sharp intake of breath and a shocked exclamation. "Shit!" Dana was standing just inside her open door. Keri stared past her and could not believe what she saw.

The office had been trashed. Furniture turned over, papers strewn about, photos that had been on the wall torn to pieces. Someone had spray painted on the wall words of warning: "Bitch" and "Get out!"

Her face ashen, Dana choked out, "Who would do this? Why?"

"I don't know. But we'll find out." Keri walked through the mess to Dana's desk and picked up the phone, instructing, "Shelley, call the police. And get security up here."

Dana was still rooted to the spot. "I can't believe this. Is it about me?"

"Probably not." Keri was searching for a logical explanation. "It's more likely to be about me."

"The security cameras." Dana swept a look toward the hall. "They'll show who it was. I'll go down there now and—"

"No." Keri stopped her with a hand on her arm. She didn't want Dana anywhere near something that might be dangerous. "Let's wait until the police arrive. Go to my office. I'll be there in a minute."

Dana seemed reluctant, but finally said, "Okay. I guess they won't let us clean up or anything. They'll be checking for fingerprints." She was talking too quickly, her mouth trembling.

Keri longed to put her arms around Dana and comfort her, but after the run-in with Kronerberg, she knew better than to try it. "Please. Go have some coffee and something to eat. You look like you need it."

Dana was numb. She'd cried most of the weekend, berating herself at her own stupidity for believing Keri could be interested in her for anything more than a fling or someone to laugh at. Now all she wanted was to curl up in Keri's arms and be comforted. She was beyond weak.

As Dana disappeared through the door to Keri's suite of offices, the elevator at the end of the hall opened to reveal a large man in a cheap gray suit and red tie and a uniformed guard. They came steaming down the hall.

Keri recognized the man in the suit. He was big and burly and bristled with attitude. He didn't look pleased.

"Stand aside, Ms. Flemons," he said, fairly brimming with self-importance. "We'll take over from here. And tell whoever called the cops to cancel the call. They won't do nothin' about a B and E."

Folding her arms over her chest, Keri stood her ground. "I'm staying right here until the police arrive. I don't want the scene disturbed. And they will do something about it, I assure you."

"Listen. As the head of security I want you out of here."

Through clenched teeth, Keri said, "And as the managing partner of this organization, Mr. Smith, I'm not leaving."

The security guy was not able to hide his surprise. "Ms. Flemons. Sorry, but I have instructions not to bother you."

"Instructions from whom?" As if she couldn't guess.

"Mr. Concannon," Smith said, with a hint of self-righteousness.

"Well, Mr. Concannon isn't here and I run this organization now. This break-in happened next to my office and to one of my personal staff, and I want answers. The police will be here any minute. Please allow them to do their job."

"Okay, okay. But, if it's just a trash job, they won't pay much attention."

She studied him, marveling at his attitude "I want to know who got in here, breached *our* security. I want you to conduct an investigation and have answers when they ask for them. If they aren't interested, I am. I'll wait for the police. I believe you have work to do. For a start we'll need the security camera footage. And I mean now."

His face red, Smith turned on his heel, summoned the guard, and the two men marched off.

Keri surveyed the damage one more time, imprinting it on her mind, then walked down the now-deserted hall and asked one of Shelley's assistants to watch Dana's office door and not allow anyone in until the police arrived. She wanted to be informed when they got there.

Shelley was just coming out of Keri's office, a grim look on her face.

"How is she?" Keri asked.

"Well, I got her some tea and a croissant. She's upset."

Giving her assistant a squeeze on the shoulder in thanks, Keri went into her office to find Dana sitting in the chair in front of her desk, staring at the photos on the long table behind it.

Keri pulled up a chair and sat beside her. Dana's shoulders were slumped and her eyes seemed defeated. She looked lost and confused. Keri sought to comfort her friend. "Dana, I'm pretty sure the words they scrawled were only meant to intimidate."

"Why would someone do that?" Dana asked, as if to herself.

She felt a warm hand slip into hers and stay there. She looked up and into Keri's incredible blue eyes. They were filled with compassion and understanding.

"Dana, I think someone is trying to scare both of us. I thought it was just me they were getting at, but on second thought, they must want you to quit too. It was a threat. I know I've been stirring up some hornets' nests around here. Perhaps they just don't want a witness. I wouldn't blame you if you did quit."

Dana focused on their hands. Listening to Keri and hearing the concern for her safety affected her deeply. And feeling her warm fingers crushed to her own was undoing what resolve she had. "Well, I'm not going anywhere."

"And they picked the wrong bitch to mess with," Keri responded. They sat in silence for a few moments.

Dana said, "They probably wanted the cameras. I stupidly left them here Friday. I thought I would pick them up before I went home but...I left in a hurry." She released Keri's hand and stood to move to the window, unable to meet her eyes.

After a moment she said, "Don't worry, I'll be ready for the vendors' meeting. If the cameras are gone or wrecked, I have a spare in the car." Quickly shoving her hand in her pocket, she located the small digital she had remembered to bring with her.

"And, if all else fails, they'll just have to be dazzled by the flash. I'll take care of it and wait for the cops."

Watching Dana, Keri was struck by her strength and beauty. She closed her eyes and savored the image. Then Shelley buzzed and the day started. She didn't see Dana again until the meeting.

❖

Carolyn threw on her sweats and grabbed her gym bag, ready to go to the Bay Club and work out. She was particularly looking forward to the punching bag, something her personal trainer had turned her on to about a month before. She was going to beat the crap out of Herb Kronerberg in effigy.

After Carolyn had left Dana and Keri at the fund-raiser, she'd found Al Phillips talking to Zander MacCauley and Dana's friend, Jim Miller. They had an instant rapport and were chatting away when Dana came hurrying out of the room.

Poor Dana had looked devastated and asked Jim to take her home. She said she was sick, but Carolyn didn't believe a word of it. She walked with Dana as they went to the car and gave her a fierce hug, one that Dana returned. She told her, "It's going to be okay, sweetie. Call me and we'll talk. I promise."

Dana's eyes reflected a deep sadness and maybe a hint of trust. Carolyn remembered that look from Dana's childhood. Well, she wasn't going to let her down this time.

When Keri came up to them looking equally distressed, Carolyn had put together some fairly simple pieces. She despised Kronerberg for his hateful destruction of so many relationships. He gloried in the scoop and didn't give a damn who was hurt. More than once he had intimated why her marriage had broken up. That rat-bastard.

Regardless of how rude Keri had been to her, she had seen genuine regret on her face over Dana, and Carolyn wanted to help her girls as she hadn't been able to when they were children. One of the most difficult things she had ever done was to admit defeat in her efforts to help Dana. Then her own life had disintegrated and she had moved out of the country. But she was back and had been given a second chance.

She might not ever be able to rebuild her relationship with her daughter, but that didn't mean she couldn't help her find some happiness. The last time she remembered seeing true joy on Keri's face was when she and Scooter had gotten permission to marry each other when they grew up. Keri was never quite the same carefree child again after Scooter was torn from her life. She was angry and despondent, then remote. She focused on being with Mike, and Carolyn's relationship with her began its downhill slide.

Despite the years of estrangement, Carolyn knew and loved her daughter. And she loved Scooter, too. Her wish for both of them would be to see the joy back in their lives. Now all she had to do was figure out how she could help.

She threw her bag in the back of her car and tipped the valet for bringing it up from the garage. It was going to be a long workout. She did some of her best thinking then.

❖

Sinking down into the leather sofa in Keri's office, Dana let out a tired groan and glanced at Keri, who was curled sideways at the other end of the couch. She was pale and drawn and looked exhausted. Dana's heart hitched a beat, and she wanted nothing more than to take her in her arms and hold her tightly.

Neither woman had eaten since lunch, and it was close to nine o'clock. The meeting had been contentious. Vendors who had been with the stadium and team for decades claimed they were getting no cooperation from Concannon and had been threatened with losing their contracts if they didn't pay more money for leases, as well as a slew of new user fees that Keri had never seen before. They insisted they were being squeezed out, and it certainly looked that way.

Late in the meeting, Keri managed to buy some time by appealing to their longtime relationship with her father and now, she hoped, her. They had reluctantly agreed and did seem mollified for the moment.

The pictures Dana had taken of some of the angry faces in the room were telling. Keri could only promise an investigation into their allegations. She had already called for a review of the contracts and was planning on asking Jim Miller's law firm to go over them. Dana was gratified that Keri took her recommendation of Jim without question.

Looking at Keri, Dana knew she wasn't supposed to care, but seeing her so weary and vulnerable made her ache to be closer. "Rough day." It was all she could come up with.

A tired smile played on Keri's lips. "I'm just glad you were there. At least I didn't have to face the lynch mob alone."

"Glad to be of service, ma'am. Really." Dana was enjoying feasting her gaze on Keri. She had worn a beautifully cut navy pantsuit and a white silk shirt, with pumps that gave her a few extra inches in height. Dana had seen it before and always admired how it made Keri look professional and sexy at the same time. But she had to admit, if Keri had worn a flour sack, she would have thought she looked sexy. Sweeping up the lovely body she stopped at her face. And Keri's open eyes.

Softly, Keri said, "Really?" The word hung suspended in air.

Dana couldn't speak. Her tongue was stuck to the roof of her mouth.

Keri hesitated. "Dana, we need to talk."

Immediately dropping her eyes to her hands, Dana said, "Yes."

She had decided after the debacle at the charity event that she needed to quit. She couldn't be a part of Keri's games. She already cared too deeply about her. She'd broken every one of the promises she'd made to herself before she took the job. It was just that, when she looked into Keri's eyes, the words were never there.

An uneasy feeling washed over Keri. "Look, we're both tired and hungry. Why don't we grab something to eat and then we'll talk. Okay?"

Dana looked up. "'Kay."

Keri studied the beautiful green, suddenly frightened, eyes. A headache was starting at the back of her head. She rubbed her neck with one hand. "We really need to eat, I'm…I can't even think."

Dana stood abruptly. Not meeting Keri's eyes, she said, "Let me go grab some things from my office and stash them in my car. I'll meet you in the parking garage. We'll eat, and then we'll…talk." She left the room.

Keri sighed and started throwing files into her briefcase. After a moment she pulled her wallet and keys out of it, slammed it shut and locked it, and stuffed it in the back of her closet. "I'm not going to be working at home tonight, no matter what Dana has to tell me. Shit." She didn't have a good feeling about it. Her headache was picking up force.

Dana numbly went to collect a bag full of papers and the spare camera she had used for the meeting. Thieves had stolen the other cameras and all the photos she had taken to date, but what they hadn't gotten was her laptop and the little digital she'd left in her pocket. She always backed everything up.

She didn't care about her office being trashed. All that mattered was the talk she and Keri would be having later. Her resolve to quit had disappeared when she thought Keri might be in danger. She couldn't possibly leave her if there was a threat to her safety. She didn't care that there might be a possibility of danger to herself. But she couldn't fall in love, and she knew that's what was happening. The talk would be about keeping her distance from Keri. Something she emotionally didn't want to do, but rationally had no choice about. The elevator rumbled open on the parking floor and she walked out, absently looking around for her car.

"Crap. Where is the damned thing?" Then she remembered she'd been late that morning. Her car was parked in a far, unlit corner of the garage. She walked over and opened the back, stashing her things. Hearing the sound of a car engine as she closed the lid, she turned to see a dark car pull in close to the elevator door.

Two people dressed in dark clothing exited and stood in front of the elevator doors, pushing the button. Something about them made the fine hairs on Dana's neck stand up. She froze in the shadow where she stood, hoping they wouldn't notice her. Her next thought made her blood run cold. Keri was on her way down.

Just then the elevator door opened and Keri stepped out. The two must have been surprised because they hesitated, then lunged for her. One grabbed her arms while the other slapped her hard across the face. Keri sagged, then tried to struggle to get free. They held her up and were yelling at her, and the taller of the two slapped her again.

Shoving her hand in her pocket, Dana pulled out the digital camera and turned it on as she hit the panic button on her car remote to activate the alarm. Pressing the shutter and holding it so the flash would fire repeatedly, she ran, yelling, toward the trio. One of the two assailants started in surprise, then shouted at the other. The one restraining Keri threw her roughly aside, and they both ran for their car. Keri's head smacked into a steel support beam, and she crumpled to the floor.

Just then the garage lit up with a search beam from the guard's SUV. The dark car roared to life, reversed abruptly, and aimed for the SUV just as Dana reached Keri. The guard swerved and the car sideswiped him, then screeched out of the garage.

Dana knelt next to Keri's inert form and frantically felt for her pulse. Keri was alive but unconscious. Blood was spreading under her head, and her face was swollen and bleeding.

The guard was running toward them. "What happened?"

"Call the paramedics!" Dana yelled. "Ms. Flemons is hurt. Hurry!"

Taking Keri's hand she leaned down next to her ear. "It's okay, it's okay, you're going to be fine. We've called for help. I love you, MyKeri. I love you. Please don't leave, please don't leave."

Dana sat back, afraid to move Keri for fear of causing more damage. She stroked Keri's arm and kept repeating, "It's okay, it's okay." She repeated it long after the paramedics had gently pushed her aside so they could work.

CHAPTER TEN

K eri was in a house and was lost. All the doors were closed; she tried one after the other, but they were locked. Finally she came to a door and the knob turned. She pushed it open and found a sunlit room. As she walked into the room, a feeling of dread seized her, and she turned to leave. She struggled but was held in place, trying to scream. No sound came out, and she couldn't breathe.

She lurched awake, heart pounding, gasping for air, to see a stranger smiling at her, shaking her gently. The many other times she'd had the dream she would usually scramble out of bed and stand by the wall until she calmed down. This time, she thought about getting away, but awareness of beeping machines and the smell of cleaning solution made the dream different and forced her into a waking state.

The stranger was a nurse, and she was talking quietly to her. "Good morning. Having a bad dream?" The nurse let her eyes drift over to a sleeping Dana in a chair a few feet from the bed. "I thought we'd let your friend sleep a bit."

Keri followed the nurse's eyes and immediately calmed down. Dana was exquisite. Her dark hair was tousled; she looked decidedly uncomfortable, but beautiful nonetheless. She had a hospital blanket thrown over her. One of the staff must have taken pity on her. *She stayed. She never left me.* Keri was overcome with relief, and she wasn't sure why.

The nurse continued with her ministrations, encouraging Keri to breathe deeply for a few minutes, checking her pulse, taking her blood pressure. Then she left the room, and Keri was free to gaze in contentment at Dana. *This is how it should be.* The thought made her aware all over again of the distance between them. They were going to "talk." She remembered that much. But it hadn't happened. Instead she had ended up here with her head aching and her mind refusing to deliver important information.

There had been an accident; she knew that much from shreds of conversation she'd heard as she slid from unconsciousness to sleep. She hadn't paid much attention, tuned only to the familiar patterns of Dana's speech, the soothing tone of her voice.

Something clanged outside the door and Dana jerked upright, then winced and gingerly eased back in her chair. All this before she noticed Keri's blue eyes regarding her.

Dana smiled sleepily. "Hi."

Her voice sounded deep and groggy. Keri thought it sexy. "Hi." She tried for a smile, but realized only then that she'd been gazing at Dana for several minutes without seeing that her shirt was covered in blood. "Oh, my God. Are you okay? What happened?"

Leaning forward in the chair, Dana put her hand on Keri's arm and watched her settle with the contact. Their eyes never parted. "I'm fine. Two guys attacked you. I was able to distract them long enough for the guard to arrive, and they tore out of there. But not before they hurt you."

Dana had relived the moment she saw Keri slump to the floor over and over, her pain just as fresh every time. It eased a little now as she studied Keri's face and assured herself that Keri was going to be okay.

"The last thing I remember was getting out of the elevator," Keri said, eyes fogging a little with the effort of thinking back. "Was anyone else hurt?"

"No." Dana kept her thoughts to herself. That the attack was premeditated. That Keri was not a random target. The assailants were either trying to kidnap her or mug her. Dana didn't know which.

"Was it…attempted rape?" Keri tried to remember some of what happened. It required a lot of effort to follow the conversation. Her head hurt and she reached up, only to run into bandages. Feeling a tug, she looked at her arm and saw that she was pulling on an IV.

"No one knows for sure what they were trying to do," Dana said. The cops think it could be linked to the break-in at my office. I wouldn't be surprised."

"They got away?"

"Yeah. But the surveillance video was working. They sideswiped the guard's car on the way out, too."

"How did you…distract them?"

"Remember that new camera with the gonzo flash? Well, I…I just set it on continuous flash and held the shutter down. Simple." Dana shrugged innocently.

Keri knew her too well to buy this meek version of events. "Now tell me what you really did."

Dana gave her a sheepish grin. "Well, I pushed the panic button on my car remote and that set off the alarm. Then I ran at them, screaming like a banshee, with the flash going off in their faces."

"Why is your shirt bloody?"

"It isn't my blood. I stayed with you until the paramedics arrived. You had to have surgery to close gashes in the back of your head and above your…" She drew a finger over her eyebrow to demonstrate. Her heart was doing double time.

Keri was silent, her gaze unwavering. Dana felt warm all over.

"Thanks. I owe you one."

"You don't owe me anything. I'm just glad you're okay. Those damned head wounds bleed a lot and I was—" she swallowed hard—"worried."

"I'm fine. Well, I have a headache."

" Then *I'm* fine, too." Dana exhaled, relieved for the first time since the nightmare had begun. "I might even consider getting out of here and giving you some privacy while I go home and shower."

Keri tried to smile, but she looked panicked. "Do you have to leave?"

Momentarily speechless, Dana repeated the words in her head. Keri was asking her to stay. Her hand was clinging tightly to Dana's, and she was staring as if Dana were the most important person in the world to her.

"No." Dana's voice cracked as she spoke. "No, I won't leave you."

Keri smiled and closed her eyes. "Thanks. I just…feel better knowing you're here. Has the media got hold of this yet? Did you call Shelley?"

Through the grin that Dana couldn't get rid of, she said, "The hospital has been running interference, but I'm sure reporters are going to be sniffing around soon. I called Shelley, and she's putting off your appointments for a week." Seeing Keri's protest forming, she quickly said, "No argument. I talked to your surgeon, and she wants you to rest for at least two weeks. I knew that would be impossible, so we compromised. And I'm going to be the enforcer. How do you like that?"

Keri's eyes were getting droopy. "I love it when you talk dirty to me."

Dana did a double take and studied the now-somnolent woman, not sure she had heard her correctly. Her entire body flushed with pleasure.

Just as she felt Keri's hand grow weak and saw her face relax into sleep, she heard raised voices in the hall, one of them familiar and distinctly male. Reluctantly taking her hand from Keri's, she eased up from her chair and made her way to the door.

Jameson Brown was standing at the nurses' station, insisting on seeing Keri. Dana tiptoed out of Keri's room and walked over to her friend, sliding a hand through the crook of his big, beefy arm.

"It's okay," she told the nursing supervisor. "I called Mr. Brown in to help with security. Until Ms. Flemons is discharged we're going to have to take some steps to make sure she isn't bothered by reporters. And I know you and the other hospital staff have more important things to do than fend off the media."

"Might be a good idea. We've already had a lot of calls." The nursing supervisor was the one who had been on duty when Keri was first brought up. She shot a steely look at Dana and Jameson, then went back to her charts.

"What the hell happened, D?" Jameson asked as they walked to Keri's room. "You look like you been in a shoot-out."

Looking down at her shirt she said, "This is Keri's blood. She had to have surgery for scalp wounds. She has a concussion, too. I'm not sure when she's going to be discharged. Either later today or tomorrow. But we need to keep this situation under control."

"Sure, I got it covered. No point me doing it. I'm no good at that stuff and I'd miss practice. I brought my cousin Huey. He's a professional."

"He works in security?"

"Bouncer at the Fifth Amendment." Jameson waved at a guy stepping out of the elevator.

Dressed impeccably, he was a movable mountain, standing well over six and a half feet tall, a solid wall of muscle. He grinned and strolled toward them, attracting a few startled stares from visitors and hospital staff. He gave Jameson a hug, dwarfing him. Both men had shaved heads and good looks, and the joint effect was formidable.

Grinning, Jameson said, "Dana, this is my cousin, Huey Brown. The family calls him Baby. Huey, this is my friend Dana. She's good people." He indicated the door to Keri's room. "That lady in there is my boss, the owner of the team. We need to keep reporters out for a while. You know?"

The large man smiled and nodded. When he spoke his voice was like rich, warm honey. "Of course. No one in except cops and people okayed by you or Dana. Nice to meet you, Dana."

Dana felt like a small child when his hand engulfed hers. But his handshake was gentle and his smile genuine and warm. He took up his position outside the door, and Dana walked Jameson to the elevators.

"He looks like he should be going to practice with you," she said. "I've never seen him around. Are you guys close?"

"Used to be, when we were kids. Then, uh, well, we kind of, didn't speak for a while. Anyway, we found each other again. Actually, I guess I looked him up. I'm glad I did. I've missed him."

Dana smiled. "I appreciate it, Jameson."

He flashed her a smile that made Dana's shutter finger twitch. "See you later. Take care of Ms. Flemons. I know you will."

As she moved away, she was surprised to see Zander and Jim exit the other elevator together. Jim had a big grin on his face and a shopping bag in his hand.

"I got your message and thought you could use a change of clothes," he announced, and hugged her firmly. "I broke into your flat to get them. Hope you don't mind."

"Thanks, Jimmy. That's so sweet of you." Dana took the bag gratefully. Inside, there were toiletries, jeans, a long-sleeve T-shirt, even a leather jacket and some underclothes.

"Well, I thought you could use the shower in her room. You are staying, right?" He gave her a meaningful look.

Dana felt her face flush. "Um, yeah. I couldn't figure out how to be in two places at once, and you've just fixed the problem." Jimmy was still looking at her intently, and when he raised his eyebrows and flicked a glance at the man hovering a few steps away, Dana caught on. "Oh!" She turned to Zander. "Have you two met?"

"Oh, yes, at the fund-raiser."

They both blushed, shyly looking at each other. She noticed that their handshake seemed to linger. *Hmm.*

Dana let out a breath. "God, I'm glad you came, both of you." Her friends' presence, combined with the events of the past twenty-four hours, made her want to collapse and weep. Seeming to sense her fragility, Jim put his arms around her and hugged her tightly.

"We should talk in Keri's room," she said, aware that they were attracting attention. All they needed was for a reporter to find his way up here and point a TV camera at them, and the place would be under siege.

At Keri's door, Huey grinned at Zander and they shook hands vigorously.

"Do you know Huey?" Dana asked as they hustled into the room.

"Jameson Garrison's cousin? Sure. He's a fine athlete. I thought they weren't speaking. Guess things have changed."

"I asked for Jameson's help and he brought Huey. Apparently he's a bouncer."

Zander's eyebrows went up. "That's a real waste."

Dana filed his response away in the back of her mind. She thought Keri might like to hear about Huey when the time was right. Her eyes were irresistibly drawn to the woman on the bed. Keri was pale and sleeping, her mouth softly parted, her chest slowly rising and falling.

"We'll keep an eye on her while you get cleaned up," Jim whispered.

"If she wakes up, tell her I'm here," Dana said, wanting to make sure Keri would know she'd kept her promise to stay.

"Don't worry. She'll know." He took the bag from her for a moment and extricated a few items. "Shampoo. Mild body wash. Decent towel and washcloth. Hospital linens can cause *injuries*."

Dana couldn't help but smile. She gave him another hug and he urged, "Go on, before you go to sleep on the toilet or something. You'll feel better."

Dana stole one more look toward the bed and was about to close the bathroom door when she froze at the sound of an angry male voice outside the room. "I'm telling you to let me pass! I have business to discuss with Ms. Flemons. Do you know who I *am*?" The man's voice was bordering on hysterical.

Signaling Jim to stay put, Dana exchanged a look with Zander, and they quickly exited the room.

Thomas Concannon, veins popping out on his neck, was standing just outside the door, trying his best to not be intimidated by Huey, and losing.

"No one goes in unless approved by Ms. Ryan. Period." Huey took up most, well, all, of the doorway. No one was getting past.

Tapping Huey on the back, Zander stepped around him, and they both made way for Dana.

Thomas heaved a petulant sigh. "Zander. Would you tell this *person* who I am?"

"Mr. Brown is here to make sure Keri isn't disturbed," Zander replied coolly. "Doctor's orders."

Concannon glared at him. "Look, if her injuries are severe, I must take over until and *if* she is ready to return. I must see her and talk with her. She has papers to sign."

"She has a concussion and lacerations," Dana cut in, despite Concannon's determined efforts to ignore her presence completely. "And she is just coming out of the anesthesia, so you will have to put off your meeting. She won't be signing anything today. I'll tell her you came by."

Concannon looked from Dana to the tall, hulking men. They weren't moving. He looked around at all the witnesses in the hall. Straightening up, he huffed, "Very well. I'll call on Ms. Flemons tomorrow."

"There won't be any need for that," Dana said. "Her mind is just fine, and she can take care of business when she returns to work."

"And what exactly does this have to do with you?" Concannon looked like he wanted to slap her.

Huey must have read the same intent in his body language, for he stepped a little closer to Concannon, forcing him to back up.

Concannon looked him up and down disparagingly. "Huey Brown. It's been a while. So, you're down to bodyguarding now. Tough break. But I guess that's what happens when you don't get drafted, eh?"

Huey answered in a quiet, menacing tone. "I'm actually in law school. I do this to pay my way through. But we could find out if I'm in good enough shape to pick you up and toss you to the end of the hall. Would you like that?"

Concannon quickly shuffled back. Eyeing Zander, he said, "Tell Ms. Flemons I'll call her."

All three of them watched him march toward the elevator. Then, as the doors closed, Zander and Huey looked at each other and laughed.

Zander said, "You should have been drafted. You were good."

"No one would draft an out gay man into the pros."

Dana kept her eyes lowered so she could hide her surprise. She knew better than to make assumptions about who might be gay or straight, but in Huey's case she'd fallen prey to the same tired stereotypes about masculinity as most people.

"Do you ever regret it?" Zander quietly asked. "Coming out?"

Huey shrugged. "Sometimes I wonder what could have been. But we all make choices, Zander. Then we have to live with them. I guess there's a price for everything."

At that moment Jim opened the door and stuck his head out. "Is there a problem?"

"Not any more," Dana said.

"Well, thank goodness for that. If you keep that shirt on a moment longer, I'll just have to leave."

Dana laughed and, thanking Huey, she stepped back into Keri's room.

❖

Thomas Concannon was fuming as he made his way through the parking garage to his car. He had parked in a space reserved for doctors, so he didn't have too far to go. As he fumbled for his keys, he caught a shadow in his peripheral vision and started to turn. Before he could make a sound he was shoved roughly against his car, causing him to drop his briefcase and keys. He almost wet his pants.

"Please, don't hurt me. Take my money, it's in my inside pocket. Don't hurt me."

A heavily accented voice said, "Did she sign the papers?" The voice was female and right next to his ear. He started perspiring. "Answer."

His sweating became profuse. "No. The woman was under

anesthetic, and she is evidently not that badly hurt. She'll be home in the next day or two, and I'll talk to her then. I promise...I'll get her to..."

"Basta! My employer is accustomed to getting results. If you wish his continued good will, you had better make something happen."

Suddenly he was alone. It took a minute to get his legs to support him. He was picking up his briefcase and keys when the parking guard made a pass in an electric cart.

"Hey, buddy, you can't park here. It's for doctors. You'll have to move along."

Thomas jerked his head up and the guard studied him for a beat, then asked, "Hey, are you sick, pal?"

He exploded. "Of course I'm not sick, you idiot! I'm moving my car, can't you see that? Now get out of my way!"

The guard gave him a long look and muttered, "Asshole." He goosed the cart along to finish his inspections.

In the shadows, Gina Pescetti watched Concannon leave. She lit a cigarette and walked away. She had another visit to make. This one, she was hoping, would be more pleasant.

CHAPTER ELEVEN

Dana came out of the bathroom, towel drying her hair. She cast a glance around the room and was relieved by its tranquility. The door to the hall was closed and Keri was sleeping. Unable to resist, Dana crossed to the bed and gazed down at her.

A shudder ran through her at the sight of the bandages and the pale hair damply matted around them. If something worse had happened the day before…She closed her eyes tightly against the image, then impulsively bent down to kiss Keri's pale cheek. As she reached her destination, Keri turned her head and their lips met, then parted.

Dana held her breath, unable to move or speak as Keri's eyes locked with her own.

A smile crossed Keri's lips. "Scooter! Where ya been?"

"I've been here, MyKeri, always."

Keri's face formed a frown. "Where's Moms?"

Words stuck in Dana's throat. Before she could answer, Keri's eyes fluttered shut as if she'd only paused in her sleep to connect with Dana.

Straightening up, Dana stood perfectly still, but her heart was thundering. She heard the soft click of the door closing and a quiet throat clearing and turned to see Jim and Zander. How long had they been standing there?

Jim walked over and took her hand. "Why don't you finish getting dressed, and we'll find some coffee and something to eat. I'll bet you haven't had anything since yesterday. Am I right?"

Dana nodded absently. "I can't leave her," she said. "I promised not to."

Jim and Zander exchanged a look, and Jim gently pulled Dana to the door. "There's a coffee cart a few floors down. They have muffins and bagels. Let's risk it."

Dana was uneasy. "I don't trust Concannon. What if he comes back?"

"You really think that piece of flab could get past Huey and me?" Zander cracked his knuckles.

"I would pay to see that," Jim said. "Come on, hon. Zander won't let anything happen to her."

Promising to return soon, Dana grabbed her jacket, and they left Huey guarding the door. As they passed the nurses' desk, a reporter was offering money to the floor clerk for information.

"The sooner we get her out of here, the better," Dana said darkly. It was only a matter of time before ten just like him would be camped out in the lobby.

After buying some food, Jim suggested a walk outside, where they found a quiet garden with some benches to sit on. It seemed intended for family and staff. With a bit of encouragement, Dana drank her coffee and munched halfheartedly on a bagel.

❖

Jim sipped his coffee pensively. "Dana? I know I've always teased you about your fuck-'em-and-chuck-'em attitude, and for that I apologize. But, have you ever been in love?"

Dana met her best friend's steady gaze and answered truthfully. "Yes. Once. Forever."

Even she could hear the pain in her voice. Jim reacted by putting his arm around her.

"With Keri." He wasn't asking.

She nodded.

"Who's Scooter?"

Looking away suddenly, Dana felt herself break out in a cold sweat.

"Dana?"

"It was Keri's name for me when we were children."

They fell silent briefly, gazing out at the fog, as hospital workers passed to and fro on their way to unknown destinations.

"Does she love you, Dana?" The question was simple and held no judgment.

"I don't think so. I think she's physically attracted to me, but I'm not going to be a rich girl's toy." The harsh words jarred and she wished she could take them back. It seemed cheap to make that assumption about the woman in the hospital bed. The Keri who had just begged Dana not to leave her bore little resemblance to the Keri she'd been angry with for so long.

Jim put his hand on her back and rubbed small circles as they sat for a while. "I don't know Keri, but I know you. I don't think you would fall in love with someone who only thought of you as a toy. You two seem...good together. I guess there's a lot to consider."

Dana snorted softly. "Yeah, made for each other. I once believed that. But stuff happens. People change."

They both leaned forward, elbows on knees, intently studying their coffee cups. Dana ventured a glance toward her friend. She had seldom felt so uncertain.

"Sometimes they change on the outside because the inside has been hurt so much," said Jim. "The point is, you're in love. Know what I think? Nothing, and I mean *nothing,* is more important than that. Not the past. Not your fears or worries. You have to find out how she really feels about you."

The silence spread between them.

"I saw how she looked at you when she called you Scooter. There was nothing but love in her eyes. Don't make the decision for her. What if you're wrong about this?"

"You don't understand."

"I understand that you've been protecting yourself for so long that trusting anyone feels like too much of a risk."

"Keri isn't just anyone. You know what she did to me."

"Yes, and I know we all do incredibly thoughtless things at some point in our lives. We all make mistakes. Dana," he took her hands in his and looked her squarely in the eye, "don't let yourself use the past as an excuse to run away from the future. Promise me you'll think about that."

Dana wanted to be angry with him, but his words hit home, and she wondered if she was sabotaging herself. She was honest enough to admit that part of her still wanted to punish Keri. Yet in doing so, she was also punishing herself.

Jim glanced at his watch and released her hands. "Damn. I'm supposed to be in court in fifteen minutes. I have to go."

Tearful, and slightly embarrassed, Dana stood with him. "Thanks for coming by…and for the clothes."

He kissed her on the cheek. "Tell her. You owe it to yourself."

Dana remained in the garden for a few minutes after he left, trying to work through her tangled emotions. She came down to some simple truths. She was in love with Keri, and she sensed that Keri felt something for her. Being in Keri's life again gave her pleasure every day. And when she thought she might have lost her, the pain was unbearable.

Feeling resolved suddenly, she headed indoors. She knew what she needed to do. But first, she had an overdue phone call to make. She foraged in her satchel and located the business card Carolyn Flemons had given her before she fled the charity event. Flipping open her cell phone, she took a deep breath and dialed.

❖

Gloria was late getting to Crush. She had been massively hung over that morning and could scarcely get out of bed, trying to get over the damage done by one too many dirty martinis. She hoped whomever the hell she was with the night before was suffering as much as she was, but doubted she would ever find out unless the woman came up and introduced herself. *Yuck. No more one-night stands.*

A few lunch patrons were in the bar, and Tiffany was busy training a new employee, so she quietly went to her office. She felt her way to her desk and turned the desk lamp on its lowest setting, plopping tiredly in her chair and immediately laying her throbbing head on her arms, on the desk.

"Good afternoon, Ms. Steeple. Not feeling well?" The voice came from the shadows in the corner of her office. It was low and sultry.

Gloria jerked upright and stifled a scream as Gina Pescetti stepped into the light and took a seat in the chair in front of her. "How did you get in here?"

With a dismissive wave the woman said, "Not a problem. I would advise a better lock for your door. In fact, this entire place could be easily broken in to and trashed. You might consider more security. At least more than that pitiful person you call a bouncer at your door."

All this was spoken with a heavy accent that made Gloria have to think to translate, thereby increasing the pressure in her head. She didn't know if the words were a thinly veiled threat or actual advice. She was still too under the weather to be coy.

"What can I do for you, Ms. Pescetti?" The smile that she garnered told her she had remembered correctly. *You know, with a little dental work, she could have a spectacular smile.* She studied the Italian woman and asked impulsively, "Did you have something to do with hurting Keri? Did you do it?"

The black eyes were unreadable. "Not that it matters, but I didn't find out about it until this morning. The answer is no."

Softly, Gloria asked, "Is Keri okay? Was she badly hurt?"

Pescetti was noncommittal. "She'll be okay."

Gloria blew out a breath. "When Thomas came to me I had no idea Bongi...Mr. Bongivanni was involved. I thought I would either succeed and get a bunch of money or go on my way. I never bargained for this."

Pescetti leaned forward and looked at her intently. "Concannon owes Mr. Bongivanni a lot of money. My boss has always wanted to own a sports team. And control of the vendors. The amount of money involved is substantial."

Gloria sat back in her chair, longing for aspirin. "What happens to me if I fail? Are you here to threaten me? Beat me up?"

Bongi's bodyguard got to her feet, and Gloria registered her height and the muscles that worked beneath her plain dark pants and white shirt. "I came here to warn you. A courtesy. And, so you know, I don't beat women. Not without an invitation."

The smile made Gloria's skin turn to goose bumps. Weakly, she said, "Good to know."

Gina Pescetti moved to the door with the lazy grace of a predator. Before opening it she looked over her shoulder. "And, you are right. My employer is not accustomed to disappointment."

After the door closed softly behind her unexpected visitor, Gloria sat for a long while staring into space. She didn't know whether to be excited or terrified. Her brain said terrified, but…

She started rooting around her desk for the aspirin.

❖

By late in the afternoon the media was hot on Keri's trail. Huey had fended off a number of reporters. The hospital was being disrupted. After some consultation with Keri's doctors, who provided strict guidelines that she swore she would follow, they agreed that she could leave with Dana.

She was not to be left alone for the next twenty-four to forty-eight hours and could not return to work for at least one week. Dana was responsible for carrying out the doctors' orders. Keri's surgeon also said she was to allow Keri no excitement for that period of time. Dana wasn't worried; she was excited enough for both of them.

They needed a distraction for the reporters so they could spirit Keri out of the hospital, so Huey called Zander, who agreed to come over straight after team practice. The distraction worked. As soon as he arrived, making no secret of his visit and looking very photogenic, he was deluged with reporters, all wanting a statement about the incident. Huey stayed by the hospital room with a no-nonsense expression on his face, while Dana and a nurse stuffed Keri in some hospital scrubs, complete with hat, and a hospital employee wheeled Keri down to the loading dock.

Dana brought her own small SUV around, and they helped Keri into it. As soon as they'd made a clean getaway, Dana called Huey, who agreed to gather some cohorts to provide security for the next few days.

"I should run by my apartment for a few minutes, Keri," Dana said, after ending the call. "I need some clothes and equipment. I'll park in the garage and leave you locked in the car, okay?"

"Okay." Keri was leaning against the seat of the car with her eyes closed. Her head bandage had been reduced to a rather bulky patch over her left temple and stitches only in the back. She looked tired.

Dana drove into the garage, found her place, and stopped. She pulled her keys out and had started to open the door when she felt Keri touch her on the back. Turning around, she could see Keri's face was pale.

"Are you all right?"

"I…yes, of course. Go on. Dana?"

"Yes?"

"Hurry. I'm…afraid."

She looked frail and her hands were shaking. Suddenly Dana was not sure releasing her from the hospital was such a good idea. She got back in the car and started the engine.

"What are you doing?"

"Do you have a washer and dryer, Keri?"

"Yes, but—"

"I can get some clothes tomorrow. Shelley will be over then and can be with you. I apologize. The doc said to not leave you alone, and I was being thoughtless."

It hadn't occurred to Dana that part of the reason the physician had given that order might have been that Keri would probably have a psychological reaction to the incident. She mentally smacked her forehead.

Keri smiled gratefully at her. "Thanks."

As they pulled out of the garage and headed toward Presidio Heights, Keri reached over and put her hand on Dana's thigh. "You are a wonderful woman."

Dana nearly rear-ended the car in front of her.

Throughout the remainder of the drive, her head spun with a relentless stream of thoughts and emotions. She kept coming back to the conversation with Jim. Her friend was more perceptive than she'd realized. He saw things she was only just beginning to see herself.

The hard truth that really stuck out was her own unwillingness to give Keri the benefit of the doubt in anything. Dana was aware that she was in the habit of second-guessing Keri, always looking for the selfish agenda, always assuming the worst, not the best. Did Keri deserve that?

She glanced sideways at the woman in the seat next to her. Keri could barely keep her eyes open. Her head was drooping forward, and Dana had an overwhelming urge to stop the car and hold her, just so Keri could sleep against her shoulder. With a flash of clarity, she understood that when it came to Keri, her mind and her heart were completely at odds. She had never stopped loving Keri, but she had stopped trusting her. Even now, when her heart was making its wishes perfectly clear, the part of her that still felt hurt and betrayed refused to be silent.

It was warning her as she halted before the stately Flemons residence, telling her not to be lulled. Keri was in a weakened state, and that meant it would suit her to keep Dana close. This was just another version of Keri having her way in all things, using whomever she pleased. Once she was done with Dana, she would discard her. *Be careful. Don't mistake her neediness for anything else.*

CHAPTER TWELVE

After settling Keri in the family room off the kitchen, Dana moved her car into the garage and quickly checked to make sure the gate and all the doors were locked. When she returned, she found Keri sitting up, asleep. Her head was cocked over in an awkward position. *Oh, that's gotta hurt.*

Dana came over and gently moved her to a prone position. She went to the master bedroom, now Keri's bedroom, and retrieved a pillow from the bed and a spare blanket from the linen closet. After tucking Keri in, she built a fire in the fireplace. It was almost dark outside. She didn't turn on any lights in the room, instead leaving it in firelight. Keri slept peacefully.

The small light over the stove was enough to allow Dana to search for something for them to eat. When she opened the refrigerator she heaved a sigh of relief. It was full of food. And Carolyn Flemons had propped an envelope on the kitchen counter with Dana's name on it. She opened it and extracted a note inked on handmade paper. Carolyn thanked her for calling about Keri, and had been in touch with the doctors to keep up with her daughter's progress. She wanted to see her, soon. She asked that Dana call her and let her know when the time seemed right.

The note ended with a sentence Dana read several times over: *I am only able to stay away because I know Keri is in your care—as she should always be.*

As quietly as she could, Dana set about boiling some pasta and making a salad. She chopped and sautéed some veggies and made a light cream sauce for a pasta primavera. After setting the small round table that was in the family room, she put the steaming food out, then turned to wake her sleeping patient.

But Keri wasn't asleep. She was watching Dana with a sleepy smile on her face. Dana remembered that smile from her childhood. She used to jump through hoops to make that smile appear. It always made her heart sing. *Guess some things don't change.* She averted her eyes and rubbed her jeans with her now-damp palms.

"Um, are you hungry?" She smiled nervously at her charge.

In a voice that was decidedly unchildlike and husky from sleep, Keri said, "Yes."

I can do this, I can do this, I can do this. But Dana's knees felt watery, and she was close to hyperventilating.

"Well, ah, dinner is served!" She did a "ta-*dah*" gesture with both hands toward the table.

Seeing Keri struggle to stand up, she hurried to her side. The softness of the contact and holding Keri in her arms were excruciatingly wonderful.

She got Keri settled and they ate more than Dana expected. She was ravenous suddenly, and it seemed that Keri's head injury hadn't affected her appetite. It occurred to Dana that neither of them had eaten properly since the incident occurred. The hospital food was, well, hospital food.

When Keri put her fork down, she gave Dana a grin. "This is delicious! I had no idea you could cook. Thank you."

Dana's cheeks burned from the compliment. "Hey, why the big surprise? And I make cookies, too."

Keri looked deep in Dana's eyes. "I'd like to taste your cookies."

Catching herself staring at Keri's mouth, Dana jerked her eyes up to find Keri watching her. "Oh! Well, sure. Soon. More pasta?"

Keri's color got a *lot* better, and she instantly dropped her gaze to her food. In fact, Dana thought maybe she was blushing too.

"No, thanks. I'm full. It was delicious. Did you go to the store?"

Dana managed, "I organized some stuff to be delivered. We can hole up in the house for a week without a problem, and Shelley will be by tomorrow."

An electronic melody sounded, and Dana swung a quick look around for her cell phone. She had left it on the counter that separated the kitchen from the family room. She reached over and grabbed it, seeing Huey's name.

"It's Huey, your temporary bodyguard," she explained to Keri. "We need to make arrangements for security for the next few days to keep the reporters out." She didn't mention the thugs who had assaulted Keri. The doctors wanted her stress free, and that was exactly what Dana planned to ensure.

Excusing herself, she greeted Huey and got to her feet. Taking a pen and some paper from the writing station near the kitchen, she strolled into another room so she could speak freely about the safety concerns.

Keri had trouble shifting her attention from Dana's departing back to the pasta. Supporting her head on her hand, and leaning against the table, she watched until Dana vanished. Then, deep in thought, she halfheartedly pushed what was left of the meal around on her plate. Even through the haze of her medication, Keri could feel a connection to Dana that was so strong it startled her. It also brought back memories.

She had felt exactly the same sense of connectedness as a child. It was as if each occupied an invisible space next to the other even when they were apart. It meant Keri had never felt lonely, even when she and Dana were apart. That was until Dana left her and never came back. That was one of the worst times in her childhood. At first she'd been sure Dana would come back, no matter what Moms said. But over time, she'd felt their connection fray until one day it was gone entirely. Keri had hated that feeling so much; all she'd wanted to do was escape from it.

In hindsight, she thought she had probably spent half her life trying to fill that terrible emptiness with anything she could find. Fun, women, fast cars. Anything that would distract her. When Moms left, the emptiness grew worse, and she had to work even harder not to care. Keri blinked sleepily, marveling that she'd never seen things quite this way before. She thought about the past few weeks with Dana. She had to admit that she was happy whenever Dana was around. She couldn't even rationalize it by reasoning that things were going well with the team. It was more than that. It felt like *home* to her. Home in a way she hadn't felt since childhood.

She knew she shouldn't be attracted to Dana. She should be grateful that they seemed to have the beginnings of a friendship. Wasn't that enough? She was angry with herself for jeopardizing the fragile new understanding between them with her behavior at the fundraiser. Why couldn't she be satisfied that Dana was always available and they were working together well. Instead, it seemed the more time they spent together, the more Keri wanted. She missed Dana when she wasn't around. Until Dana came back, she had forgotten how it felt to be contented. She had lost her certainty that all was as it should be.

Listening to the muted tone of Dana's voice, she gave a long, slow sigh and basked in that certainty once more. She knew she was drifting into sleep, but she didn't fight it. It felt wonderful to lay her head down, knowing that when she lifted it Dana would be there.

Dana slid her cell phone into her pocket and returned to the family room, smiling when she saw Keri sound asleep with her head on the table.

Gently, she put her arms around Keri and whispered, "Hey, time to go to bed."

Keri groggily opened her eyes and seemed confused at first, then relieved. "I don't want to go up yet."

Dana was captivated in the force field that was Keri. "What would you like to do?"

"Stay by the fire until you're ready to go up with me. I…don't want to be alone."

Dana quickly said, "Good idea. Besides, you can tell me where things go."

"You seemed to find everything when you cooked the meal."

Averting her eyes, Dana said, "Yeah, well, it *is* a kitchen. But remembering where everything belongs when it's time to put them back, now there's a problem."

Her grin was infectious, and Keri sat down on the couch and said, "Okay. I'll supervise."

Dana quickly cleared the dishes and set about cleaning the kitchen, wiping the counters and table. At first Keri gave a few directions, but then she fell quiet, and Dana's thoughts strayed to Mike Flemons once more.

He had found her during the U.S. Olympic trials, after her picture appeared in the paper. He came to one of the practices. He'd given her a big bear hug and asked if he could take her to dinner. Dana had been surprised but accepted anyway, unable to resist the possibility of news about Keri.

Over dinner, Mike expressed regret that their families had lost touch. Carolyn had tried to make Sean Ryan see reason, and then Mike himself had tried to make contact with Dana. Her father had refused.

Dana remembered feeling wary of Mike Flemons at the time, yet he'd been good to her. He'd asked if she needed anything and offered to help her in her sports career. She had never mentioned the meeting to her father, knowing how he would react. It was not that he particularly gave a damn about what she did. She knew now that he had always been jealous of Mike and resented her closeness to the Flemons family. How much so only became clear after he died.

As Dana put soap in the dishwasher and turned it on, her back to Keri, she impulsively said, "Want to know the final gift my father gave to me? I wrote to you, every day for a long time. But you never answered the letters, and eventually I quit writing. When I cleaned out Dad's things after he died, I found the letters in the back of a dresser drawer. He never mailed them. He didn't give a shit."

When there was no reply. Dana splashed some water on her face, hung the dish towel to dry, and walked toward Keri, softly calling her name.

There was no response. Her stomach knotted as she knelt beside the woman she'd promised to protect and love, even at risk of being betrayed again. She whispered, "MyKeri, wake up."

Keri's eyes fluttered open and they looked at each other. Their lips were so close and the heat between them...Dana forced herself back. She offered her slightly trembling hand to Keri and slowly pulled her up. Keri touched the bandage on her head gingerly.

"You can take some medicine now," Dana said. "It's been long enough. Come on."

Keri had told her earlier that she didn't want to take the prescription painkillers because they made her too spacey, but she didn't resist now. After she'd swallowed the pills, Dana firmly clasped her hand and they trudged up the stairs, Keri also using the banister for support. It had been a long day, and she seemed tired beyond words.

Dana led her to the bedroom and stood at the entrance, feeling awkward. Keri was obviously somewhat out of it, and she had been told to not leave her alone. *Just think what she needs, Dana. Leave yourself out of this. She's vulnerable; you will not take advantage of that.*

Keri sagged and Dana automatically embraced her. Taking a big breath, she managed, "Come on, sweetie. Let's get you to bed."

"No, I'm filthy. I smell like medicine and...stuff. I need a shower."

After a quick appraisal, Dana knew that Keri wasn't capable of standing through a shower, even if Dana got in with her. She pushed that tempting thought aside and decided a bath would have to do.

"No shower, you'll get the bandage wet. Come on, I'll draw a bath for you."

She put down the lid of the toilet seat and deposited Keri on it, started the water in the large tub, and found some herbal salts and bubble bath to pour in. *Lots of bubbles, Dana, so you can't see anything that might make you finally lose what semblance of control you have left.*

"I'll go turn the bed down and find something for you to sleep in. What do you usually wear?"

Keri turned to her sluggishly. "Nothing. Um, sometimes a T-shirt."

"Okay. I'll be right back."

"Dana, wait." Keri reached and grabbed the tail of her shirt. "I hate to ask, but I can't get out of my clothes and into the tub without…I really, really want a bath."

"Of course." Dana did another mental head slap, dreading what was to come. She was so hyper she couldn't think. *Big breath, let it out, feel your feet.* That helped.

She knelt so they were on the same level and, with Keri trying to help, she gently pulled the hospital scrub shirt over her head. Next, she started on her pants. When those were undone, she helped her up and peeled them down. Next, her panties. Steadying Keri as she stepped out of them, Dana made sure her eyes were anywhere but where she wanted them. Keri wasn't wearing a bra, and that alone was almost Dana's undoing. Keri had beautiful breasts. Trying not to notice them, she helped Keri settle in the bath and adjusted the water until a smile formed on the tired woman's lips.

With a very shaky voice, Dana managed, "There you go. Now, I'll be back in a minute. Are you all right?"

Keri nodded and closed her eyes.

Dana dimmed the lights and left to dig up a T-shirt. No way was she going to spend the night thinking about Keri, nude, in her bed asleep. She already knew she wouldn't be getting much sleep as it was. Keri was a *very* lovely woman. And unbelievably sexy.

After turning the bed down and locating a T-shirt, she went back in to help her patient out of the tub. If Keri was out of it before, the heat from the water had made her nearly comatose. Dana busily dried off her back and worked her way down the strong body, moving to the front and up. When she reached the top of Keri's legs she stood and handed her the towel, quickly turning and leaving the bathroom. She needed air.

Keri looked at the closing bathroom door and smiled. She managed to get into the T-shirt and slowly opened the door. Dana was putting a pillow and blanket on the overstuffed chair several feet across the room.

"It's a king-sized bed," Keri said. "You don't have to sleep in another chair tonight. I won't bother you."

Looking at the woman she had loved all of her life, the words came out unbidden. "You could never bother me."

Dana went to the bathroom and shed her clothes, quickly showering. As she dried off, she realized she had nothing to sleep in. She turned off the bathroom lights and crossed the moonlit bedroom to the drawer where she had found the T-shirts.

Hearing a noise, Keri opened her eyes and took in the sight of Dana standing naked next to the windows, a T-shirt in one hand, a damp-looking towel in the other. She was amazing. Her full breasts and caramel nipples caused Keri to lick her lips and swallow. She was a vision of grace and power, regardless of her leg.

Keri's heart pounded, and she felt more awake than she had all day. She couldn't deny her visceral reaction to seeing Dana naked. It was completely sexual. She felt her nipples harden and an unexpected moisture between her thighs. Dana dropped the towel and drew the T-shirt over her head with a weary languor that made Keri ache to get out of bed and caress her.

As Dana pushed back her hair and turned toward the bed, Keri closed her eyes and tried to breathe like a sleeping person. The mattress moved as Dana sat down on the opposite side of the bed. Air slid between the sheets as she lifted the covers and moved beneath them. Keri heard her gasp slightly, then sigh as she sank back against the pillows. The soft sounds made her even more aware of her own clamoring body. She opened her eyes just enough to see moonlight pouring in the windows. Again the image of Dana standing there, naked, occupied Keri's mind to the exclusion of all else. Weak and unwell as she was, she knew if Dana so much as touched her, she would not be able to hide her desire.

Dana shivered in the cold sheets. She had only turned on the electric blanket on Keri's side of the bed. *Damn!* She sidled over just to where the warmth began. Staring at the ceiling, she thought about her younger days with MyKeri.

They'd played in the Flemonses' backyard most days after school. Moms would call them in and feed them dinner, and they would settle in the den to watch television. One of them would always start a wrestling match, trying to see who would be queen of the mountain. They'd collapse into fits of giggles and stay curled up together, watching TV until Dana had to go home or, if she was spending the night, bedtime. Moms always called them her kittens.

Dana smiled and laughed a bit at the memory. She felt MyKeri move slightly closer and asked her softly, "Are you awake?"

"Yes." Keri's voice sounded hoarse.

"How are you feeling?"

Like making love to you. Keri controled herself. That much excitement would probably put her back in the hospital. Trying for a distraction, she said, "Can I ask you something, Dana?"

"Anything."

"The accident." There, she'd said it—the forbidden topic. "Please tell me what happened." She braced herself, certain Dana would close her out.

Taken aback, Dana paused to gather her thoughts. She wondered why Keri was asking her now. Had her own brush with serious injury got her thinking?

As if she'd read anger or unwillingness into Dana's silence, Keri quickly said, "I'm sorry. I shouldn't have asked."

"No. It's okay." Dana was surprised to find it really was okay. She wanted to talk. It was still hard to find the words, but she said, "I'd asked my dad to come after a game to meet my teammates. He never came to games and didn't seem to much care about my career, so it was a big deal in my mind." Her sad smile seemed to filter through to Keri, and a smaller hand found hers. The fingers squeezed Dana's.

"Anyway, we were all meeting at a bar after the game—first mistake. My dad never met a bottle of bourbon he didn't like. I drove with him to give him directions. At first it went okay. They asked questions about him and his coaching. He was a football coach at a local junior college. But then the topic turned away from him. He tolerated it for a while, but he started drinking faster. Things changed when a few of the girlfriends of some of the lesbians on the team joined us."

Dana explored Keri's hand in hers. It had always been a perfect fit.

She felt a tear roll against the side of her nose and swiped at her eyes with her other hand, never relinquishing her lifeline to Keri.

Keri held her breath as she listened to the agony pouring from this beautiful woman. She yearned to turn over and hold Dana tightly, but resisted the urge. Dana was finally talking to her like she trusted her, and Keri didn't want to do anything that might break that trust.

Sighing, Dana said, "My father was a mean drunk. And he'd been a heavy drinker since my mom left us. That's not true. I don't remember him *not* being a heavy drinker. I knew I had to get him out of there before he caused a scene. So I said something about practice and needing to get home, and I offered to drive him." The scene flashed through her mind vividly as she felt the anxiety of waiting to see what her father would do. "He said, 'Yeah, let's go. I can't stand to be around these fuckin' dykes any longer.' I was so humiliated and ashamed of him. I couldn't even look at my teammates."

She smiled grimly. "But I was the good daughter. I knew better than to challenge a drunk, so I helped him up and got him out of there. I tried to get the keys, but he refused to give them to me. He ordered me into the car. I yelled at him and told him not unless I drove. But he just got in the car and started it up." Tears flowed down her face, and though she tried to remove her hand from Keri's, Keri held her fast and scooted closer.

"If I'd let him drive away I guess I'd still be playing pro ball. But I couldn't. He was my responsibility. I thought I could at least keep him awake and alert and get him home safely." Dana squeezed her eyes shut.

"He started going on about dykes and women playing professional sports and said every mean thing his alcohol-soaked brain could come up with. Finally I screamed at him to shut up, and I told him *I* was one of those fucking dykes." A sob tore through her body. She barely felt Keri turn and slide an arm around her shoulders.

"He backhanded me across the face. The second that it took to do that was enough. Your car had probably drifted a little too close, and when that registered on him, he jerked the wheel hard and lost control. I barely was aware of what was happening before everything went black."

Keri could hardly stand to listen. She'd had no idea what Dana had endured. The thought made her feel physically ill. "My God."

Dana was crying silently, her shoulders shaking under Keri's touch. "He died instantly. I was told that it was a miracle I survived and kept my leg. So I guess I was lucky. Lucky me."

They lay in silence, a fog of emotion enfolding them, stranding them together in a world where it seemed all they had was each other.

Keri was silent for a moment, trying to absorb Dana's words. Her mind and body were at war with each other. Her heart ached for Dana's suffering. She wanted nothing more than to hold Dana all night and tell her the scars didn't matter. *Show her.* But she had *no right.*

"Oh, Dana, I'm so sorry." She struggled to find words that didn't sound trite. "It must have been so hard. The pain of the accident, of losing your career, and the pain of losing someone you love." *Then there was the way I treated you.*

She was the cause of Dana's pain. She was horrified and ashamed. She found herself wishing she had been there for Dana. She couldn't remember ever experiencing feelings like that for someone. She knew she would give anything to be able to reverse time and take back every cruel, senseless thing she said. No wonder Dana kept her at a distance. Would she ever be able to change that?

Dana's eyes were unseeing as she said, "The sad thing is I only lost my career that night, Keri. I guess my father had the last laugh. He made a practice of taking away anything I loved. But if I'd kept my mouth shut, maybe—"

"Maybe what?"

"There's no point thinking about what might have been," Dana said. "It's time you slept."

Keri could feel her distancing herself. Desperate to stay close to her, she moved a hand to Dana's cheek and said, "I didn't mean to make you relive all that."

"I know." Dana seemed to relax a little.

"Good night," Keri said. With considerable willpower she refrained from kissing Dana, instead moving away from her and rolling onto her back.

"Sleep well," Dana replied, relieved that Keri finally seemed ready to give in to sleep.

Her own breathing remained shallow until she heard deep, even breathing from Keri. After a while Keri rolled onto her side and shuffled back toward Dana, and they spooned together like they always used to.

Dana moved closer and decided to stay that way. When Keri didn't need her anymore, at least she would have this memory. She pulled Keri tighter into her body and felt a responsive burrowing. They slept deeply.

Chapter Thirteen

Dana's eyes fluttered open in the gray light of the room. It took her a moment to orient to the unfamiliar surroundings. Then the events of the past two days came flooding back to her. She looked down to see her body firmly entwined with Keri's. Her bedmate was snoring quietly, head bandage askew, as she lay on Dana's shoulder, close to her ear. Her damp, steady breaths sent delicious tendrils of arousal throughout Dana's body.

Not wanting the moment to end, she scanned the room for a clock and spotted one on the nightstand next to her side of the bed. It was close to eight. They had been asleep for twelve hours. She relaxed into the stolen time, hoping to enjoy it awake for a few minutes. As she lay there, she remembered that Huey would be arriving at nine, and Shelley was due, too. She didn't know what time, but Shelley had all the keys and codes to get in. With a sigh, she reluctantly sought to extricate her body from where it had always been happiest, next to MyKeri.

Keri mewled in protest at being separated from her warm pillow, but seemed still asleep when Dana slowly climbed out of bed and found her jeans. As she finished zipping them she checked on Keri and saw her stirring.

Kneeling to eye level beside the bed, she quietly said, "Good morning. How are you today?"

The silence made Dana suspect that Keri wasn't yet awake. Recalling that it always took MyKeri a while to get into her body, she walked over to the drapes, pulling them a little farther apart. Leaving the white liners in place made the room lighter, but not bright.

As she came back around the bed, she said, "I'll go down and start breakfast."

Keri stretched. "Not necessary. Sniff."

Dana stared. Keri's prolonged stretch had removed the covers from some very tantalizing body parts. Jerking her eyes to the window, she was able to focus on sniffing the air. Coffee. "Who…?"

"Shelley. Sometimes she does that. She's so nice." Keri still hadn't opened her eyes. But the stretch, catlike and graceful, had Dana flustered.

"Oh, well, I'd better get down there, then. I'll bring some coffee up. Are you okay? I mean…to be by yourself?"

Keri smiled slightly and sat up, swinging her legs out of bed to rest on the floor. She opened her eyes and focused on Dana.

"No dizziness. And I'm hungry. I think I'll live."

Dana came over and pulled the sheet over Keri's lap. Looking into her friend's eyes, she found that Keri was staring at her shoulder.

"You're hurt." She reached out to touch the dried blood on Dana's T-shirt.

"What?" Dana drew back slightly to look at the spot where Keri had placed her hand. She realized it was Keri's blood, from where she had nestled when they were sleeping. Her touch only added to Dana's state. "Oh."

"I thought you weren't hurt?"

"I wasn't. Let me get the coffee. Be right back."

Dana made a fast exit, leaving Keri sitting on the bed and looking down at the sheet discreetly pulled over her lap. *I should blush. Dana did that for me. Chivalry is alive and well, damn it.*

She took her time standing up and padded slowly to the bathroom. Once in front of the mirror, she saw her reflection for the first time since coming home. The bandage covering her stitches was almost off, and there were traces of dried blood on her skin, some slightly smeared. *You're a mess.*

She touched the skin and thought of Dana's sleep shirt. And smiled. She had slept in Dana's arms. She was sure of it. Her sleep was dreamless and deep, something she hadn't experienced in a very long time. Rationally, she could write it off to exhaustion from the incident and pain medication. But she knew it had more to do with Dana. She felt rested and her mind was much clearer.

Slowly, and not too vigorously, she brushed her teeth and rinsed. So far, so good. Without thinking she bent to splash water on her face. Waves of dizziness forced her to grab the sides of the sink. Her knees started to buckle. Suddenly strong arms wrapped around her waist, pulling her up to lean against the body behind hers. Her head came to rest next to Dana's concerned face, and they looked in the mirror.

Dana's velvet voice crooned to her, "Come on, let me change the dressing. Then I'll find you some sweats and we'll go eat. You're probably just hungry. You're okay."

Keri slammed her eyes shut and swallowed. The image in the mirror was…unsettling.

Dana's arms stayed firmly around her middle until Keri pulled away to stand on her own.

"I'm better," she announced with flimsy conviction. Already, she missed the feel of Dana's body.

"I didn't bring coffee," Dana said, apparently not sharing Keri's heightened awareness. "I thought we could have breakfast downstairs."

"Good idea," Keri said, wondering what it would take to get Dana's attention.

Dana changed Keri's bandage with diligent concentration, thankful she could distract herself from the image she'd found so stunning seconds earlier. She and Keri, framed in the mirror, looked so *right*.

Forcing herself to stay focused on the mundane, she put the cleansing agents and medical supplies away. Keri seemed much better this morning. At this rate Dana would soon be able to go home. The idea deflated her completely. Noticing that Keri had goose bumps on her arms and legs, she slid an arm securely around her waist and guided her to the bedroom. "Sit down," she said. "I'll find you some clothes."

Keri sat on the edge of the bed while Dana rummaged around for a shirt and sweatpants for her to wear. She wanted to say something about the night before, but she had the impression Dana was trying to keep their interactions on a friendly but impersonal footing. Keri was irrationally hurt by that possibility.

As she dressed, she tried not to fixate on Dana's proximity, her faint spicy scent, the arms that steadied her. They didn't speak, but Dana seemed preoccupied. Keri wondered what she was thinking about and decided she was probably wishing she could leave soon. She felt a pang of guilt. Dana hadn't left her side since the incident. She didn't even have her own clothes or toiletries here. After breakfast, Keri would insist that she was fine, and Dana could go with a clear conscience. It was the least she could do.

They made it downstairs barefoot.

Shelley was taking something from the oven and turned when she heard them come in. A look of concern briefly crossed her features when her eyes rested on Keri. Then she was bright and cheerful.

"Good morning, sleepyheads. Have a seat and we'll eat."

They all dove into the delicious pancakes and were still eating when the phone started ringing. Dana excused herself to answer it.

The voice at the other end, female, was demanding, to say the least. "Keri Flemons, and don't give me any crap. I'm a dear friend and I want to talk to her."

Recognizing the voice, Dana stiffened. "Who may I say is calling?"

"This is Gloria Steele. Hurry it up."

Keri watched as Dana's jaw muscles started working overtime.

"Ms. Steele, I'll have to…" Feeling a hand on her arm, she looked sideways to see Keri carefully nodding that it was okay to give her the phone. Reluctantly, Dana passed her the receiver.

Keri took the portable and walked slowly into another room, talking in low tones that were impossible to understand. After a few minutes Dana heard the beep of the cordless phone, ending the call. Walking into the study, she saw Keri in her father's favorite chair, leaning back against the leather. There was such sadness in her eyes, Dana wanted to gather her in her arms and love the sadness away, but she stayed rooted where she was.

"Everything okay?"

Keri sighed. "I suppose. I had to agree to meet with her this week, or she was going to come storming over here." Confusion was evident on her refined features. "Honestly, Dana, we ended our relationship just after my father died. I don't know why she's so insistent. She says she wants to try again. Why?"

Knowing nothing she said could be neutral, Dana didn't attempt an answer. Instead, she forced herself to ask, "Do you still love her?"

Looking out the French doors of the study, Keri said, "The day Daddy died he and I argued about that. He said he wanted me to find the kind of love that he and Moms had. They loved each other dearly, at least for a while. He didn't think that's what I felt for Gloria. He asked me point-blank. I had to admit that he was right."

Dana felt her body relax.

Keri rested her elbows on the armrests of the chair. "I got defensive and said he was only being that way because I was with a woman. Do you know what he told me?"

Dana looked into Keri's eyes and once again stopped breathing.

"He said since I was a kid Moms had told him I might be gay. How could she have known?"

"I guess sometimes mothers just know." She was feeling light-headed.

"I miss him so much. It seemed like life got so hard when he died. Everything just fell apart. Sometimes I feel like I just can't go on." Keri was talking to a place beyond Dana. Tears falling, she said, "I even miss Moms. I thought I didn't, but I do."

Remembering words that AJ's wife, Eva, had told her at her own father's funeral, Dana said, "You can stand anything, Keri. You're a strong, brave woman. Don't ever forget that." Those words had helped her through some of her darkest times.

Keri focused on her friend. "You make me feel that way, Dana. Thank you."

Thinking about Carolyn, Dana was about to carefully broach the possibility of a visit when the intercom sounded from the outside gate. "That should be Huey. I'll get it." She went out into the hallway and hit the intercom to verify, then buzzed the gate open.

Following her, Keri commented, "You might want a jacket or something. You'll be cold."

An odd expression on her face made Dana look down. The T-shirt she'd grabbed in the dark the night before read, "I'm with her." Between the caption and the fact that her full breasts were straining the material, she was quite a sight.

"Oh shit. Can you tell Huey I'll see him shortly?"

"No problem." Keri grinned. Her eyes never left the retreating figure. Dana from the back was almost as good as Dana from the front. And Dana in that tight T-shirt was spectacular.

❖

Huey left Dana with a detailed briefing on the security arrangements and a set of necklaces. Each had two buttons: panic and summons. The team was already in place around the perimeter of the property, and someone would respond within thirty seconds to an alarm.

Dana found Keri still in the study. Her blond hair was a mess, and the sweats Dana had found for her were wrinkled and faded. She looked irresistibly beautiful. Dana bent to gently place the necklace over her head, avoiding the bandage. Her trembling hands came to rest on Keri's upper arms, and she couldn't, for the life of her, pull them away. All she could do was look into the blue eyes of her soul mate.

Keri placed her hands on Dana's shoulders and drew her down closer until their lips were just inches away. Her eyes drifted to the soft full lips of her friend. "Oh, my."

Their mouths met tentatively at first, then melted into each other. Soon their tongues touched, causing such a strong surge of energy that both opened their eyes and flew apart.

Dana landed on her backside, gasping for air. Keri's hand flew to her mouth as she sank back in the leather chair.

Standing up immediately, Dana started to back away, absently running her palms down the sides of her jeans. Eyes wide she said, "I'm sorry, I shouldn't have…I apologize." She turned and fled the room.

Keri looked at the empty doorway and closed her eyes. To no one in particular she said, "I'm not sorry, Dana. I'm not sorry at all."

She remained in the study alone, trying to puzzle out what had just happened. She was sure the attraction was mutual. She was *sure*.

And that kiss. *The kiss.* But Dana had acted as though she had just committed a cardinal sin. Grinning at the thought that, to some people, she and Dana had done exactly that, she was struck by a painful possibility. *What if there's someone else?* No matter how she examined it, she knew that the kiss included both of them. Her head was starting to throb, making further thought difficult.

A gentle knock on the open door forced her to open her eyes, hoping Dana would be there. Carolyn Flemons smiled tentatively and walked in, holding a glass of water and a bottle of aspirin. She said, "Dana told me to tell you she had to go to her apartment to get some clothes. She'll be back shortly."

Keri burst into tears and cried, "Mama! Where have you been?"

Quickly putting the water and pills down, Carolyn knelt in front of her daughter and took her in her arms to comfort her. Keri only called her "Mama" when she was vulnerable and needy, and that evidently hadn't changed over the years. The feeling of holding her child again, after so long, brought tears of her own. "I'm here, Keri. I'm not ever leaving again. I never wanted to leave you."

Keri sobbed. "Why weren't you at the hospital? Someone tried to hurt me!"

Carolyn soothed her. "Dana called me, darling. I *did* come to the hospital. I talked to the doctors and made sure you were going to be okay. I didn't visit because I was worried that the stress of seeing me might make you worse. But I haven't slept, if that's what you're asking. The only reason I didn't burst into the hospital is that I knew Dana was watching out for you. I trust her."

They clung to each other for a few more minutes, until Keri's sobs were reduced to hiccups. Carolyn reached in a pocket of her cardigan sweater and produced a fresh tissue, giving Keri some room to gather herself. She pulled up the leather ottoman that was next to the chair and sat close to her daughter. And silently prayed that, once Keri got her emotions under control, she wouldn't send her away again. She took a risk and reached for Keri's hand. Keri took it and held it tightly.

Keri studied her through bloodshot eyes. "Mama? Why did you move to France?"

Carolyn tried to hide her surprise at the blunt question. She considered her answer and decided that if she had any hope of having a relationship with Keri, it had to be built on honesty. Protecting Mike had brought her nothing but pain.

"I couldn't deal with you refusing to see me and your father's continued unfaithfulness." She saw Keri flinch, but she didn't pull her hand away.

Her voice stronger, Keri said, "But *you* were the one who had the affair."

Carolyn sighed. *Here it comes.* "Your father had been having affairs for years, Keri. I turned a blind eye to it for a while, because he denied it and because I loved him and you so much. But the whole incident with Scooter forced me to pay attention."

Keri stiffened. "What do you mean?"

Carolyn never looked away. "Sean Ryan accused Mike of having an affair with his wife. Told me that was why she left him and Scooter. He also said that was why he'd been fired from the team."

Keri seemed stunned. "Was it true?"

"I don't know. Your father swore it wasn't true. He said he'd never touched Scooter's mother and that the reason Sean was fired was for drinking on the job and poor job performance. Even after he admitted to other 'liaisons,' he stuck to that story."

Keri didn't say a word. Carolyn continued, "It didn't matter, Keri. Sean Ryan was a hateful and violent man. Alcoholics blame others for their problems, and he certainly qualified as an alcoholic. I tried very hard to have contact with Dana, but he blocked every attempt. Eventually, and this was after talking to social workers and attorneys, I gave up. I always felt badly about not being able to help. Dana survived, but I'm sure it wasn't easy for her."

Silent for a moment, Keri said, "So, at the charity party, when you said 'retaliation,' that's what you meant? You had an affair to pay Daddy back for what he was doing?"

Carolyn nodded, fresh tears springing to her eyes. "Yes, it was the dumbest mistake I could have ever made. Mike was incensed and chose to forget about his own infidelities. You had become Daddy's girl anyway, and he was unwilling to tarnish his image in your eyes. I played along, foolishly thinking I was protecting both of you. Eventually I couldn't bear it any longer, and I moved to Paris to start a new life." She hesitated, not wanting to hurt Keri, but wanting her to understand. "I thought it wouldn't matter to you, frankly. You didn't seem to have any time for me."

Keri dropped her hand and sat back in the chair. Carolyn steeled herself for what might be next. But Keri didn't even try to defend herself. "I'm not surprised you thought that. I was horrible to you. I thought I was defending Daddy's honor, even though he never asked me to. I was so self-righteous. I didn't have a clue." Her voice full of remorse, she asked, "Why did you move back? I refused to even let you attend Daddy's funeral."

Shaking her head, Carolyn said, "Oh, I was there. In the back, heavily veiled. But the wheels of that train were already in motion, Keri. Your dad and I were going to try to reconcile."

Keri looked completely startled. The color drained from her face. "You were?"

"Yes. We'd been talking on the phone and emailing for months before he was killed. You see, I never stopped loving him. And he swore it was the same for him. Your father wasn't perfect, honey, but he was a good man." Carolyn looked down at her hands, trying to keep her emotions under control.

"I never knew." Keri was overwhelmed. Daddy hadn't said a word to her, but now that she thought about it, she was aware of a change in him in the months just before the accident. He'd seemed happier, mellower. Her head pounded. "Mama? I need the aspirin, please."

Her mother seemed relieved to be busy doing something to break the tension. Once Keri had swallowed the pills, she said the first thing that popped into her mind that steered them away from their own relationship. "Do you know if Scooter has a girlfriend?"

Carolyn's mouth opened, but nothing came out. "I don't know, sweetie. We haven't had much of a chance to talk. Why?"

Keri stared at her father's desk. She briefly thought about shutting her mother out, but the words just came. "She's driving me crazy. I know...hell, I don't know *what* I know. I just thought maybe she might have said something to you." She closed her eyes, exhausted.

Carolyn touched her daughter's shoulder. "Come on, sweetie, you need to lie down. This morning has been a lot for you. Let me tuck you in."

Keri felt the hot tears start behind her closed eyes. "You don't have to do that. I'm a grown woman."

Helping her up and putting a supportive arm around her daughter's waist, Carolyn said, "Humor me." Keri gladly dropped her façade and allowed her mother to put her down for a nap.

She waited until Keri was resting, then tiptoed quietly out of the room.

In the hallway Carolyn leaned on the door she had just closed and breathed, "Scooter, don't you dare let me down. You two need each other."

CHAPTER FOURTEEN

Numbly pulling into her parking spot, Dana sat for a moment. She had no memory of actually driving to her apartment. Keri and the kiss were the only things that occupied her mind. Just like everything else that had happened over the past two days, it seemed surreal. Her heart wanted to claim it as proof of something bigger than her mind could accept.

Making the effort to consciously loosen her hands from their white-knuckle grip on the wheel, she got out of her car and stalked into her apartment. First stop: the shower. Dana tilted her head back, letting the hot water soothe the tension that had kept her taut and on edge since Keri had been injured. Her thick, black hair was so different from how she had worn it in her playing days. She had to use more shampoo and dry it longer. She had to *think* about it. *Maybe I'll shave my head.*

But she knew she wouldn't. Keri had complimented her on her hair. End of story. *Dana, you are so pathetic. You are in love with a woman who will order you out of her life as soon as she's done using you. And worse? You can't do a damn thing about it. Even if she does send you away, you'll watch over her.*

Dana's lips were still tingling from the kiss. She put fingertips to her mouth, trying to recapture the feeling. There had been nothing friendly or childlike about it. Her own reaction was all the confirmation she needed that she was in trouble. And the look in Keri's eyes made it even clearer. "I have to confront her. I have to make her be honest. And I have to be prepared to leave."

The water was cold, and she was shivering by the time she realized the phone was ringing. Thinking it might be Keri, she grabbed a towel and ran down the hall to pick it up before it rolled over to voice mail.

"Ms. Ryan?" The familiar clipped tones of Thomas Concannon put Dana on guard.

"This is she." Keeping it formal, she wondered what he wanted.

"Thomas Concannon here. How is Ms. Flemons?" His voice was tight with barely controlled anger.

"Um, she's feeling better today. We brought her home because of all of the media attention." Dana was being stingy with details until she could figure out what he wanted.

"Are you aware that I need to see Ms. Flemons on business matters? I attempted to call on her at home a short while ago, and I was denied access!" The indignation in his voice was her first clue.

Happy to hear that Huey and his team were keeping the riffraff out, she said in a diplomatic tone, "Her doctors have issued strict orders about visitors, Mr. Concannon."

"I'm not a *visitor*! I'm the guy who manages her father's business while she plays at being an owner. I don't expect to be turned away at her gates by some hired goons. And whose stupid idea was the big security detail, anyway?"

Dana tried for damage control. "I apologize that you were inconvenienced, Mr. Concannon. Zander MacCauley was concerned for Ms. Flemons's safety, as I know we all are, and he suggested we take appropriate steps." There wasn't a shred of conviction in the small apology, but Concannon wasn't listening anyway.

"I thought MacCauley and Flemons were just friends," he snapped.

"Excuse me?"

"You heard me, Ms. Ryan. According to Herb Kronerberg, their so-called relationship is on the rocks, and Ms. Flemons has 'other interests.' I told the guy he doesn't know what he's talking about. It would be a major problem for the PickAxes if a jerk reporter like him got wind of certain preferences."

Dana drew a sharp breath at the veiled reference to Keri's sexuality and the hint of a threat. Did Concannon know Keri was a lesbian? "When were you talking to Kronerberg?"

"Twenty minutes ago when Jameson Brown's loser cousin told me to take a walk. He's out there with the other media idiots. Imagine how embarrassed I was to be denied access. *Me!*"

Great. "I don't know anything about Ms. Flemons's relationship with Mr. MacCauley," Dana said, sounding as innocent as she could. "Or anyone else."

"Well, find out! I don't want anyone taking advantage of Ms. Flemons when she isn't feeling well. You work for this organization, and apparently she likes having you around. So it's your obligation to make sure the team's interests are protected. I want you to stick like glue to her and let me know what's going on. Understand?"

No. I have no clue. "Yes, sir. Like glue. Anything in particular you want me to look for, sir?"

Sounding more confident, he said, "I want to know who visits her and what is said. And I want a daily report to my private cell phone number. There could be a sizeable bonus in this for you, Ryan. And I happen to know, where you're concerned, there's no love lost. You and I could be helpful to each other. Understand what I'm saying?"

Apparently Concannon thought he had it all figured out. Dana wondered how much he knew about her. It was no secret that Mike Flemons had picked up the tab for her care after the accident. As Mike's right-hand man, Concannon was probably familiar with the details, and it sounded like he thought Dana could be an ally. She almost laughed out loud.

He rattled off his cell phone number and hung up.

Dana stood, dripping, staring at the phone. At some point during the call her towel had fallen to the floor. "What on earth makes you think I would tell you anything at all? You sniveling little…"

The phone rang again. She stared at it before picking it up.

"And one more thing—what are you doing at your home number? Get over to Ms. Flemons's home! And take some clothes. You're staying. I'm going to tell her I want you with her at all times."

Dana was speechless. Almost. Concannon was about to hang up. "Wait! What if she is serious, or seeing someone?" She hated to even voice the thought.

After a moment of hesitation, he replied carefully. "I want you with her unless it's the woman she used to see. Um…Steeple is her name. Gloria Steeple. She always had Ms. Flemons's best interests at heart." The line went dead.

Dana was shivering. "Of all the arrogant…you asshole! You *prick!* How dare you assume I would do anything, *anything* to hurt or manipulate Keri! I ought to go over there and beat the crap out of you. I ought to—"

The phone rang again. *Now what?* She punched the button and tersely said, "Hello!"

There was a pause before, "Dana? It's Keri. Are you okay?"

All of her anger evaporated. Without thinking, she said, "No, sweetheart, I'm not. We need to talk. I'm packing some clothes and coming over. Something is going on, and we need to figure out what it is. How are you feeling?"

" I'm better." Dana could hear Keri take a big breath. "Moms is here."

"How is that going?"

"Okay…It was time, Dana."

"I thought so, too."

"She said the two of you spoke…while I was sick."

Dana hesitated. She'd felt guilty talking to Carolyn behind Keri's back, but no one should have to find out her daughter has been hurt by seeing it on television. Besides, the hospital required a signature from the next of kin before anyone would operate. Dana had kept in touch with Carolyn the whole time.

"It was very hard for her, Keri. She was desperate to see you, but she was afraid to do anything to upset you."

"I know. It's okay. Everything's okay. But…so, are you coming home soon?"

Dana had a huge grin on her flushed face. "As soon as I can throw some clothes in a duffel and get dressed. I've been on the phone so long I've air-dried. See you soon." She quietly disconnected the call and replaced the receiver.

She misses me. And she wants me to come *home.* Dana didn't even notice the tears in her eyes as she quickly dressed and started packing. She would be on her way within thirty minutes.

Keri looked at the phone. Dana's comment about being on the phone so long puzzled her. They'd only spoken for a couple of minutes, so she guessed Dana must have been talking to someone else. She felt a pinprick of jealousy, but an image of Dana naked immediately blunted it. She well remembered that beautiful body from her moonlit room the night before. Then she smiled, an expression she knew revealed every tooth in her mouth.

She called me sweetheart. Daddy used to call Moms that. An image of her parents hugging each other and laughing surged through her mind. Those were such happy times. She had Scooter, and Moms had Daddy.

A knock on the door ended her musings. "Yes?"

Moms stuck her head in. "Zander's on the phone. This is the third time he's called."

Keri grinned. "What line is he on?"

Turning down Keri's street, Dana could see a crowd blocking the front gate. As evidenced by the vans with satellite dishes on them, the media was alive and well and hoping to feed on Keri. Quickly backing around the corner, she drove around until she found a spot on the street, two blocks away. She considered that a small miracle.

Grabbing her duffels, she walked to the side gate that was manned by one of the security guards. As she approached, he spoke into his walkie-talkie. He was checking her identification against a list when Huey walked up. He seemed relieved to see her and escorted her through the gate.

"How's it going?" Dana nodded toward the throng out front. "Have they been here a long time?"

When she'd left earlier, the crowd had thinned, and people were looking lethargic and bored. She was hoping they would give up. Now it looked like they had sniffed fresh blood.

Huey shook his head. "Well, Zander came by and gave them a short interview. I think word got around because the crowd picked up after that."

Dana was relieved. Zander's arrival was very timely if Herb Kronerberg was hanging around. He'd look silly trying to persuade anyone that Keri might have a girlfriend with Zander MacCauley giving interviews. She would need to give Zander a heads-up about that.

"Man, I do not know *how* Zander tolerates it." Huey continued with the update. "Having those people around all the time would drive me postal. Oh, yeah. And your friend Jim Miller arrived a few minutes ago."

Dana thought about some of the comments Zan had made concerning celebrity. He preferred his privacy. But he was kind enough to offer himself as a distraction to spirit Keri away from the hospital. She liked Zander but wondered why he was here. And she *really* wondered why Jim was here.

Huey shouldered one of Dana's bags, and they skulked through the bushes until they could slip behind the house and enter through a utility room. Huey deposited Dana's duffel and returned to his outside duties with a wave.

Hearing voices and laughter coming from the den, Dana followed the sounds to find several of her favorite people gathered around a tray of vegetables, fruit, cheese, and breads. Relief flooded through her to see Keri laughing and enjoying her visitors. From the few words she could overhear, Zander was telling tales of evading the paparazzi. As she entered the room he greeted her with a grin.

"Hello, stranger. Looks like you made it through the welcome wagon out there."

Keri turned in her seat to give her a luminescent smile, one that Dana returned in kind. When she was able to tear her eyes away from Keri, she caught a look of amusement on Jim's face. Glancing at Zan, she saw what she thought was a wink. She didn't know what to say but could feel her ears starting to heat up.

Jim grinned. "Looks like you're here for a while. Or is that your purse?" Dana became aware that she still had a large camera bag on her shoulder.

Dana said, "Well, I...by the way, what are you two doing here? Jim?"

Reddening, Jim said, "Uh, Zander and I...met for lunch." He wouldn't look at Dana and went on in a rush. "He said he was coming to check on Keri, and I invited myself." Quickly turning to Keri he added, "I hope it isn't an imposition, Keri."

Keri smiled warmly. "I'm glad to see you both. Although Zan has a knack for always bringing the press." She seemed sincere so Dana let go of her initial feelings of protectiveness.

Dana said, "Well, in answer to your question, Jim, no, this is not my purse." She plopped the duffel on the floor beside her. "I...am going to be staying for awhile. Actually, I've been ordered to stay for a while...to report on Keri. To the general manager."

The confusion on their faces probably matched her own when she'd gotten the call from Concannon.

Keri's surprise was obvious. "What are you talking about? *I* asked you to stay here." That remark caused Jim's head to snap in her direction, but he said nothing.

"I got a call from Thomas Concannon," Dana said. "He started by being huffy. Apparently Huey and his buddies wouldn't let him in here this morning. And he wanted to know how serious you and Zander are."

Keri's mouth fell open.

Dana continued. "For some reason he thinks that if he orders me to spy on you, I'll do it. I don't know whether to be insulted or happy that he chose me instead of someone else."

"Concannon from yesterday, right?" asked Jim. "Well, if you don't mind me being an attorney right now, exactly what, beginning to end, did he say?"

Five minutes later they stared at each other.

Zander asked, "Who is Gloria and why would he make an exception for her?"

Keri grimaced. Looking only at Zander, she said, "She and I had a...relationship. We ended it shortly after my father died. Lately, she's been trying to get together again. But why that would matter to Concannon, or how he would even know about it, I can't imagine."

"That's what I'm concerned about," Dana said. "I got the impression he thinks he can use it somehow. He mentioned Herb Kronerberg."

"I can't hear that little snake's name without wanting to do him physical harm." A voice floated across the room, and Carolyn Flemons entered with another tray of finger foods.

Keri's face softened as she looked up at her mother, and Dana felt her eyes prickle. She could sense a completely different energy between them. It made her smile to see Moms brush Keri's shoulder lightly.

"I wonder what he's up to," Keri said.

"You said, 'we' ended it." Jim wiped his fingers on a napkin. "Is that accurate?"

Looking at her hands, Keri replied, "Not entirely. I ended it. I realized I...didn't love her. Daddy knew it. We had talked about it the day he...it was more honest that way."

"So, Gloria wasn't happy when you broke things off?" Jim asked.

"I thought she was fine about it," Keri said. "We both knew it was over. There was nothing...*there*."

Hanging on every word, Dana became aware that she was grinning when Keri admitted that she didn't love Gloria. She changed her face to neutral, but not before she caught a look from Jim. She gave him one of her own, and he glanced away.

Zander asked, "When did she start calling you?"

Keri had to think about that. "Shortly after I moved back to San Francisco and took over the team operations."

Jim popped in, "How often have you seen her?"

Keri shifted uneasily. "Well, once for dinner." Eyes darting to the window, she added, "I kind of let things get out of hand that night." She quickly added, "But I made sure she understood it was just a...one-time...thing."

Dana didn't know where to look. She met Moms's eyes, and something in the older woman's expression calmed her. The thought of Keri with Gloria...*with anyone*...sickened her. She tuned into Keri once more, trying to tell herself that the past was the past, and right now, she couldn't afford to get hooked in to her emotions. Something was going on with Concannon, and it seemed Gloria had a role in it. For Keri's sake, they needed to figure this out.

"She and another woman showed up at minicamp the other day," Keri continued. "The one where I gave the interview on the field. Then she called this morning and insisted that we see each other again. She keeps saying we were meant for each other."

Quietly, Jim asked the question that was foremost in everyone's mind. "How do you feel about that? About getting back to her?"

Dana felt nauseous but stayed glued to her seat and kept her eyes on Keri. Her ears were pounding so hard she could barely hear.

Without hesitation Keri replied, "There is no chance we'll be together again. I don't love her. I never did." Dana felt her stomach untwist a bit.

Leaning forward, Keri said, "But the odd thing is, I don't really feel it from Gloria either. She's been persistent, though, and...I don't know, *urgent,* I guess. It's strange. Why on earth would she want to reconnect, especially since I'm so involved with the team now? She always made fun of it, thought it was a waste of time. Except for the money, of course."

"Bingo," said Jim.

Keri asked, "What do you mean?"

Jim sat back and put one arm on the back of the sofa. "Keri, did Concannon know about your relationship with Gloria?"

"Well, I didn't make a complete secret of it. She came with me to several team functions when we were together."

"It sounds like Concannon and your ex are in this together, trying to manipulate you out of the team."

"But why?" Keri looked pale.

Dana hastened over and stood behind Keri, placing both hands on her shoulders and gently kneading some of the tension from them.

"The most common reasons are money and power," Jim said.

Dana added, "You know Concannon wasn't happy about you taking over the team. He's tried to disparage and block your movements whenever he could. And I'll bet he's talking loud and long to all the chauvinists on the board."

Zander asked, "Keri, who let Gloria Steeple in the closed practice?"

Keri opened her eyes and thought about it. "I asked her that and she never answered. I'm going to make a call and find out."

"Did your father trust Concannon?"

Jim's question caused a ripple of tension to cross Keri's shoulders. Dana kept working the muscles.

"No. That last…day…I asked him why he didn't fire him. He said that he was a genius with numbers, and he'd rather have his enemies closer, to keep an eye on them." Keri closed her eyes. "God, what a mess."

Carolyn, who had been leaning against the sofa, listening in silence, cast a thoughtful stare at Keri. "From what Mike told me, your friend Gloria likes the good life. Do you think she could be bribed to do something that might not be in your best interests?"

Dana slid down beside Keri and put her arm around her shoulders. It wasn't an easy question for anyone to be asked about an ex. She could sense that Keri was struggling with it.

"I just don't know." Keri leaned into Dana, seeking her warmth.

After a few moments, she sat up and, without thinking, took Dana's hand. "I'm sorry to involve you, Zander. You, too, Jim. I don't know what's going on, but perhaps you should distance yourself from me until this is resolved." To Dana, she said, "I don't think it will be so easy for you, Dana. Perhaps this whole idea of the book is wrong. I could fire you and you'd be safe. I don't want you in the middle of this."

Keri glanced down at the hand she was holding and tried to release it.

Dana held on. "I'm afraid it's too late for that. I'm here and I'm staying. Just following orders, of course." The look of gratitude from Keri made her heartbeat double.

"Sweetie," Carolyn said, "I don't think anyone in this room is going to allow a small-time upstart like Thomas Concannon to dictate terms. In case you've forgotten, you were physically assaulted. If that man had anything to do with it, I want to find out. And I'll see him in a cell for it."

Keri blinked and her mouth curved with delight. "You really don't like him, do you, Moms?"

"I have my reasons," Carolyn said.

Jim spoke next. "I'm for going after him. I might even be able to help."

Zander added, "Me, too. Whatever I can do."

"Are you sure?" Keri looked at each man seriously.

In unison, they replied, "Yes."

"And I think we all know where Dana stands," Carolyn said, clapping her hands together like it was a done deal.

Dana laughed. "I'm the one he seems to think he can trust. Let's figure out how we can use that."

CHAPTER FIFTEEN

The next hour was spent discussing possibilities. Keri would have Shelley get copies of the vendor contracts and past years' tax returns to Jim to go over as an outside consultant. She would also find out who had put Gloria on the list for the closed practice. Zander would ask around to see what he could find out about conversations Concannon had been having with various members of the team. Dana would play along with Concannon's request to spy on Keri. And Carolyn said she wanted to "handle" Herb Kronerberg personally.

When it became obvious that Keri was flagging, they tacitly agreed to wind up their strategy session, and Dana saw Jim and Zander out to their cars. Zander left first, taking most of the reporters with him.

As Jim opened his door he said, "Wow, she's really something. You two look good together, Dana."

"She's amazing. She always has been."

"Talk to her, Dana. She cares about you, I can see that. Take the risk." Jim gave her a gentle hug, then settled into the car.

Dana knocked on the window and he slid it down. She leaned close to him and said, "You and Zander look good, too. Guess I don't have to worry that Zander will try to sweep her off her feet, eh?"

Jim turned an amazing shade of magenta in just a few seconds. "Just between us, I'd come out wearing a rainbow-colored Armani suit if he was by my side."

"I don't want to see you two on the cover of *The Advocate* before we've dealt with Concannon," she teased.

He winked and raised the window.

Dana watched the car leave, and a feeling of rare contentment washed over her. Keri was waiting for her. She was *home*. Whatever else was going on, whatever Concannon was up to, nothing seemed to matter but that simple fact. Smiling, Dana went indoors.

She found Keri in the den lying on the sofa with her eyes closed, dozing. Dana cleared away the dishes and straightened up the kitchen, idly wondering where Moms had disappeared to. Hearing Keri stir, she took a breath, tried to still her fidgeting hands, and turned from where she had finished putting dishes in the dishwasher. "How are you feeling?" She absently dried her hands on her jeans, forgetting the towel on the counter.

Keri watched her a moment, then smiled. "I'm okay." Patting the cushion next to her, she said, "Sit."

The time had arrived; Dana could feel it. She slowly hung the dish towel on a hook to dry and walked over to sit on the ottoman. "Where's Moms?"

"She went out. Something to do with her part of *the plan*." Keri chuckled softly and reached to take Dana's hand. "You seem nervous. Is something bothering you?" There was just a trace of teasing in her eyes. "That kiss—should I say I'm sorry?"

"Are you sorry?" Dana couldn't tease in response. This was too important.

"No." Keri reached for her and they were in one another's arms.

Dana held her soul mate, protecting her from the outside world as she always had.

They clung to each other. Keri felt soft kisses on her head and forehead, a cheek pressing against her own. The strength of the hug, given from the heart, made Keri feel safe and warm in a way she hadn't felt since before Dana had been torn from her life.

Keri looked up into the beautiful face and eyes so close to hers. The kiss seemed the most natural act she could imagine. She leaned up, a whisper of connection, then incredible softness on her mouth. She put her arms around Dana's neck and pulled her closer as the kiss deepened. They stayed that way forever or a minute, she wasn't sure. What she was sure about was that she had never felt anything so intense.

When they finally parted slightly to sip some air, they looked at each other in wonder.

Dana whispered, "You are so special to me."

Her eyes were a deep emerald. Keri was sure Dana could hear her heart beating. "Let's go upstairs."

Dana searched her face uncertainly. "I don't want to sleep," Keri said. "Not right away."

"I'm not sure…Keri, you're not well."

"Are you turning me down?"

Dana rose and took both of Keri's hands. The silence that followed was palpable. Dana stopped breathing. "I—"

"Please don't make me beg." Clear blue eyes held nothing but certainty.

Dana forced air into her lungs. "Keri, the doctors said no excitement."

"Maybe all I want is you beside me. Naked. We could work on not *too much* excitement."

Dana's mind raced to keep up with her hormones. She'd promised the doctors, she'd sworn to herself, she had to take watch over Keri. What if something happened? What if it was a huge mistake? What if it was all a lie?

"But I promised to watch out for you."

Smiling, Keri said, "Dana, you're a very beautiful, caring, loving woman. And I want you in my bed. More than that, I need you in my bed. I need to feel you, make love to you, have you make love to me. That is what would take care of me best. Please, Dana, please."

Staring, Dana finally whispered, "Anything."

Holding hands they climbed the stairs slowly. Once inside the bedroom, Keri closed the door firmly. "I need a shower." She entered the bathroom, leaving the door ajar.

Dana heard the water running and felt a jolt of energy from the top of her head to her toes. She murmured, "Go slow."

Walking over to the bed, she turned down the spread, then went to the chest of drawers to pull out two sleep shirts. She hesitated, then dropped them back in the drawer and walked over to sit heavily on the bed, staring into space.

Keri called, "Dana?"

The blood pounding in her ears, Dana stood with some effort and walked slowly to the door, leaning around it to answer. Any thought of speaking became impossible at the sight before her eyes.

Keri had stepped out of her jeans and was dressed only in her panties and shirt. Dana couldn't help but admire Keri's legs and blushed when her eyes rose to meet the blue ones smiling at her.

With a hand on her shirt to unbutton it, Keri raised an eyebrow in invitation. She dropped her hand and said, "Help me."

Dana swallowed hard and walked to her, reaching for the shirt with trembling fingers. Keri did the same for her, both of them fumbling shyly with the clothing. When both shirts were unbuttoned they stood before each other.

Dana's voice was husky. "Keri."

A tender kiss that reached right into her soul was the only response. The kiss dissolved any doubt she had. She returned it with every fiber of her being.

Within minutes they were naked, each in awe at the beauty of the other. Holding hands they stepped into the shower and stood under the water, their senses alive with anticipation. Dana reached for the liquid soap behind Keri and squeezed some into her hand, her eyes never leaving her. "Let me."

Keri moaned when Dana touched her. Her hands slid over Keri's body, grazing hard, erect nipples, sliding down her belly, around to her back. She longed for Keri's lips again and they were there, her tongue seeking entrance. Keri's arms wrapped around Dana's neck and held her, their skin sensitive to the close contact. They explored each other's mouths with exquisite tenderness.

Keri moaned and released one hand from behind Dana's neck to trail down her strong body and brush the side of a breast. Dana gasped at the touch, her nipples beginning to ache.

Keri's hands explored Dana's body, unable to stop seeking the pleasure. The soft skin with firm muscles beneath was intoxicating. Dana slid a hand around to Keri's blond curls and brushed her hard center. With a sudden movement, Keri pulled her mouth from Dana's and looked into the emerald pools of light.

She said, "Not…"

Dana pulled back and looked at Keri, a question in her beautiful eyes.

Keri grabbed her shoulders and pulled her close. "I meant, not *here*. Not for our first time. Don't you dare leave me now, for *any* reason."

Dana could only nod. She slid her hands around to cup Keri's buttocks and lifted her. Keri instinctively wrapped her legs around Dana. Her eyes were fire emeralds.

Keri turned off the water and pushed open the door for them. She grabbed a towel on the way to the bedroom. Dana seemed to hold her effortlessly. She dried Dana's face and neck and dabbed at her own before Dana turned to deposit her on the bed.

Keri watched through eyes filled with lust as Dana retrieved the towel, bending as if to help dry her more.

She said, "Drop it."

The towel fell to the floor.

Keri looked deeply in her eyes. "Do you want me, Dana?" Tugging on her hands, she pulled her down to the bed.

Dana stopped, dead still. Keri held her breath, afraid Dana would once again run. Then Dana gently settled onto the crisp sheets of the bed, placing her body over the smaller woman and lowering herself until she was resting on top of her.

Keri breathed, "You are so beautiful." Fire consumed them both.

Dana explored the beauty that was Keri. Her hands roamed her body, feeling the swell of her breasts, the taut nipples. She kissed her neck and along the line of her collarbone. Keri's gasps and moans guided her.

She rose, straddling Keri. When she cupped her breasts and allowed her thumbs to lightly graze the beautiful nipples, she was lost. Keri ran her hands up the strong thighs and grasped Dana's waist, pushing her to the side and throwing a leg over her.

Keri was the first to taste her lover's breasts, sucking and teasing one with her mouth and tongue while kneading the other with her fingers. They moved together urgently, and Dana slipped into Keri's wetness to find her swollen center, almost coming at the touch. Keri rose to kiss her but stopped midair, eyes hazy with desire. Dana entered her with her fingers, her thumb massaging the pulsing clitoris.

"Oh! Oh...Dana!" Her head arched forward as her pelvis ground into Dana. Keri moved with the waves surging through her, Dana never stopping until her lover lay limp on top of her. Slipping her arms around Keri, she held her tightly. Dana slowly became aware of the tears seeping from her own eyes.

Then Keri was there, kissing the tears, exploring Dana's mouth with her tongue and her body with her hands. Keri moved to separate

Dana's legs, working her way down to feel the slickness waiting for her. Keri settled between her legs and sat back, eyes hazy with lust. She lifted Dana's legs at the knee and pushed them farther apart, placing Dana's hands on the knees.

Keri said, "So lovely." She leaned in to taste the wetness and stroked her lover with her fingers and tongue, seized her clit between her teeth, and gently began to suck on the object of her desire. Dana moaned. Keri entered her, matching the rhythm of Dana's body, using her tongue to bring her to a pounding climax within minutes. The two fell exhausted into each other's arms and slept.

CHAPTER SIXTEEN

Stirring and stretching under the coolness of the sheets, Keri became aware that she was alone in the bed. She heard clothing rustling and the sound of a page turning. *There she is.*

Opening her eyes she was momentarily disappointed when Moms looked up and met her gaze with a warm smile. She tried to cover it with a yawn.

Moms wasn't fooled. "You know, between the two of you I'm beginning to feel unwanted."

Keri pulled the covers over her head and moaned, "Oh gawwwd." She was flushed and her hormones were in overdrive, but she stifled the urge to scream. She flapped the covers down and sat up, only slightly woozy from the sudden switch in positions. "What do you mean, 'between the two of you'? Did Dana say something?"

"She didn't have to. She was in the kitchen when I arrived, and I guess she was expecting you. Let's just say her face fell just like yours when I walked in."

Keri grinned widely. "Okay. So much for keeping it to ourselves." It occurred to Keri that she had just admitted to having made love to Dana to her *mother*. Somehow she wasn't embarrassed.

Carolyn drew the curtains. "How are you feeling this morning, other than very pleased with yourself?"

Laughing, Keri said, "Oh, much better, actually. I think I'm over the worst. Hopefully the headaches will stop soon."

"I'm sure they will, sweetie." Carolyn strolled to the bed and slowly surveyed her daughter's face. The dark rings under her eyes and yellowed hairline told their own story. Profound maternal rage swept her. That some thugs had dared to do this to her daughter made her angrier than anything in her life.

She had spent several hours discussing the case with the police the previous evening. They were no closer to coming up with a list of suspects, even with all the publicity. The people who had shared the elevator with Keri had given confused descriptions of the assailants, and no one had managed to get the plate number of their car. Evidently they had obscured it so the security cameras wouldn't pick it up. At this rate it seemed more likely that Keri's friends would solve the case.

"By the way," Carolyn said. "Dana says she needs to go in to Jim's office. They were on the phone a few minutes ago."

"Oh, is there some news?"

"I'll let her fill you in. But I don't want you rushing out. Let her go and do whatever has to be done."

"Oh, Moms." Keri rolled her eyes. "I'll be careful."

Carolyn sat down on the edge of the bed and regarded Keri tenderly. Taking her hand, she said, "I'm so happy for you."

Keri blushed. "Me, too." She hardly dared believe it. Part of her had expected to wake and find Dana had run screaming into the night. "She still here?"

A soft alto voice answered from the doorway. "It would take a helluva lot more than changing your bandages to get rid of me, Keri."

The look of joy on both their faces gave Carolyn a lump in her throat. "If you'll excuse me, I need to go call my hairdresser. He really enjoys hearing from me."

Dana came into the room tentatively, watching Keri for some sign that last night had not been just a one-night stand. Keri beamed at her and opened her arms.

The softness of Keri's lips stole what few thoughts Dana had been able to muster. She slid her arms around Keri's slender waist and pulled her into an embrace, never letting go of her mouth.

With a soft moan, Keri broke the kiss and burrowed into Dana's neck. "So it wasn't all just a wonderful dream. It *was* real. You *are* real."

Smiling, Dana said, "And you aren't just going to send me away saying, 'Thanks, I needed that'?"

Keri studied Dana. "No, I won't do that." Her heart ached.

Moms called from downstairs. "Jim is expecting you both in one hour. Get going, ladies."

Keri and Dana grinned at each other and answered in unison, "Yes, Moms!"

❖

Huey created a distraction by having one of the guards pull the Range Rover out in front of the house and wait with the motor running. The remaining reporters were busy focusing their lenses on the car as Dana and Keri slipped out the back way. They walked the few blocks to Dana's car and drove to Jim's law office in downtown San Francisco. Huey was following them to provide security in and out of the building.

The drive over gave Dana a chance to get her left brain back in control. Even now, she couldn't even glance at Keri without feeling giddy. They were *lovers*. It didn't seem real. But it was.

Zander was already there when they arrived. He took them to a conference room where a light breakfast was laid out and explained that Jim was finishing a phone call and would join them soon. His eyes were dancing, but he wouldn't offer any explanations.

A few minutes later, Jim hurried through the door. "Okay, things are starting to make sense." He went to the buffet and started to fix an elaborate plate of lox and bagels.

Dana, recognizing Jim's style of making a short story long, said, "Jim, so help me, if you don't give us some information very soon, I'm going to make a mess of that Hugo Boss suit you're wearing." She caught surprise on Keri's face and a grin on Zander's.

Whirling around, Jim shot her a wounded look. "Dana, I'll have you know I've been up all night working on this stuff." He glanced coyly at Zander and added, "Almost." His face took on a rosy hue.

Intensely aware of Keri sitting just inches away from her, Dana said dryly, "Just throw us a crumb to consider while you eat, okay?"

Jim put his plate down on the table. "Okay. Consider this. The contracts I've gone over are very different from the ones the vendors have been bound by traditionally. The new contracts demand outrageous cuts of the profits and make unreasonable demands on the businesses. They seem designed to force them out rather than keep them affiliated."

That said, he went about designing and constructing a bagel, cream cheese, lox, onion, and caper extravaganza. They all stared at the food in silence.

Once he had carefully quartered his creation, Keri asked, "What else?"

The corners of Jim's eyes crinkled in delight. "I contacted a friend of mine whose life partner is a forensic accountant named Patrick Hideo. After talking with him, I called Shelley and obtained a copy of the books and tax returns for the two years preceding your dad's death and since Concannon took over. In my limited experience they look...unusual. I want your permission, Keri, to send them to Hideo and have them examined. Something's up."

He took a huge bite and waited.

Without delay she said, "You have my permission. What looked unusual?"

After munching for what seemed like a very long time, Jim managed, "The numbers are out of whack. Things don't add up. I only noticed because the ratios are very different since Concannon took over, and it's odd to see much variation in certain statistics year to year."

"I have no idea what you're talking about." Keri had never had to look at a balance sheet in her life and relied on experts to translate the sheets of mysterious figures that seemed unavoidable when there was a business to run.

Concannon had waved various financial summaries in front of her at meetings, and she was too embarrassed to admit she had no idea what they meant. She'd been thinking about enrolling in some business courses just so she could ask intelligent questions.

"Is this just recent?" Dana asked.

"Probably not," Jim said. "According to Pat Hideo, if there is a problem and Concannon is the reason, it probably started some time ago. Maybe on a small scale."

"He's been embezzling from the PickAxes as well as creating problems with the vendors?" Keri frowned. How could Daddy not have known?

Putting down his bagel, Jim looked at Keri steadily. "It's possible and, if he is, I think we can assume Concannon probably has a problem that requires money to fix."

"Like what?" Dana asked.

Jim wiped his mouth with his napkin. "With guys like him, it's usually some kind of addiction. Drugs, sex, gambling, something like that. There could be another component. Maybe he cheated on his wife and is being blackmailed."

"Does he even have a wife?" Zander looked doubtful.

Keri shook her head. "I don't think he's on drugs, and I've never seen him remotely interested in women or men. People seem more like *things* to him."

"Gambling would fit." Dana could easily imagine Concannon at a high rollers' table.

Jim blew out a breath. "Well, that would answer a lot of questions. If he's in debt—"

"But he makes a lot of money." Keri was at a loss.

Zander shook his head. "It makes no difference, if he's addicted. I've seen players lose millions because they can't stop, and they won't admit it's a problem."

Dana stared at the wall behind Jim, her mind ticking at double time. "The people who hold those markers don't mess around." Sitting straight up, she said, "Wait a second. Remember the Italian woman who was with Gloria that day. I told you I thought I recognized her."

"Gina something," Keri said.

"Yes. The one who didn't like her photo being taken. I think she's an enforcer or bodyguard or something for one of the big crime bosses. I helped Jake, my friend at the *Gazette*, do some layouts for an organized crime feature a few months ago, and I'm sure she was in a couple of the photos we were cropping."

"I still don't see where Gloria fits in, even if she is hanging around with a woman like that. It's probably just a coincidence."

"I don't think it's a coincidence that Concannon knows more than he should about your relationship with Ms. Steeple," Dana said. "Even if they had met at a team function, it's a pretty big assumption to make—that you and she were lovers."

"Gloria's timing is interesting," Jim said. "Let's say Concannon was using the PickAxes as his personal bank account. Suddenly, you enter the picture, Keri, and he has to figure out a way to either distract you or get you to sell your interest in the team. Voila! He remembers Gloria and tracks her down. He offers her money to lure you away from work."

Jaw grinding, Dana muttered, "Why that little..."

Keri slipped her hand into Dana's and gently squeezed. Without looking at her, she addressed Jim and Zander. "I know we parted but it was mutual. She's impulsive sometimes, but I've never known her to be malicious. Gloria might agree to something without thinking it through. But I can't imagine her doing it if the Mafia is involved. She's not stupid."

"We have no proof, only supposition," Jim said. "We need some hard facts."

"I'll check in with Jake at the *Gazette*," said Dana. "At least we can find out who Gina works for."

"Keri, do you think you could get Gloria to admit to anything?" Jim asked.

"Possibly. What do you have in mind?"

"See if you can find out whether Concannon has offered her money. Maybe scare her a little. Don't forget. The police are involved in this."

"Until the forensic accounting is done, we need to play it cool," Jim said quickly. "Maybe we can gather enough on paper to take to the cops and let them handle it from there."

Relaxing, Dana said, "That's better. Remember, Concannon thinks I work for him. Maybe I can find out some things too."

"I'm not sure I like the sound of that, at all," Keri said.

Dana retorted, "About as much as I like the idea of you talking to Gloria with Ms. Muscle standing by."

Breaking the semiplayful standoff between the two women, Jim said, "Look, the report is being rushed so we should have something within a week. Meantime, you two stick to each other like white on rice, and Huey can be the gravy." He looked pleased with the analogy, but the rest of them groaned.

Keri looked at her watch. "Oh! We have to go. I have an appointment." Everyone stood, and after quick good-byes, Dana and Keri left the room.

"An appointment?" Dana asked.

Keri smiled. "You'll see."

Chapter Seventeen

"A re you sure she'll fall for this?" Dana asked, as they strolled into the lobby of the Mark Hopkins Hotel. Keri had arranged to meet Gloria for a late lunch at the hotel's Nob Hill Restaurant.

"I know her," Keri said, brushing by a huge potted palm. "She won't be able to resist the idea of being immortalized in print. Just flatter her. She likes a lot of attention."

Dana groaned. She had no idea how she was going to sit through lunch with Keri's ex, let alone feign breathless admiration.

Gloria had dressed to be noticed in a tight lime-green dress cut low enough to display more cleavage than Dana wanted to know about. At first, Gloria was annoyed by Dana's presence and didn't bother to hide her feelings, asking Keri, "What's she doing here?"

"Thomas insists I have her with me." Keri managed to sound like this was a chore. "Just some added security."

Gloria sniffed. "Oh, yeah. She'd be a big help if you were mugged again."

"The police don't think it was a mugging," Keri said.

"Like they'd know."

Keri wondered if she detected a faintly guilty expression on Gloria's face, but her ex swung her eyes away, scanning the restaurant, before she could be certain. She was looking for celebrities, her habit at every upscale establishment.

Dana opened the case she was carrying and took out a camera. She made a show of testing the flash. With a glance at Keri, she said, "Perhaps I should mention to the staff that we're going to be shooting a few photographs in here."

A frown disturbed Gloria's careful eye makeup. "What's going on?"

"Dana's starting work on a book about prestigious women of the Bay Area. Photos, a biography." Keri shrugged. "She thought it would be nice to get the two of us in the same photo. Would you mind?"

"It would be a big favor, Ms. Steeple." Dana managed to say it with some saliva escaping on the Steeple part.

Gloria's demeanor underwent a remarkable change. Instantly, she slinked toward Keri and struck a pose, sliding her arm over Keri's shoulders.

In response, Dana lifted her camera, framed a shot, then shook her head. "No, from that angle, the light emphasizes Gloria's nose." Politely but firmly, she arranged them across the table from each other.

Keri gave her an amused look and noticed with some satisfaction that the muscles in her jaw were working overtime.

Dana fired off several shots, then said, "Would you mind a close-up, Ms. Steeple? In case we run with a feature page about you and your business interests." She was almost gagging.

"No problem." Gloria adjusted her neckline for full eye-candy effect and thrust her chest out.

Dana suspected she would probably have climbed on the table if she'd been asked. Resisting the temptation, she angled Gloria's head a little and said, "Good. Nice jawline. A subtle smile now?"

Gloria obliged by wetting her lips and producing a smoky look. Dana wondered what Keri had seen in her, beyond the obvious physical charms. As she took a few tight shots, Keri spoke quietly to Gloria.

"I really wish we could get beyond all this and just have a friendship." Keri sighed. "I just don't think getting involved again would work, Gloria. I mean, for a start we couldn't be seen *anywhere* together. I can't be outed now that I'm running the PickAxes."

"No one's going to out you." Gloria struck another pose.

"Actually, I'm worried that Thomas Concannon is. He's been dropping hints."

"What?" The smile fell from Gloria's face.

Perfect timing. Dana lowered her camera. "If you'll both excuse me for a moment, I need to sort through these shots and see what I can use."

"Sure." Gloria pasted on a glitzy smile. "And I want to talk about that book with you afterwards, too." As soon as Dana moved a few paces away, she scooted closer to Keri and said, "What do you mean? What's he been saying?"

"He's dropping hints about talking to Herb Kronerberg. And you know what that means."

Gloria looked confused, then angry.

Before she could speak again, Keri said, "I'm not surprised. I know he wants me out of the business. The thing is, it looks like he's been breaking the law, too. I don't know what kind of trouble he's in, but it's all going to hit the fan pretty soon. The police are getting involved. They think he might have arranged for me to be attacked."

"They do?" Gloria looked genuinely appalled. "That's terrible."

"Seems like he's gotten mixed up with some dangerous people." Keri looked Gloria directly in the eye. "I'm telling all my friends to keep their distance from him."

"I hardly know the guy," Gloria said. Her voice sounded thin and a little shaky.

"That's good to hear. Because if I thought you were a friend of his, I wouldn't be able to see you again."

"I'm not," Gloria asserted grimly. "I hope he gets what's coming to him if he had anything to do with hurting you."

"I'm sure the truth will come out. If you hear anything, make sure you let me know. Then I can keep your name out of things."

They fell silent as Dana returned. The lunch conversation was lame. Though Gloria proclaimed herself an ardent suitor, the effort seemed halfhearted, and she appeared anxious to leave. Surprisingly, she invited them both to drop by her bar later that week. She actually seemed relieved when the meal was complete, even joking with them as they waited for the parking attendant to bring them their cars.

After she'd driven off, Dana slid her hand into Keri's and asked, "Well?"

Keri smiled. "She got the message. By tomorrow, I bet she'll call and tell me everything."

❖

Gloria drove back to Crush, her mind whirling and the meal she had picked at souring in her stomach. She barely remembered what they talked about. It had been pleasant. Vaguely registering that there was much more heat between Keri and the photographer than she'd ever had with Keri, her smile was fleeting.

Jesus! She didn't want to be with Keri. And she didn't want her to get hurt. *This is crazy! I've got to get out of this. Gina's going to kill me.*

She knew the scary, sexy Italian woman would be there sometime during the day or night. She'd been visiting more frequently. There was a tension between them. She was so…dangerous. Gloria could feel herself getting wet thinking about her. *Damn you, Steeple! You might know you'd be attracted to her.* Keri was just a challenge and a toy. This woman was much more to Gloria's liking. *Crap!*

She sped up and screeched to a halt in her parking spot, inches from the brick wall of the building. Her car rocked for a moment, and Gloria stared into space, lost in thought. A shadow falling over her brought her attention back to the moment. Gina Pescetti was smiling down at her, sunglasses masking the dark, almost black eyes. She opened the car door for Gloria, and they walked in silence into the bar.

Hardly anyone was around, and Gloria led the way directly to her office. Gina closed the door and leaned against it. Gloria heard the lock slip into place. Gina was quiet, studying Gloria with an intensity that made her feel weak.

"What?" Gloria said. To her surprise, her voice came out husky.

Gina's voice was silken, seductive. "The meeting. How did it go?"

Gloria tried for nonchalance, but Gina's presence was having its effect. And it wasn't fear she was feeling. "Oh, it was fine. She brought a woman with her. That photographer from the other day. Beautiful woman, really."

The silence hung between them.

Never moving, Gina said, "What's your progress?"

Gloria arranged papers on her desk and started fiddling with a pencil. "Well, I've invited them to the bar later this week." She wouldn't look up.

"That's it? You invited *them* to the bar?"

Gloria threw the pencil on the desk. "What do you want from me? Look, there's…well, there's nothing between Keri and me anymore. Hell, she seemed more interested in the photographer than me. And frankly…" She rubbed her face with both hands and sat back.

Suddenly right beside her, Gina growled, "Frankly what?"

Gloria knew she should be afraid. She was trembling, but…She stood to look up at Gina. There it was, raw need, matching her own. The scent in the room was of leather and wet lust, overwhelming her. Gina moved like a panther, pulling Gloria up into an embrace. Her tight black leather pants had a definite bulge.

Gloria lost her breath. "God. Gina!" She grasped Gina behind the neck and pulled her into a searing kiss.

With one hand Gina cleared the desk, sending everything flying to the floor. Effortlessly, she lifted Gloria and laid her across it, pushing her dress up to her waist and ripping her panties off in one motion. Her tongue masterfully circled Gloria's belly before she moved up and demanded entrance to her mouth. The kiss ignited both into a breathless heat. Gloria spread her legs as she reached for Gina's zipper.

Reaching in, Gloria purred, "What do we have here? How do you get around with this strapped on? It's really, really big."

Gina bent to cover Gloria's wet center with her mouth, licking the length of her, sucking and nibbling on her clit. Gloria moaned, her heat growing,

Raising her head, Gina challenged, "I wear it for special occasions. Do you want it? Can' you handle it?"

"Yes! Can't you tell?"

Gloria gasped. Gina was kissing her breasts through the flimsy material of the dress as she entered her and began a steady rhythm. Each stroke took her deeper, and Gloria rode the waves of the buildup, delirious. "Harder. More."

Gina dropped her pelvis and weight, thrusting against Gloria's clit with every sliding motion. The motion rubbed Gina's clit, too, and they were both lost in sensation. The sounds of wild abandon rocked the room as both women came, again, and then again.

Eventually, Gina pulled out and slid to the side of Gloria. "Magnifico."

Gloria was about to reply when the sound of banging on the door brought her out of her haze.

"Gloria? Are you okay in there? Should I call the cops?" Tiffany sounded frightened.

Irritation on her face, Gina raised her head to look at the door.

Gloria sucked in air. "Tiff. I'm okay! Go back to the bar!"

"I got a baseball bat if you need help!"

"Tiffany, go *away*!"

There was no more knocking.

Feeling cold air on sensitive tissue made Gloria aware of her compromising position. She tried to lower her dress but Gina's hands were there before hers, gently pulling the dress down to cover her. Then she helped her sit up on the desk.

Gina gingerly arranged herself and zipped her pants. "I must go."

She turned to leave but Gloria caught her arm. Looking her in the eyes, she grabbed her crotch and squeezed. "You were wonderful."

Gina smiled at her. "I enjoyed you too, baby." She walked to the door and paused there, looking back. "When will you be home tonight?"

Suddenly wet again, Gloria said, "About two. Let me write the address for you."

She started to open her desk drawer when a low voice stopped her. "I know where you live."

Watching the door close behind her, Gloria muttered. "Yes, you do."

CHAPTER EIGHTEEN

Dana waited in Thomas Concannon's outer office for her appointment. Sitting on the opulent leather sofa with a magazine open on her lap, she stared at the writing without seeing it. She wanted to be at home with Keri. Despite Huey and his big-necked buddies standing guard, Dana still felt uneasy leaving Keri in the house alone. She couldn't stand to have her out of her sight, for fear something would happen to her.

And it wasn't just worry about Keri's safety that distracted her. She spent almost every waking moment in a mix of lust and painful anxiety. The passion was so strong she marveled at the woman Keri had unleashed in her. She had never before experienced the unquenchable thirst that Keri evoked, often with no more than a look or touch. Just thinking about Keri naked in her arms made her body react. The rapid opening of Concannon's office door put an end to that.

His assistant, Alison Herndon, stood in the doorway and smiled as she motioned Dana in. As though Alison could read her thoughts, Dana stood abruptly, spilling the magazine on the floor. Her face grew warm as she bent to pick it up and return it to the table in front of her. Telling herself to get serious, she marshaled her thoughts to the problem at hand and aimed for Concannon's office.

As she walked past Alison, the secretary quietly said, "Careful. He doesn't miss much."

Dana snapped her head up and met Alison's even stare. This woman saw everything. She probably knew her boss was up to no good. And it seemed as if she was hinting that she was not entirely on his side. Wondering how they could use this shaky loyalty, Dana nodded slightly, schooled her features to neutral, and stepped through the doorway.

Concannon was just hanging up the phone with the usual scowl on his face. Today he was wearing a hand-tailored, navy pinstriped suit that was cut to hide his obvious gut and his spongy body. The neck on his bright white shirt was too tight, attesting to his continued gluttony. The knot on his tie was too small, adding to the uncomfortable picture. *Maybe he's a nervous eater.* He glared at her when he apparently noticed the slight grin on her face.

Without preamble he leaned back in his chair, steepled his fingers, and demanded, "What's your report?" His small eyes bored into her.

Fighting the urge to fidget, Dana said, "Not much. Ms. Flemons has spent most of the time in bed...recuperating from the head injury. She's gone out to a few meetings, and Shelley has brought work to her. I think she's expecting to have her first day at the office very soon. Maybe tomorrow."

"Did you monitor her phone calls? Were you present when people met with her?"

"I monitored as best I could, without being obvious. And I've been with her all the time."

He sat forward, a vein pulsing in his forehead. "Has there been any discussion of matters relating to the team, for example, the vendors?"

Meeting his eyes, she lied. "Not that I know of."

He sat back in his chair. "What about MacCauley? Were you with them? Do you think that Flemons's relationship with him is romantic?"

"He came by the house to see how she was doing, but I'm pretty sure they are not romantically involved."

"Did she talk to Ms. Steeple?"

"Yes, sir. They went to lunch today. Actually, I was asked to go, too. By Ms. Flemons."

The look of irritation on his face was very satisfying. "Uh, Ms. Steeple invited Ms. Flemons to visit her bar."

That seemed to mollify him. "Good. Good. When is she going?"

Dana slowly said, "Well...a definite date wasn't—"

"You suggest it. Get her down there as soon as possible. Don't leave her side unless it's to leave her alone with Steeple. Understand?"

"Yes. But, um, may I ask why? Perhaps I could help if I knew—"

"Just do it and don't ask questions. It's for the good of the team. That's all you need to know. Now, our appointment is over. Good-bye, Ms. Ryan."

Dana gratefully exited, trying not to speed walk. As she passed Alison's desk she whispered, "Thanks."

Alison grinned and winked, then returned to her computer screen.

❖

Keri was resting in the den when Dana arrived. Just hearing the gates open and the car engine made her heart start drumming. She smiled and went to the window, grinning at the speed of the vehicle approaching. It literally screeched to a halt.

Dana tore out of the car and bounced up the steps, rapping on the door. Keri made it by the third knock. Pulling Dana inside, she slammed the door and threw her arms around Dana's neck, kissing her thoroughly. When they separated they were breathless.

"Now that's a greeting I could get used to," said Dana. "Damn, I feel like I've been gone a year." She dipped her head and went for an encore, slipping her arms under her lover's shoulders and knees and whisking her up in her arms.

A surprised Keri exclaimed, "My, oh, my, Ms. Ryan. Those workouts with our star wide receiver have definitely paid off. Where are you taking me?"

Grinning and waggling her eyebrows, Dana growled, "Someplace we haven't *been* before. Living room." She marched them off to the huge room with the oversized furniture. Selecting a loveseat easily longer than the two of them with twice the depth of a normal sofa, she tossed her love onto it.

"Anyone else around?" she asked.

Keri's mouth parted softly, just waiting to be kissed again. "No."

"Any appointments due?"

"Not here."

"Strip."

"I beg your pardon?" Keri's blue eyes were dancing.

"Strip. Here, I'll show you." Dana was topless in less than ten seconds.

Keri feasted her eyes on Dana's breasts. Her breath hitched watching the nipples tighten, and she moved the tip of her tongue over her lips. She purred, "More. Slowly."

The tables had suddenly turned. Dana swallowed and unsnapped the top part of her jeans, her body tingling under the unabashed gaze of her lover. Watching as Keri's eyes grew hazy with desire, her own need grew as she pushed her jeans down and stepped out of them, standing naked before Keri.

Keri breathed, "You are so beautiful. Come here, I need to feel you."

Dana stepped closer. She bent to kiss her true love and felt her breasts cupped as Keri groaned. Their lips met in softness and fire. Keri rubbed Dana's breasts with her palms. She broke the kiss to use her tongue to flick a nipple and make it harder.

Dana gasped, "Ah…it won't take much to make me come. I've been thinking about you all day. Lunch made me crazy. That woman."

"That woman means nothing to me." Keri eased back a little. "I want to see you. Please."

Looking into the eyes she trusted as no other, Dana stood beside the loveseat, then put one leg on the other side of Keri, opening herself to her lover.

Keri gazed in Dana's eyes, her love and desire unmistakable. "Closer."

Dana moved so she was straddling Keri, just above her face. She could feel Keri's warm breath on her center, and when the blue eyes left hers and studied her, she felt a wave of desire flush through her.

The swollen tissue inviting her, Keri reached to feel the wetness and delicately trace the length of it. She heard Dana moan.

"My legs…I'm not sure…"

Her voice husky, Keri said, "Closer. Come for me." She put her hands on Dana's hips and pulled her down.

Dana was trembling. When she felt Keri's tongue on her clitoris she fell forward to grab the arm of the loveseat. She wasn't sure who groaned in pleasure, but she was way beyond caring. Keri slowly entered her and began to match her tongue and stroking to Dana's hip movements.

The orgasm came in waves, and Dana cried out as Keri held the bundle of nerves between her teeth, the tip of her tongue unrelenting. After the first waves subsided, Keri suddenly filled her and pulled up, pushing her face against Dana's clitoris as she held for the second, stronger orgasm.

Dana curled over her lover's head, trying not to smother her but not trusting her now-weak body to behave. She felt a tongue flick and she spasmed.

"Ah...no more...I...gods." Dana sagged to the back of the loveseat, gasping.

After a few moments she heard Keri murmur, "Thank you."

Finally able to speak, Dana managed, "You take my breath away."

"Do you think you could lie beside me?" Keri replied with a muffled chuckle. Or...?"

Dana jerked when a soft tongue connected with a still-tender nipple. "Wait! Help me get my legs..."

Keri gently assisted her rubbery lover into a comfortable position beside her. Gazing into slightly unfocused green eyes, she said, "There. By the way, you take my breath away, too. And you have the most wonderful taste and perfume. I'm not washing my face today. Maybe never."

Hearing this said so matter-of-factly, Dana focused to regard her lover. She studied the beautiful eyes, perfect features, full mouth. She noticed that Keri was still fully dressed and squirming slightly.

Dana licked her lips. "I'm naked."

Keri turned on her side to face her lover. "Yes, you are. Beautifully so."

"You aren't." Her alto voice was rough.

Breath catching in her chest, Keri said, "That's true, too."

"I want you."

Keri wondered how Dana's simple words evoked such a strong physical response. "Yes. I almost came when you did. You just..." Keri reached for the smooth pale breast so close to her. A hand stopped her.

"No. *I* want *you*."

The look in Dana's eyes only made Keri's condition worse. She was jumping out of her skin. Dana gently pushed her on her back. She unbuttoned the silk shirt and pulled it from Keri's slacks, trailing her fingers up the center of her stomach as she reached for the front opening of her bra. Keri arched to her.

Releasing the opening with one hand, Dana cupped a firm breast and leaned to bring it to her mouth, gently closing her lips on the taut nipple, then pulling it deeper, sucking and nipping with her teeth. Her hand covered Keri's exposed breast and teased the nipple, and the need to taste that one as well grew with each moment.

The sounds Keri was making let her know she was welcome. Her mouth savored each breast as her hand roamed down to the clothing that covered what she so needed to feel and see. She unzipped Keri's slacks and let them fall open, then flattened her palm against the finely muscled belly and slid her hand under the cotton briefs until she felt the warmth and arousal waiting for her.

"You are so wet." Her fingers parted the lips and felt the prominence of Keri's clitoris, slick and hard, waiting for her touch.

Keri gasped, "I need you...so."

"Yes." Dana pushed deeply into her lover. Each time she started to crest, she pulled back, only to go deeper and harder when Keri calmed. When she knew her lover could stand it no longer, she plunged inside and slipped down Keri's body to use her mouth to send her over the edge. She held her as wave after wave coursed through her, gently turning to pull Keri on top as her breathing returned to normal.

After several moments, Keri said, "I've thought about making love with you ever since we left this morning. I'm wet all the time. That's a first for me. You make me crazy."

Dana's deep voice murmured in her ear. "Me, too. I was in heat during my chat with the charming Thomas Concannon. My orders are to get you to your ex's bar." They thought about that for a moment.

Keri sighed. "Tonight. Later."

"No, tomorrow." Dana lifted her head and looked at the dark blue eyes of her soul mate. "Do you suppose you could finish undressing? I want to feel your skin next to mine."

Keri grinned and struggled to her feet, settling back down within a minute and groaning in pleasure at the contact. "In heat?" she asked. "Do you think he caught on?"

"I doubt it. He focuses on himself, exclusively. But he might have if his assistant hadn't warned me. To quote, she said 'Careful. He doesn't miss much.' And when I thanked her for the warning after the meeting, she winked at me. Do I have some sort of sign stamped on me? 'I want it nonstop'? Do I know her?"

Keri chuckled and reached down, pulling an afghan located on the arm of the loveseat over the two of them. She snuggled closer to

Dana, noting with satisfaction how well their bodies fit together. "Was it Alison?"

"Yeah. That was her name. Is she family?"

Keri thought for a moment and replied, "I'm not sure, could be. But she and Shelley are good friends, and I'm pretty sure that's who is helping us get the contracts and other information from his office. So at least she's on our side."

"Phew! I was worried I'd never be able to show my face again because I'm so obvious. As it is, it's hard to be around you without getting completely turned on and brain-dead."

Keri looked at her lover. "I love you, you know. I'm madly in love with you, Dana."

Dana's breath caught in her throat. "You…you are?"

Her eyes bright with the truth, Keri said, "Yes."

Swallowing hard, Dana tried to absorb the enormity of what had just happened. "I love you, too. I've always loved you."

Keri let a slow smile cross her lips. "Then show me."

With a grin and an eye roll, Dana moaned. "Now, see? It's happening again. The way you look, dressed or undressed. The way you feel, or the *memory* of how you feel. Your eyes, your hair, your skin, your *teeth*, for God's sake. I'm going to have to be shut away. Just pull me out to do your bidding when you need some, ah, attention."

"Well, I'm pretty much in the same boat. Since I'm never going to wash my face or hands again and all."

Dana grinned. "About that. Go ahead and wash. There's lots more where that came from. But," she abruptly flipped so Keri was under her, "I think I need some perfume and dessert of my own." She reached down and pulled her T-shirt off the floor, laying it across Keri's eyes.

Keri raised her head and peeked out at Dana. "Nonstop, eh?"

Grinning, Dana rumbled, "Relax. I'll be back soon. Think about how I want to do this to you twenty-four hours a day, every day. Bandaged head or not."

Starting just below her ear and working her way steadily south, Dana made sure Keri knew just how much she loved her, for quite some time. But all the while, the thought she wouldn't let surface was whether Keri would ever love *her* the same way or whether she was just kidding herself.

❖

Dana lay prone, unable to move. *What have I done? It was too soon. "Follow my heart." Look where it got me? If she discards me now, I won't survive.* After what seemed like hours in an awkward sleeping position on the sofa, she got up and put on some sweats. Her stomach was tight and throat dry.

Quietly she went to the kitchen. Staring at the coffeemaker, she tried unsuccessfully to still her sudden panic while she brewed a pot. When the coffee was ready she poured two cups and walked into the room, putting the cup on the table close to Keri.

The sound woke her and she asked, "Dana?" Finally she looked in the beautiful blue eyes of her hopes and dreams. Clearing her throat, she said, "Hi." Nothing else came, her mind a blank.

Keri studied the woman a few feet from her. She reached to pick up her coffee cup, took a sip, and put it down again. Lying back against the pillows, she sighed and ran a hand through her hair, still wild from their lovemaking. There was an odd expression on Dana's face.

"Dana, is something wrong?"

Staring at her cup, Dana said, "No. Everything's fine. But I was just thinking maybe we should slow things down."

Keri gazed at her for a long moment. "Is this because you told me you loved me?"

"Maybe," Dana conceded.

"Did you mean it?"

Dana spoke straight from her heart, but was unable to raise her eyes from the cup. "I've always loved you, Keri. But if you're asking if I've fallen in love with you, the answer is yes. Yes."

"Please, look at me. Come on, I need your eyes."

Dana finally found the courage to meet the eyes of her beloved. What she saw pushed all rational thought from her mind.

"I love you, too. I'm in love with you, too." The blue eyes that had occupied all of her dreams and nightmares for so many years held only truth in them.

Dana sat back heavily, not noticing the coffee slosh on her sweatshirt. "Keri I…"

Keri shook her head. "I, Keri, fell in love with you, Dana. I didn't expect it. I didn't plan any of this. All I know, all I can think about, is how much I want you. I don't know what the future holds, but I have to believe this is not just a passing enchantment. It was meant to be. I'm willing to give it a chance if you are."

Bracing her hands on the sofa, Dana looked deeply into Keri's eyes. "I have no choice, Keri. I'll take any chance I can to have a future with you."

Keri opened her arms.

Dana barely remembered to put down the cup she was holding. She moved to settle into the arms of her soul mate. They quietly held on, not wanting the moment to end. The tears flowed freely down both of their faces.

Keri registered her new lover moving away and opened her eyes to see the woman she had just given her body to. The entire experience took her breath away.

Dana asked, "What do we do now?"

Their kiss started softly but quickly grew in intensity.

Gasping for air as they parted, Keri managed, "Can I answer that question later?"

All thought quickly left her mind as Dana covered Keri's face and neck with soft kisses. Her hands grazed the fullness of Dana's breasts through the thick material of the sweatshirt.

Dana mumbled, "Maybe we should go upstairs."

"What time is it?" Keri was fast losing control.

Trying to think, Dana said, "After midnight."

Pulling at Dana's clothing, Keri growled, "Take this freaking thing off."

Abruptly sitting back on her heels, Dana swept the shirt off her body to land on the floor beside them. Keri had explored their feel but wanted to visually absorb Dana's breasts. Her arousal grew as she watched the nipples pucker.

Dana removed the afghan she had covered Keri with, doing some admiring of her own. She felt wetness begin to wash down her leg.

"Is it possible to come just from looking?" Dana's voice was husky and her eyes slightly out of focus with need.

Sitting up, Keri pulled the tie on Dana's sweatpants and reached inside to place her hand between her lover's legs. "Almost possible."

Dana felt Keri slip inside and begin to stroke, eyes never leaving her own. She put her hands on her lover's shoulders to keep upright as her body swayed. "I'm ready. Don't stop...don't..." The orgasm hit hard and explosively.

Keri quickly wrapped her free arm around Dana's waist to hold her tightly, as her body melted into pleasuring Dana. Finally, she settled Dana on top of her.

After several minutes Dana breathed in her ear, "You...are a magical lover."

A self-satisfied sound was the only response. Dana rose on her elbows and kissed her love. Then she grinned and moved down the beautiful body, capturing a nipple with her teeth, tasting the arousal. Keri groaned, rising to kiss the mouth that had claimed her breast. Their bodies moved together as Dana sought to taste all of the silky skin beneath her.

"You are so much more than any fantasy." She moved lower, savoring her beloved's sweetness. Her mouth was infatuated with the delicate taste that was Keri. Once again, she gazed at her lover's arousal. "My God, you are so perfect, so delicate."

Keri growled, "Now, Dana, *now.*"

Dana entered her as she took her into her mouth, tongue and lips concentrating on the throbbing she felt beneath her. Matching the rhythm of her lover's body she took her over the edge quickly. Keri called her name as she came and bucked without control.

Dana held her, crawling up Keri's body to claim her lips, her hand never leaving its safe haven. Dana sleepily grinned and said, "Amazing. I can come just by looking. Or feeling. Or tasting. You." She leaned to capture the soft lips of her soul mate. "Only you."

Breathless from the kiss, Keri again reached inside Dana's sweatpants and crooned, "I love you. Take these off. I have plans."

CHAPTER NINETEEN

It was early in the morning, and they'd been awake for as long as it took to want one another again. Through the haze of desire, Dana vaguely registered some electronic tones. Reluctantly pulling away from her tender ministrations, she said, "The security system. Someone's here."

With that she abruptly sat up, the image of her lover, aroused and swollen for her, almost making her forget everything else. Quickly slipping on her sweatshirt and pants, she heard a sound outside the door and crossed the room to open it.

"Shelley! What are you doing here so early?" Dana plastered a bright-eyed smile on her face and tried to control her breathing.

Shelley looked her up and down. "Well, I thought I would make breakfast for you two." She continued to stare. "I also brought some papers for Keri to examine. They're in my car." Two more beats and, "Maybe I should go get them." As she started to close the door she stopped and added, "Oh, and Dana? Your sweatshirt is inside out." She winked and was gone.

Rolling her eyes, Dana returned to the bed and lay down next to her lover. They started giggling.

"'Your sweatshirt is inside out!' She never misses a thing!" Keri was in full guffaw.

"Yeah, well, she must have heard you panting, because she got the hint to leave."

Hands flying to her mouth, Keri said, "Oh, my gawd. Talk about coitus interruptus! And by Shelley! I'm so embarrassed!" She rolled onto her side and buried her face in Dana's shoulder.

"Are you really? Embarrassed?" The whisper in her ear made all thought fade.

"Well...I..."

Dana drew back the sheet and resumed exploration of Keri's body, pausing after a few caresses. "You know, when an orgasm has been interrupted, the one right after it is twice as strong."

The words were followed by a kiss, then playful sucking on Keri's earlobe. Gasping at the touch and words, Keri felt her body instantly ready. "Ho...how do you know that?"

Dana was moving down her body, covering her with nips and tugs and butterfly kisses. She paused before burying her face in her favorite place and grinned at Keri, who was barely able to focus on her. "I'll show you."

Within seconds Keri was coming hard and long for her lover. Lying in Dana's arms later, she said, "I see what you mean. I'll file that one away."

❖

Three hours later, Keri and Dana, escorted by Huey, knocked on the door of Zander MacCauley's home. Jim had called to deliver Zander's invitation, and it was he who opened the door and motioned them in.

He said, "Zander will be out in a minute, he's back from practice."

They followed him into his study, a large, warm room. A rich mahogany desk was the centerpiece. The matching leather sofa and love seat complemented the warm colors, Persian rug, and bookcases. The room seemed perfect for reading and relaxing. As they sat on the wine-colored sofa, Zander walked in, looking freshly showered and shaved. As a matter of fact, they both looked freshly showered and shaved. Keri and Dana gave each other an inquiring look.

Zander and Jim sat across from them, sharing the love seat. There was something different about the two.

Keeping her question neutral, Dana asked, "So, what have you got? The call sounded urgent."

Jim smiled. "Well, first, Zander has something to say."

Blushing, Zander said to them, "I want you to know...that I'm gay."

Dana could read the delight on Keri's face.

"Zander, thank you for telling me, us," said Keri. "I know that took a lot of trust." She reached over and squeezed his hand.

Dana grinned. "So, what prompted this sudden confession? Anything I should know about?"

Jim and Zander stole shy glances at each other. Jim said, "We're… seeing each other. Seriously dating." He was looking hopefully at the two of them, especially Dana.

"I'm so happy for you." Dana got up and hugged both men. Zan grinned, giving her a pop on the shoulder. Dana almost yelped.

"You're the first to know," Jim said.

Zander added quickly, "The *only* ones to know…at least for now." .

Jim cocked his head and looked pointedly at Dana. "Is there something you want to tell *us*?"

Blushing, Dana said, "Um, well, yes. I…that is, Keri and I…" She looked at Keri for permission.

Keri grinned at the men. "Dana and I are in love."

Zander quickly offered his congratulations, and Jim's eyes were tearing up when he reached over to hug Dana. He whispered in her ear, "I'm so glad for you, sweetie. Is it all good?"

Dana said, "I love her, Jim."

He hugged her again and then did the same to Keri. Once they were settled down, he said, "Well, we're beginning to get some interesting data. Maybe we can draw this to a close so we can all get on with the happily-ever-after trip."

He took some files from a coffee table nearby and flipped through them, withdrawing several sheets of paper. "I have here a preliminary forensic accounting report that says money has been systematically drained from the team accounts for the last three years. If we go back further, we may find more, depending on when Concannon started with the team. The activity really picked up after your father's death, Keri."

"How much are we talking about," she responded tightly.

"Pat Hideo says several millions are missing. And that's what can be accounted for at this stage. There could be other areas of fraudulent record keeping."

Keri's eyes narrowed. "Can we trace the missing money to Concannon?"

"Pat's pretty sure that the trail leads directly to him," Jim said.

"And I've had a couple of agencies run a detailed investigation. He's in debt up to his eyeballs."

Keri took Dana's hand and squeezed it. "Well, at least we have some hard facts to work with now."

"That's not all." Zander picked up where his new lover left off. "I asked around, and some of the equipment guys who are close with the stadium employees came back to me with some interesting information. Frank Owens says a lot of the people who have worked there for years are frightened. Some guys have been beaten up and warned off the job. He's seen what he calls 'hit men' trying to intimidate a few of the concession employees."

"Hit men," Dana echoed, picturing the thugs who'd attacked Keri. In her gut, she'd known Concannon was behind the assault all along, in some way or another, and a call she'd had earlier from Jake at the *Gazette* made her even more certain. The thought made her coldly determined to bring Concannon down.

Keri seemed to avoid making the connection. "I've met Frank. And his son. Mike, right?"

Nodding, Zander said, "Yes, you have. They describe the meeting at great length to anyone who will listen. They both admire you very much."

Keri blushed, and Dana had the urge to kiss her.

To Jim, Keri said, "I don't understand. If he's funneled off millions, why is he in debt? Surely he couldn't have gambled it all away."

Frowning, Jim said, "I can't answer that yet. We're still unearthing Concannon's private financial dealings."

Keri leaned forward. "Is that legal?"

Dana snickered. "It has to be more legal than what he's doing to you."

Shaking his head, Jim said, "We're not the cops. We're basically going to hack and snoop. Law firms have ways of doing that without leaving a trail. All we need is enough to point the law in a direction, and they can pick up the investigation."

Keri asked, "What are you looking for?"

"Private offshore accounts, mostly. A money trail. It's almost impossible not to leave one. Concannon gambles with team money, but keeps some for himself for a rainy day. Thinks he can always pay it off, but gets in too deeply."

Dana sat back on the sofa. "So Concannon is an ass, but this kind of firepower with the vendors is from the guy he owes money to."

Keri looked thoughtful. "You know, Gloria invited us to the bar, and Dana and I are planning to go late tonight. Her bartender, Tiffany, and I get along pretty well. She's a sweet person, but she has no idea how to be discreet. She's always innocently giving out information that Gloria doesn't want to be public knowledge. Maybe a chat would be in order."

"By the way, on the subject of Gloria, I found out who that Italian woman works for." Dana had been putting off telling Keri about the phone call from Jake, but with everything moving so fast, it now seemed unavoidable. "Rollo Bongiavanni."

"Rollo Bongiavanni?" Keri repeated. "Mafia?"

"Extremely," Jim said, his face sober.

"Does that mean there's a hit out on me?"

Everyone fell silent.

"I doubt it," Jim said finally. "I think if Bongi wants someone dead, they're dead. Concrete boots."

Keri lifted her eyes from the photographs on the table to Dana. "Your friend is completely certain?"

Dana nodded. "I'm afraid so."

"If Bongi's involved, it means Concannon is into them for a pile of cash." Jim folded his notes away. "Maybe the big guy's calling in his markers."

"You really think Concannon is trying to bring a Mafia family into our operation?" Keri was stunned. The evidence was becoming pretty clear, but she was having trouble believing it. If Concannon had his way, their vendors would no longer be the independents who'd been loyal for years; they would be fronts for a crime family. The PickAxes would be home to an organized crime money-laundering operation.

Gloria had phoned not long after their lunch, just as Keri had expected. She'd mumbled something then about Concannon owing money to bad people, but she'd claimed her life would be in danger if she said too much.

"It all fits," Dana said.

Zander said, "Yes, and it means visiting that club could be a dangerous idea."

"Look, Huey can wait outside and Dana will be with me," Keri said. "We'll both carry those panic-button thingies around our necks. It'll be perfectly safe."

Dana shot her a worried look, but shrugged. "It probably is safe with Huey close by. Maybe the bartender will give us something Gloria won't. It might be worth it." She didn't want them anywhere near Gloria and her damned bar, but she did want this nightmare to end. If they could get enough on Concannon to have him arrested, it would be worth an uncomfortable evening.

Jim said, "One more thing. Dana, who knows about you and Keri?"

"Only you guys and Shelley."

"And Moms," Keri added.

"Listen, it's pretty obvious how you feel about each other. Other than this close circle, it would be safer if no one else knew. We're still not sure what we're dealing with here. Until then, Dana just works for Keri and secretly for Concannon. Do you think you can pull that off?"

Keri said, "Of course."

Jim looked skeptical. He asked Dana, "When do you meet with him again?"

"I guess, when he calls me into his lair. So far, I don't think he has any idea we're suspicious of him. He still thinks he has this scam under control."

"Good. Keep it that way. Concannon is shrewd. I'm calling in the cops as soon as we have enough. I have a friend in the D.A.'s office who can help us nail him." He exchanged a quick look with Zander before adding, "And keep your hands off each other. At least in public." The wry smile on his face didn't quite hide the concern in his eyes.

"That isn't going to be an easy task. Now that I've found her, well, it won't be easy." Keri smiled sheepishly.

"Don't worry," said Dana. "We'll be careful."

Jim's eyes softened. "Thanks. If it's any consolation, we have to pull off the same ruse."

Laughing, they all rose and hugged their goodbyes.

"Call us if you need anything," Zander said. "And congratulations."

"And to you," Keri said, and she and Dana left their friends standing in a loose embrace at the door.

❖

Herb Kronerberg slid his window down and informed the big guy in charge of the Flemonses' security of his name. "Mrs. Carolyn Flemons is expecting me," he announced loudly enough for the hacks nearby to get the picture.

While the bonehead was phoning in, Herb craned up to check his teeth in the rearview mirror and took a puff of spearmint extra-strength breath freshener. He dusted the shoulders of his brand-new Italian suit for dandruff, checked his belt and zipper, and revved the motor of his Lexus.

When the gates opened before him, he benevolently waved the bonehead over and palmed him five bucks. "Anyone asks, remember the name. Kronerberg. I'm here for an exclusive interview with Mrs. Flemons."

He was still in a happy state of disbelief over the phone call that had summoned him to this elite address. Evidently, Carolyn Flemons had decided the past was water under the bridge. Not that Herb had any reason to apologize for his exposé articles on Mike-Womanizer-Flemons and his cheap tramps. Carolyn had married beneath her, and what does a woman expect when she steps down the social ladder so dramatically?

Obviously the poor thing had fallen for Flemons's bad-boy charm. They all did. Herb had witnessed Flemons in action, suckering every female from waitress to duchess. Oh, yes. The man had no control over his urges. Herb had considered it a personal triumph when Carolyn dumped her philandering husband and moved to Paris. He had even followed her there, hoping for a candid—the ex-wife tells all. It had been too soon for her. She wouldn't take his calls. But his photographer had snared some great shots. One thing he would say for Carolyn—she had style. Paris was the perfect setting for her.

Herb parked his car and stepped out, peering up at the lifestyle home. He almost wished he was writing for *House & Garden*.

Carolyn Flemons received him at the door in person, an intimate touch Herb thought said a lot about her class. She was not the kind of woman who had to be pretentious, although he found it a little odd that there was no maid or butler to be seen. He made a mental note to drop that into the piece, just a subtle point. The discreet presence of household staff said so much about status.

As he accompanied Carolyn into a gracious living room, he

decided her print dress was Escada and her shoes were Ferragamo. As always, she looked elegant. Herb was perspiring slightly by the time he sank down into a sofa that positioned him at a lower level than he enjoyed.

"Would you care for tea, Mr. Kronerberg?" Carolyn asked.

His preference would have been a shot of bourbon, but in the interests of good manners, he said, "Yes. Thank you. Very nice." He glanced toward the doorway. Finally, the maid. Not even a uniform. He noted that as well.

To his surprise, his hostess said warmly, "Shelley, let's talk while I make some tea." She excused herself, and with a casual wave toward the coffee table opposite the sofa, said, "Help yourself to reading material."

Herb gave her his best smile and surveyed the items on the table. *National Geographic* magazines. *Really*. Beneath those a file protruded. Accustomed to making the most of his opportunities, Herb quickly plucked the out-of-place item from the pile and flipped it open.

Sitting right on top of a stack of papers was a photograph of him chained to a wall, naked, a tall dominatrix standing in front of him with a whip. It was obvious he was aroused.

He almost had palpitations. Losing no time, he flipped through the file and found a collection of photographs and reports from a private detection agency. Everything was a photocopy, the originals no doubt filed in a huge safe for the day this vindictive and dangerous woman planned to destroy his life. She must have been angrier than he thought, seeing her husband's character assassinated. Some women were strangely loyal. Stand by your man, no matter what.

He closed the file and shoved it back into the heap. Had she intended for him to find it, or was it left in the room by accident? He wiped his hands on his pants as Carolyn returned and took a long, hard look at her face. His journalistic instincts told him this woman didn't leave anything lying around by mistake.

Carolyn could tell from the wet blinking, and the perspiration gluing Kronerberg's dyed mahogany hair plugs into hideously discrete spikes, that he had just seen his whole life flash past his eyes.

"Milk. Lemon. Sugar?" she inquired, pouring tea into two cups.

"Yes," her guest croaked. "I mean, no. Nothing. Just black for me, Mrs. Flemons." He took out his cassette recorder, then, after a brief but pointed look from Carolyn, put it away again.

She handed him his tea and sat down on an overstuffed chair across from him. For a few delicious seconds, she allowed herself the long-awaited pleasure of seeing her nemesis squirm like the snake he was. Then she said, "I'll get to the point. I want something from you, Mr. Kronerberg."

"Yes?" He spilled a little tea.

"My daughter has a right to her private life, just as you do to yours. And as my husband and I did to ours."

A dull flush invaded Kronerberg's cheeks. He was silly enough to say, "It was never personal, Mrs. Flemons. I was just doing my job…a man has to make a living."

Carolyn sighed. "And I was just trying to make a life with the man I loved. My husband never did you any harm. He could have, but he didn't. He was a bigger man than that."

A person with an ounce of conscience would have been shamefaced by her honesty and her loss, but Kronerberg simply stared resentfully in her direction. "Put your cards on the table, Mrs. Flemons."

"I want something from you."

"Go ahead."

"I want you to leave my daughter alone. You know what I'm talking about. If anything ever comes out that traces back to you, I'll find out."

"I think we understand each other," he said stiffly.

"There's something else."

"I'm listening." He gnawed on his thin lower lip.

"I have a story for you. No one else in the media has it yet."

At this, he looked like a rat trapped in a grocery store. "And this involves?"

"Thomas Concannon hiring thugs to beat up my daughter."

"Just say the word, Mrs. Flemons, and he is destroyed. You have my personal word."

"And I know exactly what that's worth." Carolyn stood and handed her eager enemy an envelope full of information she'd received from Jim Miller. "This will make up for a lot, Mr. Kronerberg."

"Yes. Er…I'm sorry for your loss." Having articulated this belated sentiment, he snatched the envelope. "If I may ask…certain original documents…"

"Are safe and secure and will never see the light of day, unless you give me reason."

Carolyn walked the nasty little man to the door and smiled as she closed it behind him. Being sensible meant trying to make an enemy useful. Mike had taught her that. She glanced up at a portrait of him Keri kept in the hallway and felt what could never be buried with him. *I love you.*

CHAPTER TWENTY

The bar was already smoky when they walked through the doors at nine o'clock that evening. All eyes gave them an appreciative stare. Keri was dressed in leather and Dana in denim and cowboy boots. They made a striking pair.

Both leaned on the bar and scanned the faces in the room. Keri noticed the bartender was smiling at her.

"Hey, Tiff, how are you?"

"Keri! I thought it was you. You look tewif…terrific!"

Grinning, Keri said, "Thanks. So do you. What's that flash of silver I see in your mouth?"

Tiffany proudly displayed her tongue stud. Keri almost blanched but managed an interested stare. "Nice." Resting her hand on Dana's arm, she said, "This is my associate, Dana Ryan. Dana, Tiffany. She's been tending bar here for several years. I don't know what Gloria would do without her. Right, Tiff?"

Dana extended her hand and the two gave each other a friendly shake.

"Yup. No one else would put up with her," Tiffany said. "Nice to meet ya, Dana." Turning to Keri once more, she guilelessly inquired, "So, what are you doing here?"

Casually, Keri said, "Gloria invited me down. I thought tonight would be fun so I asked Dana to come along. Always a lot of good-looking women here."

Dana chimed in, "Yeah. I've never been here. Lots of good-looking…ouch!"

Shooting her a look, Keri said, "What is it?"

Dana scowled and returned the look, rubbing her foot on the back of her other leg. "Um…cramp. Guess I've been working out too much."

"Perhaps you haven't been working out enough," Keri said, as her eyes swept up and down Dana's body. "That can cause cramps, too."

Tiffany seemed oblivious to their teasing rapport as she stared across the dark room toward the front door. Wiping the bar vigorously with her towel she muttered, "Here comes trouble."

Turning with the rest of the customers, Dana spotted Gina and, at the same time, heard Keri catch her breath. She quickly turned back to Tiffany, hoping Gina hadn't noticed them. Tiffany's eyes followed the woman across the room, and she automatically started preparing some drinks to give to the barmaid. Two single malt scotches made their way to Gloria's office.

Sneaking a peak, Keri watched the waitress knock on the office door. She was in and out of the door within thirty seconds, a satisfied look on her face as she examined her tip and stuffed it in her bra.

"Interesting," Keri said.

Tiffany shrugged. "Yeah. Gloria's picked up another one." She blushed instantly and added, "I don't mean you, Keri. You were the best. But she's up to her old tricks. I think she might be in over her head." She nodded to the barmaid and moved to fill another order.

Dana tried not to stare at Keri. She wanted her so badly, if she allowed herself another long look, she wouldn't be able to keep her hands to herself. She started to lean in and whisper that very thought to Keri but suddenly stopped herself. Things were moving so quickly; when did the other shoe drop? Keri told her she loved her, but what if Gloria could lure her away again. What if Gina Pescetti became violent, or was ordered by her boss to harm Keri? This was a bad idea. She had the urge to take Keri and run, get her to safety and turn over what they had to the cops and hope for the best.

Tiffany returned and said, "Sorry to ignore you, ladies. What can I get you?" After setting two drafts in front of them, she took the money Dana put on the bar and started to move away.

Keri hastily asked, "Are they involved with each other? Like, romantically?"

Tiffany hesitated, then leaned in conspiratorially and said, "Well,

I'm not sure romance has a lot to do with it. The other day there was enough noise coming outta there that I thought she was getting beat up. I banged on the door, ready to use my trusty bat. She just screamed at me to go away. And every day that woman comes in here, about this time, the same thing happens." She leaned even closer. "I think that gal is packin'."

Keri's eyes went round. "A gun?"

Dana and Tiffany exchanged a look. The bartender shook her head and said to Dana, "You explain. I got customers." She went back to work.

Keri eyed Dana's current shade of red and took a sip of beer. "Well?"

Dana was vaguely surprised by Keri's lack of knowledge on the subject. Maybe all her lovers were of a definitely femme variety. Whatever, now she was charged with explaining it to her. Searching for a vague euphemism that would not embarrass both of them, meaning her, she said, "Um, well, she meant that the tall one was, uh, was… had…it means…"

Watching Dana struggling, Keri was nonplussed. "Dana, spit it out. What on earth is so hard? What does 'packing' mean if it isn't about a gun?" She whipped her head around when she heard some snickers behind her.

Taking her by the arm, Dana steered Keri to the dance floor. There was slow music playing, and she took Keri in her arms. Close to Keri's ear, she said, "'Packing' means she's wearing a dildo."

Keri stopped in her tracks, almost stumbling over Dana's feet. Looking up into her lover's eyes, she said, quite clearly, "A *dildo*?" The crimson on Dana's face was truly a sight.

Others around them broke out in unrestrained laughter. Keri blushed and buried her face in Dana's chest. *So much for not drawing attention to themselves.* Dana maneuvered them to another part of the dance floor and kept them moving, thankful Gina Pescetti was in Gloria's office, otherwise engaged.

Keri finally dared to look at her and squeaked, "I'm so sorry. I didn't mean to be so loud. I was just…surprised. I mean, I should have gotten it."

Looking at the closed door of Gloria's office, Dana commented disingenuously, "I wonder what they're doing in there?"

From wide-eyed embarrassment, Keri's eyes suddenly narrowed. "Yeah. I wonder." She pulled away and headed for the office door. Looking over her shoulder she winked at Dana and motioned for her to follow.

Dana muttered, "This won't be good."

Hesitating long enough for Dana to bump into her, Keri tried the door handle and found it locked. She took a breath and loudly started banging on the door.

"Gloria? Hell-oo-hoo! Open up, dear! It's Keri! Didn't you ask me to drop by?"

She kept it up for several moments until the door was suddenly thrown open and a very flushed, panting Gloria greeted them. Between her gritted teeth she said, "Keri! What are you...two...doing here?"

She eyed them suspiciously as Dana tried on her most naive smile.

Taking a breath, Keri swept past her ex and entered the office in time to see Gina Pescetti still arranging her clothing and zipping her pants. She fought the overwhelming urge to stare at her crotch.

"Oh, hi! We met the other day. I'm Keri Flemons." She started to hold out her hand but suddenly dropped it and gave her a friendly grin. Pescetti at least had the grace to blush slightly as she folded her arms over her chest and leaned against the wall behind Gloria's desk, unsmiling. Her chest was heaving slightly.

Looking around at the disheveled office, Keri sidled over to a chair, brushed some papers off it, sat down, and crossed her legs. Dana stood behind Keri, declaring who she was with. She glued her eyes on Gina.

Gloria, nervously smoothing her hands over her tight skirt, walked over and sat down behind her desk. Without preamble she said, "I thought you would call before you dropped by, Keri. I wasn't expecting you."

Leveling her with a look, Keri responded, "Obviously."

Pescetti stood up from the wall and seemed to grow in height and mass. Dana tried to match the effect but was sure she was woefully inadequate. The tension in the room was thick enough to cut.

Keri sought to diffuse the situation and said, "Gloria, what's going on?"

The honesty of the question seemed to catch Gloria off balance. She colored and said, "What do you mean?"

"Cut the bullshit, Gloria." Keri watched her former lover's normally cool exterior fail her.

Gloria looked away and cleared her throat. "Why, Keri, what happened to that innocent young girl I used to make love to?"

Dana stiffened, then realized Gloria was only trying to get control of a situation she was hopelessly entangled in. Gina moved away from where she had been standing and stood next to Gloria, giving them her most menacing stare.

Keri swept the two women with an intentionally bored look. "I've grown up. I wish I could say the same for you." When Gloria bristled, Keri preempted with, "Do you really want to get back together with me, Gloria? Be honest."

Gloria's mouth opened but nothing came out. No one moved. Finally, she said, "No."

The four women let out a collective breath. To Dana, it suddenly seemed warmer in the room.

"You sounded upset when we talked on the phone," Keri said more gently. "So the next question—is Thomas Concannon at the bottom of this?"

The look on Gloria's face told the story. Gina quickly said, "You don't have to answer that."

Studying her former girlfriend, Keri said, "Gloria, I've been mugged and put in the hospital. Millions of dollars are missing from the team. It's important."

After a moment, Gloria turned her back on Keri and Dana and took Gina's hand. She looked up and said, "This woman never hurt anyone. She's…a friend."

Gina looked down at the fiery redhead. She nodded slightly, her face an unreadable mask.

Turning back to Keri, Gloria said, "Concannon owes Rollo Bongiavanni a bunch of money. And he owns paper on the bar, as collateral for a loan. He wants me to get you to sell him the team. In return for the debt, Bongi gets control of the concessions at the park. Gina is here to make sure that happens."

Keri was quiet. She felt the solid presence of Dana behind her and noticed that Gina had drawn Gloria to her, almost protectively.

"Will you help me get Concannon?" Keri directed her question at both of them. When Gloria and Gina tensed, she quickly added, "All you would have to do is make a statement."

Gina growled, "Bongiavanni would not be happy if he found out she turned him in. It could be dangerous to her. You would do this?" She glared at Keri.

"Of course not!" Keri said with conviction. "I had no idea of Mr. Bongiavanni's interest in this. Damn. What can we do?"

Dana picked up her cue and said, "I don't understand. How much money does Concannon owe your boss, Gina? He's drained several million from the team. Doesn't that mean he's paid his gambling debt?"

Gina pondered that, then suddenly laughed, a not entirely unpleasant sound. "Perhaps Mr. Concannon is playing both parties for fools. I know his markers total over half a million. From what you say, he could pay this, but he chooses not to. Maybe he thinks he needs Bongiavanni to take control of the team. Or maybe his greed prevents him making wise choices. No matter. My employer does not like to be played with."

Gloria piped up, nervously, "So, maybe I can get out of this?"

Her emotions fully masked again, Gina said, "I will talk to him. You will not be harmed. I will see to it." She lifted her bold, dark eyes to Keri. "Mr. Bongiavanni intends you no physical harm. The offense to him is not yours."

Keri said sincerely, "Thank you, Gina. But does that mean that Bongiavanni will still come after the team? Because when I have the auditing numbers, I'm going to the police. I can probably demonstrate that he's trying to take over the concessions already."

Gina considered the information. "Let me talk to him. Maybe we can find out where all this money is. At least two million? Maybe you will get some back, maybe you won't. But you will be rid of Concannon and the problem with your hot dog people."

Keri stood. "Can I trust you?"

Gloria quickly said, "If Gina says something, she does it." The affection in her voice was obvious. Keri thought she saw a ghost of a smile flicker across Gina's mouth.

"Please call me when you've talked to him, Gina. Gloria has the number. I'll be gathering my evidence, in case."

Dana and Keri left the office and the bar. Once on the street they turned to each other and Dana said, "Phew. That was intense. I think you may have solved a boatload of problems."

Keri shook her head. "I hope Gina isn't blowing smoke. I know Gloria really likes her, but she doesn't have the best track record. I guess we keep an eye out and hope for the best."

They held hands and started walking toward the car.

Dana said, "Oh, and she *was* packin'."

Keri stopped and considered the information. "Yeah. Sexy."

Dana blurted, "What?" but Keri took off like a shot, and she chased her all the way to the car where Huey was waiting for them.

He opened the rear passenger door, his eyes tracking a group of beautiful women headed for the club. As they collected themselves, he said, with mild wonder, "You sure have a number of fine women playing for your team. My compliments."

Keri laughed. "Thanks, Huey."

"You're welcome." With an eloquent roll of the eyes, he got into the driver's seat and said, "Where to, boss?"

Dana quickly said, "Could you drive through Golden Gate Park and take the long way home through the Presidio? We can see the Golden Gate Bridge and Sea Cliff that way. And turn up some nice music, will you, Huey?

"Not a problem!" He found a station that played love songs and turned up the music.

Keri turned and looked in Dana's eyes, surprised by the request. "We could just go home, you know. We have a lovely bed."

"You know, when I was a teenager, I always heard about making out in the backseat of a car. But then I thought you had to do that with a boy, and I never did it. Come here."

Dana held open her arms and Keri slid into them. Keri said, "Did you dream about having a driver, too? Kinky."

Sheepishly, Dana said, "Well, no. But it's too dangerous for us to go and park right now and, besides, I just want a kiss."

Their lips met in a sweet and chaste kiss. Keri pulled back and whispered, "More." And she deepened the kiss. When their bodies started to respond she murmured, "Want to go to second base?" She took Dana's hand and placed it on her breast, and hearing Dana's gasp only emboldened her.

Dana explored both of Keri's breasts through the material of the silk tank she had worn under her leather jacket. She pulled the tank up and unbuttoned the pants, moving Keri to sit in her lap. Close to Keri's ear she said, "I want a triple." Laying her hand flat on Keri's soft skin, she slid into the wetness waiting for her.

Keri's eyes flew open in surprise and she gasped, "Dana!"

Thankful for the darkness in the back of the car, and the fact that their driver was a gay man, she fought to keep her body from moving so as not to make too much of a scene. But Dana was torturing her with the slow stroking she was doing. When she stopped and then started flicking Keri's already swollen clit, Keri grabbed her and ground out in a hoarse whisper, "Hold me tight, I'm coming." She felt herself implode and liquefy without a sound. The shuddering lasted a long time.

When she could talk again, Keri looked at Dana and could see the need in her eyes. "Darling, do you want some of what you just gave me?" She fairly purred in Dana's ear.

Dana's voice was husky "Yes. God, yes."

"We're almost home, sorry."

Dana grabbed Keri's hand and placed it between her legs to feel the damp denim. "Let's have Huey make another round. I'm so hot for you."

Smiling sweetly, Keri crooned, "Remember, when you're interrupted, it's twice as good later."

Dana could barely see Keri through the lust. "No, don't do this to me."

But it was too late, the gates were already swinging open. Dana gathered herself, wanting to at least be civil to Huey before he left her and Keri to run to their bedroom.

❖

They drove through the gates and Huey stopped the car. Before the automatic gate could close, Dana first heard, then saw a black SUV quickly pull into the driveway behind them.

"Keri, get down. Call the cops."

Keri craned around and her fear turned to curiosity. "It's Gina. She's getting out of the car. What's she doing?"

Gina walked around to the other side of the car and opened the door. She reached in and pulled a disheveled-looking person out of the vehicle.

"Is that Concannon?" asked Dana. "He looks like he's had the crap beaten out him."

Keri could only stare as Gina hauled him up to the front door of the house and looked at them expectantly. A slight head jerk was all that was needed to get Dana and Keri scrambling out of the car.

Asking Huey to park, then wait at the door in case they needed him, Keri fumbled for her keys and said to Gina, "What happened?"

Concannon croaked, "I'll tell you what hap…"

"Silence!" Gina unceremoniously shoved him into the door frame headfirst. Eyeing Keri, she demanded, "You have called the police?" When Keri shook her head, she smiled and purred at her charge. "Good. Mr. Concannon would like to talk to you. Let's go in."

Once in Keri's office, Gina kept Concannon standing while she ordered Dana and Keri to sit. They had no problem following orders.

When Concannon remained mute, she raised a hand and he started talking to Keri. "I've…decided to make restitution for the monies I borrowed…" A smack on the back of the head made both Dana and Keri wince.

Concannon corrected, "I embezzled from the PickAxes. I have…" Gina feinted toward him and he amended, "Ms. Pescetti has a check for the entire amount to give to you. A cashier's check."

Gina reached into a jacket pocket and removed a piece of paper, placing it on the desk with gloved hands. She stood back, slightly behind Concannon.

Keri looked at the check. Astounded, she said, "Over two million dollars? What about your debt to Mr. Bongiavanni?"

Dana watched in fascination, marveling that Keri could be concerned about the crime boss and paying debts when she had to be bursting to have a turn with Concannon. And if she didn't want one, Dana did.

"It seems Mr. Concannon had a little more stashed away than he would have preferred revealing," said Gina. Mr. Bongiavanni has been paid his debt, with substantial interest."

Dana interjected, "What about the vendor contracts? Is your boss still—"

"Not at the present time. Though he regrets not being involved with the team, now is not a good moment to invest. Not with criminals like this man."

The disgusted grunt from Concannon was met with another blow. He shut up.

Keri looked between Concannon and Gina. "What's going to happen to him?"

Gina shrugged. "What would you like to have happen? As long as my boss is not brought in to it, I can do as you wish."

All eyes in the room were on Keri. Dana suppressed the urge to say, *"Whack him."*

"Let him go," Keri said.

He sighed in relief. Gina abruptly turned him around and slapped him hard across the face, making him sag. Then she hauled him up again and growled, "You will leave town. If I ever hear of you again, *I* will decide your fate. And I am not as kindhearted as your former employer." To Dana she said, "Walk us out."

Dana and Keri glanced at each other, but Dana obligingly escorted them out the door. They walked Concannon to the side gate and watched him scuttle down the street and around the corner.

"Vermin. I grew up with men like him," Gina said, and walked back toward the SUV, Dana keeping pace with her.

Feeling awkward, she said, "Gina, thanks. I mean it. You helped Keri solve a huge problem. Both of us really appreciate it."

Gina smiled widely for the first time, and in the porch light Dana saw clear braces on her teeth. Seeing her try to hide her surprise, Gina chuckled, "Ah, Gloria, she wants me to have the Hollywood teeth. So, why not, eh?"

Dana stuck out her hand and shook Gina's vigorously. "Yeah, why not? I think she really likes you."

Beaming, Gina climbed into the car. "You and Keri, made for each other, yes?"

Dana's smile slipped a bit, but she said, "I've always thought so."

Gina looked at her seriously. "She loves you. You love her. The rest? Is just stuff. Mark my words."

She closed the door and started the engine, driving slowly out of the gate and down the street.

Dana watched as the car disappeared. "Gina Pescetti, from your mouth to the goddess's ears."

Her mind working overtime, she returned to Keri's office and found her still staring at the check. She walked over and kissed her love on the forehead, took her by the hand, and guided them to sit on the leather couch by the fireplace.

Keri was in awe. "I still can't believe it. We've been so worried, and now it's all fixed."

Dana nodded and stared into the empty hearth. Keri noticed her expression and reached for her hand. Her gut started to churn. "How are you?"

Returning the warmth, Dana looked in her eyes. "I'm good. Tired."

"You look…like you're somewhere else."

Letting her eyes drift back to the fireplace, Dana quietly said, "I'm thinking I should quit."

CHAPTER TWENTY-ONE

Quit?" Keri felt short of breath.

Dana studied the woman who had occupied her dreams since preschool. "I…need some time to catch up with myself, Keri. I've spent my life longing for you. These past weeks have been a miracle for me. I know, without a doubt, that I love you beyond all measure."

Puzzled by the anxiety in Dana's eyes, Keri sat back and said, "I feel exactly the same way. This is so wonderful I can't believe it's real. But you don't have to quit. If you want a few weeks of time for us, we can do that."

Dana took her hand and squeezed gently. She felt oddly drained. "I can't put things in perspective with you so close to me every day. All I can think about is being with you. Making love with you."

Keri's eyes glittered with mischief. "Is that a *problem*? I mean, I know it's a distraction, but it's a nice one."

Dana rubbed the back of Keri's hand with her thumb. The soft skin of her love. She felt inexplicably sad. Keri was right. What they had was wonderful. Why couldn't she simply relax into it and be contented? Everything was falling into place. Concannon was all but out of Keri's life, and the risk to her safety had vanished with him. There was no way a coward like him would do anything to entice the likes of Gina Pescetti to hunt him down.

As if Keri suddenly sensed her train of thought, she said softly, "You know, both of us are in this. I have just as much at stake as you. If there's a reason you don't feel happy and secure about us, please tell me. I have a right to know."

But Dana was silent. Keri could almost see her struggling for words. Tumblers started to fall into place. "It's the accident, isn't it? You still don't trust me." She didn't say it accusingly. It was painful to acknowledge.

Dana's tortured eyes met hers, bright with tears. "I want to. You've no idea. This is everything I ever dreamed of. The truth is, I'm not even sure if it's you I don't trust or myself. I love you, and it clouds my thinking so much, I feel disoriented."

"What will it take?" Keri pleaded, terrified suddenly. What if she couldn't prove her love enough that Dana would trust her and stay with her and give the future they deserved a chance. What if she lost her again? All the misery of her childhood loss flooded back, and Keri felt a strange tremor, almost like a seizure, wrack her body.

Desperately, she dropped from the leather couch to her knees in front of Dana. "Don't leave me," she begged. "I think I would die. Can't you see…you weren't the only one who felt lost all those years. I did, too. Only I was so lost to myself without you that I didn't even know it."

Dana stared down into the face she loved. Tears washed like a torrent down Keri's cheeks and dripped from her chin. Her nose was wet. Her mouth shook uncontrollably. Eyes candid with emotion shone up at her. Keri was concealing nothing. Her love was right there for Dana to see, if she would let herself.

Remorse swept her. What was she thinking? How could she, for a minute, cast doubt on what they shared. Keri was not the problem here. *She* was. She reached down and pulled Keri into her arms, cradling her close, kissing her tears away, loving the damp weight of her pressed close, where she belonged.

"Sweetheart, I'm an idiot. I don't doubt you for a moment. Forgive me." She crushed her cheek to Keri's. "I love you more than life. I just think so much has been taken from me in the past, I'm afraid to be attached to anything or anyone. But I promise I'm not going anywhere." She could feel Keri's frantic sobs easing into shudders. Her body was beginning to relax.

Dana kept talking. "You're right. If there's a problem, we can solve it together."

Keri took a deep breath, her pulse slowing at last. She huddled into Dana, wanting nothing more than the haven of her arms and the comfort of her familiar scent. It wasn't all bad, she told herself—Dana had just been amazingly honest with her. She hadn't closed Keri out. She had bared herself. To do so meant trust was there. It had to be.

Encouraged, she said, "You were at Daddy's graveside the day he was buried, weren't you? It was you who took me home. Your hair was shorter and you limped more. And you wrote the note."

"Yes." Dana slowly nodded.

"And it was you who took that picture of Daddy and me that's behind my desk, wasn't it?"

"How did you know?" Dana sounded surprised.

Keri mopped at her own wet face with both hands. "I've been looking at your work for the first year project. I just didn't connect the dots. Your photographs of me feel so intimate, like you're touching me. That picture always gave me the same feeling."

Sadness in her eyes, Dana admitted, "It was the only way I *could* touch you, Keri. It kept me together."

Keri leaned to capture Dana's lips for a soft kiss. They lingered, each memorizing the other. Breaking the contact, she said, "I don't want you to go. I want you with me, always. We've just found each other…again." Her voice faltered. Leaning closer, she said firmly, "I need *you*. I won't let you go. You can take some time, but you can't quit the project and you cannot leave my life. Understand?"

The love that glowed in Dana's eyes gave Keri hope. "You know, we have a lot of talking to do, memories to reconstruct. Could take a lifetime."

Dana's heart soared. Cupping Keri's face between her hands, she said, "I hope it does. Meantime, I want to ask a favor of you." Seeing the concern on her lover's face, she said, "Keri, we will solve this together, but I can't put this on you. I know this is something very old and ugly I just need to deal with. I'm sure it's about my father. Do you understand?"

"What do you want to do?"

"Nothing scary." Dana trailed kisses over her forehead and cheeks "Walk on the beach, go to some of my 'thinking' places…that will help. I'll see you in five days. Please?"

Eyes brimming with tears, Keri said, "I'm afraid."

Taking her in her arms, Dana held her tightly and they sank back onto the couch.

"Tell me." Dana stroked the blond hair of her love. Her resolve was starting to crumble.

"I'm afraid you'll disappear. That I'll wake up and discover this was just another one of my nightmares. I used to have them all the time. We'd be playing and then you weren't there. I couldn't find you anywhere." A sob tore through her. "Oh, God, what if I lose you forever?"

Dana rocked Keri for a long while. When she had calmed down, she looked deep into Keri's blue eyes. "I'm not a dream. We are real and so is our love. But I want to come to you as a whole woman, with no fear and no expectation other than your love. I want to be able to accept whatever happens and not be a frightened child about it."

Keri closed her eyes and nodded, feeling much more the frightened child at the moment. "Do you think that's possible?"

"Yes," Dana replied, without a shred of doubt. Wanting to instill confidence, and to lighten up a little, she said teasingly, "I survived a fatal car crash. This is child's play."

Keri nodded into Dana's shirt, but kept silent. She knew Dana was right. For their future, this needed to happen.

Dana finally said, "Um, one thing. Could I call every night to make sure you're okay? I don't think I can stand not to talk..." The speed with which Keri covered Dana's mouth with her own gave her the answer.

❖

The next five days seemed an eternity. Keri dove into work and dealt with the fallout from Concannon's unseemly exit. She had lunch with Moms most days and was comforted that her mother seemed to understand exactly why Dana needed some time to think, and had no doubt she would come back.

She would wait for the phone to ring each night, unable to sleep until she heard Dana's voice. They usually talked for close to an hour, but neither asked for more. Keri was determined to give Dana what she needed. But she would lie awake long after they had hung up, analyzing every word, nuance, and tone. She was driving herself crazy. And trying *not* to think about it only made it worse.

Dana spent a lot of time in her darkroom, walking on the beach or visiting Mike Flemons's grave, a place she found comforting for reasons she was not quite clear about. She spoke to no one other than Keri. She longed to be in Keri's arms, touch her, comfort her, and love her. But she needed distance and, slowly, she found what she was looking for. On Friday morning, she called Keri and asked her out on a "date."

Keri couldn't concentrate on anything at work. She had barely slept the night before—any night since Dana had left—she was a wreck.

She gave up on working about noon and left the office. Shelley had given her a worried look as she left, but said nothing. She drove to her favorite florist and bought a bouquet of bright flowers, then drove to the cemetery.

Parking her car, she absently took the bouquet and started toward the plot her dad was buried in. She came up short when she saw a figure sitting on the grass, seeming deep in conversation. Tears came to her eyes when she recognized Dana.

Not wanting to disturb her, she turned and began to walk back to her car. She saw a young man in the uniform the maintenance workers wore and went to where he was carefully clipping the grass around a headstone.

She caught his eye and quietly asked, "Excuse me, would you do me a favor?"

His deep brown eyes were warm, and his long hair was tied neatly behind his head. He smiled and said, "Sure. What can I do for you?"

"I…don't want to disturb the person by the Flemons gravesite. But I'd like these flowers to be placed there when she's gone. I'd be happy to pay you to do that."

He looked beyond her to the site and saw Dana. He smiled.

"No problem. She's been there every day this week. Must need to puzzle out a big problem this time." His eyes lingered then came back to see Keri's questioning expression.

"I've worked here for a couple of years. She's always been a regular." Cocking his head to one side, he said, "I think I've seen you here, too."

Nodding, Keri said, "It's my father's grave."

He studied her for a moment. "Is she your sister?" His eyes drifted back to Dana.

Keri looked at Dana and said without hesitation, "She's my soul mate."

❖

Late afternoon on Friday, Dana got a call from an old client. He was desperate to find some shots she had taken of him several years before. She tried to get out of delivering them to him until the next day, but he begged and had a deadline, so she relented. She dug out the negatives, and as they were printing she called Keri on her cell phone.

Smiling at the sound of Keri's voice, she said, "Hi! Are you still coming over tonight?"

Keri immediately answered, "You bet. I've been looking forward to it all week." Suddenly unsure, she asked, "Why are you calling? Are we still on?"

"Absolutely! But I got a call from an old client and have to drop off some pictures. He begged and he's a nice guy. I called to tell you where the spare key is and ask you to just come in and help yourself to anything, in case I'm late. There's beer and wine and stuff. I was going to cook, but maybe I'll pick up a pizza." Her voice dropped three or four notes. "I've missed you."

Feeling her anxiety drop a notch, Keri answered, "Not as much as I've missed you. See you soon. Dana? Hurry."

The tone of her voice made Dana swallow hard. "I will. Promise." After telling her where the key was, she rang off.

❖

Keri opened the door and called for Dana. With no answer she came in and put her things down, wandering through the flat. She was impressed with the attention to detail in the restoration of the Victorian. It was spotless, and she wondered if Dana had cleaned it just for her. She grinned at the thought.

Finding some small bottles of sparkling mineral water in the refrigerator, she opened one and continued the tour, stopping in Dana's office. The furniture was utilitarian, she decided. File cabinets, desk, closet, and a door labeled "Darkroom" that she imagined was a converted bathroom. The door was ajar, so she opened it and turned on the light. A venting fan came on with the light.

An impressive array of trays, bottles, and equipment were neatly arranged on the tables and shelves. One bar stool was placed to allow Dana to reach everything easily. The wall behind the stool was full of photos.

The shot of Keri and her dad was there, in the center. She smiled at that. Others were of Keri playing high school and college sports. She took one down and turned it over, to see a younger version of Dana's neat handwriting labeling the date and event. Keri would have been sixteen. It was a better photo than all of the ones that had appeared in her high school yearbook or the newspaper. The same held true for several college shots. Keri's smile was bittersweet at the idea of Dana watching over her, but unable to contact her. So many years.

There were also photos of a younger Dana, taken during her soccer career. The short hair and strong legs, the expression of intense concentration made Keri react physically to the raw power she saw in the picture.

She chided herself. "Oh, Keri, you have got it bad."

Making a mental note to ask Dana about the photos, she left the darkroom and wandered to the living room, sitting on the sofa. The television held no appeal. She decided she could spend the time waiting for Dana by making notes for the attorneys and accountants. She was lost in the mountains of paperwork that arrived daily.

With Concannon's disappearance had come a huge administrative headache in separating him from the team. She'd been working on that process all week, as well as meeting with the board to update them on the situation. When she'd wandered out of the office, she'd left her PDA. She thought if she could concentrate, the time would go faster.

There has to be a tablet of paper around here somewhere. She got up and went to the office, settling herself behind the desk. Feeling a little like a snoop, she promised herself she would find a pen and some paper and go to the living room to write.

The pen was easy, as the center drawer had several. But there was no paper. She hesitated and then opened another drawer. Her eyes found a yellow pad of paper, and she grinned at her success. She reached in and pulled it out, but stopped just before closing the drawer.

Under the pad was a large manila envelope. And on the envelope, in large block letters, was written *MyKeri.*

Keri sat perfectly still, staring at the envelope. Her heart rate started to climb, and she was flooded with fear. She had to remind herself to breathe. Trembling, she reached for the envelope labeled with the childhood nickname. At first she felt guilty. These were Dana's personal papers. But she opened the clasp and slid the contents onto the desk.

Most were letters, addressed to MyKeri. The handwriting was a childish scrawl. They were in unopened envelopes, now yellowed with age. The ink was faded. She picked one up and held it to her nose. It smelled musty

After testing the glue that sealed the envelope, she opened it without much effort. Trying to still the trepidation running through her, she reached in and pulled out a piece of lined school paper. It was folded three times. The childish handwriting went straight to her heart.

> *Dear MyKeri,*
>
> *I hope you are better. My dad says he will mail this to you. He said you were in the hospital and really sick. I asked him to take me to see you but he said they don't let little kids in the hospital because they are noisy. I said I would be so good but he said no. I can't sleep at night because I worry about you. I miss you so much. Moms always tells me to take care of you. I promised her. How can I take care of you if I can't see you?*
>
> *Please write, I love you. Moms said we could get married. Now we only have to ask your dad.*
>
> *Love, Scooter*

Tears seeped from her eyes as she opened the next one at random.

> *MyKeri,*
>
> *I'm really lonely. I cried all day and night and my dad got mad. Are you okay? I'll try to come and see you.*
>
> *I get scared sometimes. I miss you.*
>
> *Love, Scooter*

She reached for a third envelope, and a faded photo fell out of it, along with the letter. She gasped when she saw the picture of the two of them the day Moms told them they could marry. The day Dana was ripped from her life. Wiping her eyes with the back of her hand she read,

> *MyKeri,*
>
> *We are moving. Dad told me today. He has a new job. I haven't heard from you and I think you hate me. I want you to*

*have my picture of us. Maybe you will remember our promise
that day.*

    *I hope you are okay. I wish I could run away but maybe
you hate me. Please write to me. I'll come one day. I promised
and I will keep my promise.*

    I love you, Scooter

Keri couldn't read anymore. Sobs tore from her throat, and she
held the letter to her breast. Still clutching it, she wandered into the
living room, lying down on the sofa, crying.

❖

"Keri? Honey? MyKeri? Talk to me. Look at me, please?"

Keri opened her eyes to see Dana, kneeling beside her, a worried
look on her face. She smiled and whispered, "Hi, Scoot. I've missed
you." She opened her arms to Dana and pulled her into a tight
embrace.

She cried, "I'm so sorry. I didn't realize. I was so miserable that
I couldn't see what it must have done to you. You lost everything that
day, too. My Scooter, I'm so sorry."

Dana ignored the tears that had sprung to her eyes. She clung to
Keri for dear life. "I never heard from you. I was so frightened."

Whispering in her ear, Keri said, "I know. I remember. I didn't
know where you were. I just made it make sense to *me*."

Dana had trouble finding her voice. Finally, she said, "I tried, Keri.
I wrote every day. But I didn't know your address so I asked my dad to
mail the letters. I couldn't believe it when I found them all after he died.
I couldn't believe he knew how much it meant to me but his revenge
meant more. He just dumped them in a drawer."

The pain of betrayal in her voice was wrenching to hear. "Oh,
Scooter, why did he do that?"

Dana pulled back to see her beloved sharing her tears. "Maybe he
already knew I was in love with you. He was always jealous of your
family. I knew better than to mention the fun I had with you and Moms,
but sometimes I think it just spilled over. I never wanted to come home
to him. And, later, when I came out to him just before the accident, he
was a typical homophobe."

Keri hugged her again. Dana buried her face in Keri's shoulder.

After a few moments Keri struggled to her feet, never relinquishing her hold on Dana. She held her hands at arms' length.

"I need to know what you decided this week."

Dana put her hand to Keri's face, touching her softly. She held her gaze and offered simply, "I love you. Only you can fill the emptiness in my arms."

Keri sighed, transfixed by her lover. "We can't bring those years back, and we can't pretend the past didn't happen. But we don't ever have to be apart again."

❖

Later, in the stillness of the bedroom, they touched each other. There was wonder in both of them.

"Every touch is new," said Keri. "When I put my hand on your breast I feel so much more than desire. I can't explain it."

Dana gasped, "Let me feel it."

Keri covered Dana's breast with her mouth, releasing all thought and letting her heart be her guide. There was a fire moving through them, a fire that the word *passion* failed to describe. "I want to take you slowly, but I don't think I can control myself."

"Don't try to control anything," Dana said.

Her words released a flood of desire, Keri moving to coat Dana's thigh with her wetness, whispering, "See what you do to me."

Dana opened her legs, allowing Keri to settle between them. She cried, "Do you feel that? Do you feel how we fit?"

Their hips rocked faster, Dana putting her hands on Keri's hips and pulling her closer, eyes never leaving her. The fire burned through all that was not real, all that was a barrier to the freedom of their love.

Keri cried, "Come with me…now."

The explosion fused past, present, and future.

Bodies in perfect rhythm, hearts a perfect match, souls forever found.

About the Author

JLee Meyer utilizes her background in psychology and speech pathology in her work as an international communication consultant. Spending time in airports, planes, and hotel rooms allows her the opportunity to pursue two of her favorite passions: reading and writing lesbian fiction. When she was recently booked into a gay brothel instead of a Las Vegas hotel and was delighted at all the plot and scene possibilities, she realized she really had become a writer.

JLee and her life partner celebrate their lives together in both Northern California and Manhattan.

For news of upcoming releases and author appearances, visit JLee's website: www.jleemeyer.com

Books Available From Bold Strokes Books

Forever Found by JLee Meyer. Can time, tragedy, and shattered trust destroy a love that seemed destined? When chance reunites two childhood friends separated by tragedy, the past resurfaces to determine the shape of their future. (1-933110-37-6)

Sword of the Guardian by Merry Shannon. Princess Shasta's bold new bodyguard has a secret that could change both of their lives. *He* is actually a *she*. A passionate romance filled with courtly intrigue, chivalry, and devotion. (1-933110-36-8)

Wild Abandon by Ronica Black. From their first tumultuous meeting, Dr. Chandler Brogan and Officer Sarah Monroe are drawn together by their common obsessions—sex, speed, and danger. (1-933110-35-X)

Turn Back Time by Radclyffe. Pearce Rifkin and Wynter Thompson have nothing in common but a shared passion for surgery. They clash at every opportunity, especially when matters of the heart are suddenly at stake. (1-933110-34-1)

Chance by Grace Lennox. At twenty-six, Chance Delaney decides her life isn't working so she swaps it for a different one. What follows is the sexy, funny, touching story of two women who, in finding themselves, also find one another. (1-933110-31-7)

The Exile and the Sorcerer by Jane Fletcher. First in the Lyremouth Chronicles. Tevi, wounded and adrift, arrives in the courtyard of a shy young sorcerer. Together they face monsters, magic, and the challenge of loving despite their differences. (1-933110-32-5)

A Matter of Trust by Radclyffe. JT Sloan is a cybersleuth who doesn't like attachments. Michael Lassiter is leaving her husband, and she needs Sloan's expertise to safeguard her company. It should just be business—but it turns into much more. (1-933110-33-3)

Sweet Creek by Lee Lynch. A celebration of the enduring nature of love, friendship, and community in the quirky, heart-warming lesbian community of Waterfall Falls. (1-933110-29-5)

The Devil Inside by Ali Vali. Derby Cain Casey, head of a New Orleans crime organization, runs the family business with guts and grit, and no one crosses her. No one, that is, until Emma Verde claims her heart and turns her world upside down. (1-933110-30-9)

Grave Silence by Rose Beecham. Detective Jude Devine's investigation of a series of ritual murders is complicated by her torrid affair with the golden girl of Southwestern forensic pathology, Dr. Mercy Westmoreland. (1-933110-25-2)

Honor Reclaimed by Radclyffe. In the aftermath of 9/11, Secret Service Agent Cameron Roberts and Blair Powell close ranks with a trusted few to find the would-be assassins who nearly claimed Blair's life. (1-933110-18-X)

Honor Bound by Radclyffe. Secret Service Agent Cameron Roberts and Blair Powell face political intrigue, a clandestine threat to Blair's safety, and the seemingly irreconcilable personal differences that force them ever farther apart. (1-933110-20-1)

Protector of the Realm: Supreme Constellations Book One by Gun Brooke. A space adventure filled with suspense and a daring intergalactic romance featuring Commodore Rae Jacelon and the stunning, but decidedly lethal, Kellen O'Dal. (1-933110-26-0)

Innocent Hearts by Radclyffe. In a wild and unforgiving land, two women learn about love, passion, and the wonders of the heart. (1-933110-21-X)

The Temple at Landfall by Jane Fletcher. An imprinter, one of Celaeno's most revered servants of the Goddess, is also a prisoner to the faith—until a Ranger frees her by claiming her heart. The Celaeno series. (1-933110-27-9)

Force of Nature by Kim Baldwin. From tornados to forest fires, the forces of nature conspire to bring Gable McCoy and Erin Richards close to danger, and closer to each other. (1-933110-23-6)

In Too Deep by Ronica Black. Undercover homicide cop Erin McKenzie tracks a femme fatale who just might be a real killer...with love and danger hot on her heels. (1-933110-17-1)

Course of Action by Gun Brooke. Actress Carolyn Black desperately wants the starring role in an upcoming film produced by Annelie Peterson. Just how far will she go for the dream part of a lifetime? (1-933110-22-8)

Rangers at Roadsend by Jane Fletcher. Sergeant Chip Coppelli has learned to spot trouble coming, and that is exactly what she sees in her new recruit, Katryn Nagata. The Celaeno series. (1-933110-28-7)

Justice Served by Radclyffe. Lieutenant Rebecca Frye and her lover, Dr. Catherine Rawlings, embark on a deadly game of hide-and-seek with an underworld kingpin who traffics in human souls. (1-933110-15-5)

Distant Shores, Silent Thunder by Radclyffe. Dr. Tory King—along with the women who love her—is forced to examine the boundaries of love, friendship, and the ties that transcend time. (1-933110-08-2)

Hunter's Pursuit by Kim Baldwin. A raging blizzard, a mountain hideaway, and a killer-for-hire set a scene for disaster—or desire—when Katarzyna Demetrious rescues a beautiful stranger. (1-933110-09-0)

The Walls of Westernfort by Jane Fletcher. All Temple Guard Natasha Ionadis wants is to serve the Goddess—until she falls in love with one of the rebels she is sworn to destroy. The Celaeno series. (1-933110-24-4)

Change Of Pace: *Erotic Interludes* by Radclyffe. Twenty-five hot-wired encounters guaranteed to spark more than just your imagination. Erotica as you've always dreamed of it. (1-933110-07-4)

Honor Guards by Radclyffe. In a wild flight for their lives, the president's daughter and those who are sworn to protect her wage a desperate struggle for survival. (1-933110-01-5)

Fated Love by Radclyffe. Amidst the chaos and drama of a busy emergency room, two women must contend not only with the fragile nature of life, but also with the irresistible forces of fate. (1-933110-05-8)

Justice in the Shadows by Radclyffe. In a shadow world of secrets and lies, Detective Sergeant Rebecca Frye and her lover, Dr. Catherine Rawlings, join forces in the elusive search for justice. (1-933110-03-1)

shadowland by Radclyffe. In a world on the far edge of desire, two women are drawn together by power, passion, and dark pleasures. An erotic romance. (1-933110-11-2)

Love's Masquerade by Radclyffe. Plunged into the indistinguishable realms of fiction, fantasy, and hidden desires, Auden Frost is forced to question all she believes about the nature of love. (1-933110-14-7)

Love & Honor by Radclyffe. The president's daughter and her lover are faced with difficult choices as they battle a tangled web of Washington intrigue for...love and honor. (1-933110-10-4)

Beyond the Breakwater by Radclyffe. One Provincetown summer, three women learn the true meaning of love, friendship, and family. (1-933110-06-6)

Tomorrow's Promise by Radclyffe. One timeless summer, two very different women discover the power of passion to heal and the promise of hope that only love can bestow. (1-933110-12-0)

Love's Tender Warriors by Radclyffe. Two women who have accepted loneliness as a way of life learn that love is worth fighting for and a battle they cannot afford to lose. (1-933110-02-3)

Love's Melody Lost by Radclyffe. A secretive artist with a haunted past and a young woman escaping a life that has proved to be a lie find their destinies entwined. (1-933110-00-7)

Safe Harbor by Radclyffe. A mysterious newcomer, a reclusive doctor, and a troubled gay teenager learn about love, friendship, and trust during one tumultuous summer in Provincetown. (1-933110-13-9)

Above All, Honor by Radclyffe. Secret Service Agent Cameron Roberts fights her desire for the one woman she can't have—Blair Powell, the daughter of the president of the United States. (1-933110-04-X)